CW01657764

The Vampires of Alfama

by

Pierre Kast

Translated from the French
by
Peter de Polnay

W. H. ALLEN · LONDON
A Howard & Wyndham Company
1976

© Olivier Orban, 1975

English translation © W. H. Allen & Co. Ltd, 1976

This book may not be reproduced in any form whatsoever without permission in writing

Printed and bound in Great Britain by
Butler & Tanner Ltd, Frome and London
for the publishers W. H. Allen & Co. Ltd,
44 Hill Street, London W1X 8LB

ISBN 0 491 01997 1

To Vinicius de Moraes
and, naturally, to Boris Vian

Author's Note

The action of the novel *The Vampires of Alfama* takes place in Lisbon towards the middle of the eighteenth century. But this is a Portugal of fantasy, let us say of a dream. No real historical personage can be found in it, either by transposition or in any disguise. The King, the Cardinal Prime Minister and the policemen have never existed and will never exist. But it is a history parallel with real history, a universe parallel with the one in which we live.

This tale aims only to re-create the colour of the eighteenth century, the colour and above all the architecture of Portuguese baroque, the smell of Alfama and its Brazilian twin, Pelourinho de Salvador.

The christian name 'João' is pronounced like Jean in French. São José is San José, and the villa of Azeitão, Azeitan.

Part One

Chapter 1

On the low table near the hammock the chocolate was keeping warm in a jacketed saucepan, a very complicated work of art in wrought silver, on which black bearers held up slender naked nymphs at the point of puberty: it was a present from the Corporation of the Silversmiths of Ouro Preto. The singular taste that the master of the house had acquired in Brazil was evident everywhere. A stuffed snow-leopard, crocodile skins, a berimbau from Salvador, and a young Negress, even more fragile than the nymphs, asleep in the hammock.

A panelled door into the vast library revolved without a sound, revealing a dark, vaulted staircase. João mounted the last steps, taking off an apron and asbestos gloves. Behind him the embers of the fires still glowed. Their dying glimmer was reflected in the retorts, earthenware crucibles and containers of every size. Eussa opened an eye, saw or rather guessed the alchemist's laboratory, and full of vague terror immediately pretended to be asleep.

João carefully closed the door behind him, and almost absent-mindedly caressed the little body in the hammock. He sat down behind his enormous writing table overloaded with files. Sighing, he put on his wig, and got down to work. The pen grated. He wrote rapidly.

Eussa jumped out of the hammock, poured the chocolate into a large precious cup, and brought it to him timidly. João drank, letting his hand slip down from the waist to the loins of the little girl.

Then he rang.

A lackey appeared at the other end of the immense room, his eyes downcast so as not to look at Eussa's exciting nakedness.

'Your Eminence?'

'Pedro, have the horses harnessed. I am leaving in half an hour.'

The lackey vanished. Helped by Eussa, João dressed in silence. The heat was insufferable despite the blinds, the cool flagstones, the glazed tiles on the walls, the garden, the ponds and artificial waterfalls. João submitted with bad grace to the hours of the siesta, that too short interval, leaving only two or three hours for the laboratory.

A knock on the door, and the lackey reappeared.

'The carriage is at the door, Your Eminence. Dom Manuel would like to have a word with you. Also Meninha wants to see you before your departure.'

João nodded. A young priest entered without waiting. With a pleasure that long habit had not dulled, he gazed lengthily at the little black figure.

'Go and play, Eussa,' said João.

The little girl glided into the garden. The two men watched her go, and smiled at each other.

'Whenever you like, Manuel,' said João.

Slightly unsure of himself, the young priest gave the Cardinal a brief glance. The double meaning of French phrases invariably frightened him. Maliciously João prolonged the silence. Then he sat down abruptly.

'I am listening,' he said.

Dom Manuel sighed, and sadly opened a briefcase he carried under his arm.

'But sit down,' said João. 'I loathe inappropriate marks of respect.'

The young priest obeyed. He opened a file.

'I have an informer who has just arrived at the house of the Marquis. He is a certain Dom François, a Jesuit Father who has a high position in Paris. It appears that he has brought a number of documents that concern you.'

João smiled.

'You know very well that nothing my Minister of Police ever plots against me can escape my attention. Heresy, black magic, corruption, various perversities—there is a file about each of my small vices.'

'Very dangerous,' said Manuel.

'Not at all. I inform His Majesty one by one about the reports I receive, concerning the reports others receive about me.'

'The principle of Mithridates.'

'Exactly. I hold the King.'

'You think you hold him.'

'He has agreed to change his confessor. You will say that all depends on the new one. I have designated you as the best candidate.'

'Am I not a little too young for it?'

João laughed, and stood up.

'You are certainly a little too handsome . . . I fear that the influence you are bound to have over His Majesty won't be limited to religious matters.'

Imperceptibly Manuel blushed as he also stood. Familiarly João put his arm round the priest's shoulders.

'I will be the confessor's confessor,' he said. 'You receive my absolution in advance.'

He did not notice the flash of anger in Manuel's furtive eyes.

'Are you accompanying me to the Palace?'

The young man hesitated; João smiled, and turned for an instant towards the garden.

'I perceive that if you do not much appreciate the male penitents I supply you with, you won't have the same opinion of a new female penitent . . . '

His arm restrained the young priest's involuntary jump.

'Do remain,' João continued. 'She must have joined her sister in the little pavilion at the bottom of the garden. You will find me later at the Ministry.'

With a quick, light step João made for the door.

'Your Eminence!'

'Yes?' said João, stopping.

'Take care. The Marquis knows about the little house in Cascais.'

'I know that he knows. I had the whole troupe embarked for Salvador last night. As if by chance, the dear Marquis organised a shoot near Cascais for His Majesty early this morning. All his trouble was wasted. My police are better than his.'

'For the moment.'

João shrugged his shoulders, and went out. Manuel waited an instant, in fear that João had not really left. Then he started for the garden. To his surprise the view changed as he advanced. A tiny secluded pavilion suddenly appeared. Eussa and her sister (who was neither much older nor more fully dressed) were playing at knuckle-bones. They raised their eyes at the approach of the handsome young priest, and rose gracefully. Docile already.

The carriage was in the courtyard. A woman on horseback waited beside it. João approached, and gave a brief sign of intense pleasure on seeing that Alexandra had not yet left. When she saw him arrive she dismounted and her riding skirt, with its sly but brazen slit, opened fully. João never tired of that long, tapering marble thigh. Alexandra threw herself into his arms.

'Have you arrived or are you just leaving?' he asked.

'I want to ride Penelope as far as Cascais—we must get accustomed to each other.'

'Do you love her?'

'Madly. Tell me, dear uncle of mine, are you seeing the horrible Marquis?'

João's arm, which had automatically slid round her waist, twitched as if in recoil. She held on firmly to her uncle. They would talk more easily clasped in each other's arms, and what she had to say was not at all easy.

'He wants me, does he not?' she said.

João sighed. Alexandra's profile was exactly like that of a young lioness: a seed-plot of freckles, nearly transparent eyes, the complexion phosphorescent. Very ugly, according to the standards of the Court which had been inherited from the late King of France. But the handsome and still young man enthroned in the place of that dirty, sordid and old King would undoubtedly appreciate the young girl. The effect of her beauty was always staggering.

'Yes,' said João. 'And he will do all he can to possess you.'

'I know. What interests me is to find out what you can do to prevent him.'

'Practically nothing. He holds me completely in his grasp. My only consolation is knowing about all his movements minute by minute. Pretty meagre.'

'I shall never marry him. Even the idea of his touching me makes me vomit. On top of that, I do not much care for the police.'

'They are needed. I have them too,' said João.

'You do not go to bed with them.' She laughed. 'Indeed, they and I are the only people with whom you do not go to bed!'

'That is true. Incest is not part of my repertoire.'

'If you wanted it you know I would not be cruel.'

'A fine education.'

'Your sister . . .'

'Your mother . . .'

'Before her ridiculous marriage she had much to endure. Are you sure I am not your daughter?'

'No,' said João.

They laughed happily. João dropped his arm, opened the carriage door and got in. Alexandra put her head in through the window. As she moved her riding coat opened. She had nothing on under the jabot made of Malines lace. An admirable breast pointed directly at the coat's lining. Small for the fashion of the times. João could not resist touching it tenderly.

'Do you never wear a chemise?'

'It is not for you to complain!'

'Let us continue,' said João. 'It is like a chess problem. The chief of police has weapons against me by which he hopes to obtain my niece.'

'Against her wish.'

'How can I refuse without losing the game?'

'Gain time.'

'It's not so simple. It is a political problem. Inch by inch I am moving towards expelling the Jesuits and putting the Inquisition into mothballs.'

'French politics. That is what my stepfather writes. He asks me to return.'

'Never,' said João. 'He will end up raping you.'

'Certainly, but with a great movement of his soul, and in an admirable landscape of forests, fir trees, mountains—do you see it?'

'I see it. The mists of the north.'

'They are dreadful, those little German princes. Provincials sick with vanity, mad about Paris fashion.'

'How is your mother?'

'She adores music. Your brother-in-law's orchestra is the most renowned between the Rhine and the Oder. As a matter of fact, mother loves the musicians too. Joking apart, there is something in German music that moves me profoundly . . .'

'I distrust it.'

'I know. Our friends the Encyclopedists are for Reason. So am I. But I believe that Reason serves to open the doors to unfathomable chasms. The music of the Germans runs towards these chasms. I will go with them at full gallop.'

'Bravo!'

Regretfully his hand left Alexandra's breast which it had almost forgetfully caressed, teasing the hardened nipple like one strumming a guitar, and buttoned the riding jacket.

'A means of parrying him must be found,' João concluded.

'I am good at chess. I will help you.'

She turned the mare round, and flew off on her. An athlete, a female centaur, João said to himself. Her grace and physical strength fascinated him. When he saw it combined with moral strength, as in Alexandra, despair overcame him. As a young man he had loved the idea of action and of fighting. They had made a priest of him, the destiny of younger sons. His elder brothers having died without issue, the Duchy fell too late into his hands. Today he was Prime Minister, but waging war he left to others. During the last ten years all his energy had been concentrated on the useless struggle to give direction to the weak and miserable caprices of a king who, terrorised by superstition and the remorse caused by his as yet unadmitted pederasty, was like a puppet in João's hands. But João himself had reached the stage of knowing no longer what he wanted, and remembering no more what he had desired. Diderot wrote to him, and he subsidised d'Alembert in secret. Alchemists and astrologers lived in his shadow. It was believed that he was all-powerful. He was the only one to know what incredible weakness lay behind the façade. But for how long?

He sighed.

'Let us be off,' he told his coachman.

The customary audience with the King had been insufferable. In his lack of will-power, taste for caprice, and a total surrender to immediate pleasures João saw reflected all his own inclinations, all his cherished faults as if multiplied by a deforming mirror. It was evidently the secret reason he had such influence on that weak spirit. A Caligula without madness or greatness, hence without breadth, João would sometimes say to himself. The cruel necessity to manipulate that jellyfish often made him sick. He left the small royal apartments almost out of his mind, red-faced, sweating, his wig awry. Two hours of subtle strategy with but one result: Manuel was accepted. In truth, no great result.

He crossed the gardens. A young Italian architect had conceived the exquisite little palace built betweeen two ravines. Hundreds of prisoners had to be used for the earthwork, but the result did give some satisfaction. A canal traversed the park. The banks were entirely covered with glazed tiles, depicting the conquest of Brazil, and under a little bridge some slightly risqué scenes, almost invisible, caused ladies and more than one young girl to cluck. Youthful pages from provincial families would blush, thus giving the King a perfect opening, and also the means of combining the pleasures of safe navigation with his favourite vice. João had invented a parable about Henry the Navigator which he often repeated—a hardly innocent joke that would have proved fatal to him if repeated to the King. That was all that was left for him of the pleasures of war.

So he smiled as he crossed the bridge over the canal. Outside the park he had had a chancellery built for him, which was reached through the gardens and gave on to a little square. He had wanted it to look as Italian as possible. Three ministries, stables, outhouses, a church, a small replica of the Trinita de Monte, turned it into a stage set for Italian opera. Concerts for the court and visiting foreign monarchs were given there. He entered a gate hidden by a mass of orange trees, and started to undress in the miraculously ventilated cool passages. A smart maid-servant took his garments as he shed them. His bath was ready. He spent but thirty seconds in it, was dried and dressed in a moment. Scent of jasmine.

'Mariette,' said João, 'is there anybody waiting?'

'The Marquis, Your Eminence. He frightens me.'

'I hope he has not touched you.'

'I'm private property,' laughed Mariette.

Vigorously smacking the ravishing little behind, picked out as it were by a too short dress and the absence of a hoop petticoat, João laughed too.

'I want my carriage in an hour's time,' he said.

He was swallowed up in a spiral staircase that led straight to his office, where he appeared to lock himself in in order to work. Opening the door to the waiting room, he admitted the Marquis in person.

Da Silva had his profession written all over him. Were he even presentable the King with all that he knew would immediately have put him in João's place. Luckily the King found him repugnant, which he truly was, and thus João could resign himself to the inevitable.

They worked fast together. Da Silva had no political convictions. He followed João's supervision of the Jesuits, keeping his distance from the Inquisition, retaining ties with France, and tolerating the printers of French books. Portuguese books were another matter. Correspondence with d'Alembert to be sure, but rigorous prisons. Da Silva appreciated those aspects of policy.

He would not have to make any changes once he got João's skin.

All over again Da Silva weighed in against Alfama. A town within the town, sloping down to the waterfront of the Tagus, where it had its own private port. A warren of alleys, terraces and dark passages, where the roof of one house was the cellar of the one above it. The whole hill resembled those Swiss cheeses full of holes.

Da Silva, who had been to Algiers to ransom slaves, described the Casbah, comparing it with Alfama. The police did not dare enter it. No fugitive could ever be caught there. News travelled even faster than people. In the centre were four or five mansions, some of them up for sale; Da Silva spoke of buying them, to turn them into fortresses. The municipal police, controlled by police chief Ricardo, were a reserved domain that had to live in symbiosis with Alfama under the pretext of supervision. Ricardo was the *bête noire* of the Marquis.

'You know as well as I the state of our finances,' said João.

'I thought perhaps that *you* might make an effort.'

'You know better than I the state of *my* finances . . .'

'I know a very accommodating Jew,' said the Marquis, 'and I have the means to bring pressure on him.'

João sighed. No means of escaping the confrontation. He sat back like one on a long journey, while imperceptibly the Marquis made himself comfortable too.

'My dear sir,' said João. 'At chess one would call it a stalemate. You hold me in your hands. Let me quickly repeat your advantages. The reports of your spies about my relations with my little girls from Bahia. The little house in Cascais.'

He could not resist being dazzled by images one following another, almost in crowds. Alexandra entering the room with the light against her, not at all embarrassed by the two orphan girls playing truant from their orphanage—exquisite stuff. On horseback with her under olive trees. His monologue did not stop, though it might have slowed down somewhat.

'You intercepted some of my correspondence,' he continued. 'Let me enumerate. I know which of the letters are missing. Three to the French King's Prime Minister. One with handwritten marginal notes by the King himself. The minutes of a conversation with the Grand Inquisitor. In fact, I saw his file. Your services are as easily penetrated as mine.'

'You forget,' the Marquis said softly, 'the authentic and clear proofs of your Brazilian administration. The bogus sugar, cocoa, tobacco, inventories of the ore that arrived here. The same with the Achilles heel of an immense fortune, quicker spent than made.'

'I have not forgotten them, but you interrupted me. Your relative integrity, let us say your prudence, not to speak of your avarice, will protect you.'

'I could check-mate you in two moves,' said the Marquis. 'Perhaps in one.'

'Not really. The King will never listen to you. If you attack me you will lose. You are my protégé whether you like it or not. You overthrow me, but you kill yourself at the same time.'

'I could try. I have my own ideas about it.'

'Very amiable of you to warn me,' said João. 'But very useless. If you hold me I hold the King.'

After a little silence the Marquis added:

'Evidently, but I embarrass you.'

'To be sure.'

'There could be other means . . .'

'Alexandra?'

The Marquis looked at him.

'She would never agree,' said João.

'You have great influence over her. I would leave her free and very rich. But do not say anything. We are not in any hurry.'

João sighed again, and stood up. The Marquis remained obstinately seated, tense and silent, so João pulled up a chair and sat down beside him.

'Right,' said João. 'What else is there?'

'Public matters. I am very worried. Your peace treaty with the Grand Inquisitor, a masterpiece, has dangerous consequences. There have never before been so many alchemists, astrologers and magicians in Alfama.'

'There is a tacit agreement that they must not come out, and we—and you—do not go in.'

'Oh yes, that's true. But it does not apply to their clients. I could point to ten mansions where the furnaces burn day and night. Everybody does not have screens on his chimneys like you.'

'You know that too?'

'And a lot more.'

The Marquis had won. He was the first to rise. Fortune had

changed sides. João rose too, a little dazed. When the Marquis took his arm he did not dare to push it away.

'Dear friend,' said the Marquis, 'you are my master. Accept it. I admire your politics. I am a man of order and tradition. But I know that one must let a little steam escape. I do not believe that scaffolds and dungeons will save us in the long run. I detest as much as you the imbeciles who want the iron hand without the velvet glove. What I reproach you for is the weakness inside your glove.' They had reached the door. The Marquis crossed the threshold and turned round.

'I am willing to tolerate well-educated people reading French libels printed in Holland, but I do not care for the people who write them, and I will prevent their being printed.'

João returned to his office, and dropped into his armchair. Despondency. Bitterness. His hand grasped a bottle almost automatically. He poured. He drank from a tiny silver cup five times at least. *Batida de maracuja*, a drink made of alcohol of sugar cane mixed with a small fruit of the Amazon. Euphoria. He chewed a brownish tablet reduced to crumbs. A moment's respite. Then his mind went on a journey. In sweet semi-consciousness he took a white sheet of paper and a quill. Fast and uncontrolled his quill moved along the paper stopping after sixteen lines of unequal spaces. He floated for an instant between two waters before surfacing. Methodically he counted the spaces and drew figures. Then he drew the small geomantic emblem. The ballet of the figures arranged itself with the majestic harmony of ritual consultation, geomancy being the algebra of occult sciences. In each house corresponding to astrological houses the figures found their place full of significant secret messages. He took from a drawer a treatise hidden in the binding of a Missal. He concentrated on finding the interpretation. *Rubeus*, lewdness, the glowing embers for him. Danger, *carcer* in House VII, that of the adversary. And *Fortuna major* for the judge. Not so bad.

For some time geomancy had governed his whole life. He consulted it before every decision. The contradiction between that superior form of divining and the rationalism of his French friends did not trouble him. He did not feel it. Thus many mathematicians were astrologers too. They had decided that it was a sign of their times.

Chapter II

The afternoon had been very hot in the alleys of Alfama. At nightfall cool air rose from the river Tagus. The town within the town came to life. The night sky had never been so clear. The moon was full, almost as light as day. Burghers and noblemen slipped into the admirably specialised brothels. Drinkers in different stages of inebriety collapsed under the melancholic influence of *fados*. The whole night long the *fados* would sob for the unlikely return of King Sebastian from beyond the seas. Mysterious shadows moved about. At midnight Alfama was like a big city at market time.

Above Alfama, in the streets and squares of Graca, a furtive shadow moved from an alley to a small square, and stopped in front of an ordinary house. It was on two storeys, the façade covered with glazed tiles, the roof with raised edges, a style imported from Macao. The house was on the brink of an abyss, hiding from view two more storeys lower down and some terraces. The front door was in the square below. And at an angle two sections of the wall hid a tiny door. Thus on one side, namely at the top, the house gave on to the Graca, and on the other side lower down on to Alfama. Convenient. Clara pushed open the nearly invisible tiny door, which opened noiselessly, and drew the bolts. On a console table she placed an inlaid box, a medical chest, and briefly checked its contents, the little drawers that contained herbs, a silver mirror, and instruments, then after closing the lid she turned the key in the secret lock, and entered the antichamber of dimly lit drawing-rooms, which were the formal part of the house.

She touched a spring. An entire decorated panel swung round, to show stairs that led to the two secret storeys below. She went down, and the panel closed hermetically. The two lower floors of the house contained a laboratory on the first, and a 'scientific' closet on the one beneath. Geography, astronomy, astrology. There were two terraces on each level.

On the lower terrace a telescope had just been erected by a young girl who was more of an assistant than a servant.

'Thank you, Ursula,' said Clara.

'What is the news?'

'Nothing can be done. She will die in ten days, twenty at the most. Her insides are eaten away. The poor family.'

'That will be your first defeat.'

'Anybody would have failed. I have no spell against death. Besides, you know very well that I have no spells whatever.'

'That is not what the police say,' said Ursula.

'That is true . . . At the moment they are being quiet, but I shall remain cautious. If they can arrest me, they will certainly burn me.'

'Not here. This is not Spain.'

'For the moment, no. His Eminence João, Duke of Queluz, is considered to be very liberal. But he is a *Janus bifarons* with an official face and a private face. Which is the true one? At this moment His Eminence indulges in a philosophical whim.'

'The Elder Brother of the Lodge of Lapa boasts of having been received twice,' said Ursula. 'They conversed about the great Albert, Paracelsus, and our Roger Bacon.'

'If the Brother gets himself caught His Eminence won't raise his little finger. And in a month, in a year perhaps, His Eminence of Queluz himself will be the one to have him arrested. It's high politics. His Eminence is a queluzist before anything else.'

Clara went into a storeroom near the terrace. Out of habit Ursula followed her. With an effort the two women pulled a strange contraption to the middle of the flagstone marked out by mosaics, a complex moon-dial adorned with figures and symbols. It was an enormous globe made of Bohemian glass, with a diameter of at least one metre. The symbols drawn on the floor were also engraved on the surface of the crystal globe, which rested on a cradle of exotic wood, hard, dark, almost like a mineral, and displaying more symbolic carvings and divisions. The globe could revolve like a globe of the earth or a map of the two hemispheres. Legs made of the same wood reached down to a frame mounted on small wheels, so it moved easily about. The moon beams played on the crystal, throwing sparks of light in every direction. Ursula left the globe in the middle and Clara, who had gone out for a second, came back with a magnifying glass attached to a jointed stick which she fixed to the wooden cradle. Ursula slowly moved the globe while Clara, whose eyes were focussed on the image enlarged by the magnifying glass, began to concentrate. The combined movements of globe and jointed stick allowed the magnifying glass to explore every inch of the surface. Ursula brought a chair, and then withdrew like a shadow.

Slowly, as though it emerged from the world of shadows, an image materialised. Clara's hands moved the globe, making the image larger and clearer. The young woman kept her eyes glued to it. She could make out a study. With miraculous clarity she saw a window, a yard, snow-covered mountains like the endless inside courts in a Dutch painting. A very old man, with a majestic bearing and a white beard, his long hair white too, was seated in front of a table, a crystal globe and a magnifying glass smaller than Clara's before him. Their eyes never left each other's. Without a doubt they were speaking to each other—beyond language and tongues, a sort of consultation. Dona Clara had the greatest respect and veneration for Master Swedenborg. The image became blurred.

Clara threw herself back exhausted, but a kind of signal brought her forward again. Her expert hands slowly moved the globe and the stick. Another image took shape, and became clear. A terrace in a small market-town on top of the cliffs of the Rhine, a reflection of the moon on the old river. Another globe, and before it an ascetic, tense young man. He stopped his globe, waiting for Clara's image to become clear. They gazed at each other. His was a sort of distress signal, a call for help, a message: a friend of the magician was in mortal danger. His glance seemed to give Clara geographical indications, co-ordinated ones without a doubt. Feverishly Clara turned her globe, also taking her bearings at moments from the numberless stars in the night sky of Lisbon.

Another image took shape in a still thick fog. She saw the pointed roofs of a gothic town, but also a succession of baroque façades.

'Prague,' murmured Clara. 'A bank of the Vlatva.'

An enormous, heavy, bearded man appeared, enveloped in magnificent furs. He fixed his globe, his eyes searched for Clara's. They found each other. Above words their spirits spoke of dangers, stakes, persecutions. Clara trembled. His name reached her: Count Kotor. She knew only a small number of the initiates: the Swede, the German, one Irishman lost that night, an Italian she had not looked for. This was her first contact with Bohemia, though her globe came from there. She gazed intensely at the Count. He asked for a place of refuge, security for himself and his own, a secret, closed-in, well-guarded spot. Clara accepted at once. She would find it in Alfama. Kotor appeared to understand. He would set out immediately, the voyage would take a fortnight, twenty days at the most, and they would arrive at nightfall. Clara described the quays of the Tagus at the bottom of Alfama. Every night she would be waiting there with a Berlin drawn by black horses.

They were six in all, the count, his daughter Barbara, his son Laurent and three servants, more friends than underlings. There was a guide too, a disciple. Clara did not comprehend very well, and tried in vain to catch his words. The image became blurred. Danger. Far too long already. Thank you. *Au revoir*.

She collapsed, dropping between sleep and unconsciousness into a limitless torpor which lasted for hours. Ursula wheeled the globe back into the storeroom without her giving even a stir. Already dawn lit up the Castle of São Jorge above Alfama. The market-gardeners were shouting in the alleys. At last she awoke, weighed down by tiredness, still in a dream. The communication this time had been more exhausting than ever before.

Towards the end of the afternoon Clara bravely tried to reassume the usual course of her peaceful daily life. In the rooms above thronged the patients whom Ursula endeavoured to keep quiet. Clara appeared preceded by a muffled murmur. Women kissed her hands, embraced her legs. As was her custom she was dressed like a cavalier: black breeches, high boots of Villafranca de Xira, a lace shirt, a short leather jacket, her hair pulled back and tied with a flame-coloured ribbon. She locked herself in, taking a long time to decide to receive the pushing crowd. She took a brown pill from the drawer which, reduced to powder, she quickly swallowed. Her vigour returned, and the fruit of the cola gave her new strength: her mind was now sharp and detached, her intuition flashing. She should think of renewing the provisions. If Felipe's ship, which brought her drugs, was late in returning from Peru by Cape Horn and Salvador, she was in for a bad time.

The crowd left in small groups. Fever, deformed backs, all the illnesses caused by the wrong food, bodies underfed and overworked. Two cases of leprosy. Hers was the labour of Sisyphus. Ursula dismissed any late comers, for the hour of visits was approaching. At dusk, enveloped in the black cape of the fishermen of Nazare, Clara stole along the alleys. They were waiting for her wherever she went. The souls and the spirit were often sicker than the bodies.

She nursed one and the other, advised, took their confessions, expelled violence, the wish for power, jealousy, the spirit of lucre, the lure of profit in which coupled with poverty, dirt and greed she saw the secret roots of nearly all the illnesses that came her way.

Eventually she arrived at the Fonseca household. She adored the father and the mother. He was a printer's mate in the low town, she embroidered the shawls of the *fado* singers. They had but two daughters, Fernanda and Lavinia, lovely, strange girls, perhaps with a little Mulatto blood. The grandfather, a widower, had brought their mother from Brazil. Nobody had questioned the exact colour of the grandmother. He had been a smelter in Ouro Preto, and one day he arrived in Lisbon with his iron ore, and a girl, the mother of his present grand-daughters. Fernanda, a musician, sang and danced, the younger one remained at home, devoured by a merciless illness which Clara could not halt. In a corner sat her fiancé, eating his heart out. Clara backed away every time she brushed past him, in fact even when he looked at her. He was not bad, but he was a bigot and a hypocrite. He made the sign of the Cross when he saw Clara leave. However, Lavinia loved him, and Clara kept quiet.

That evening she saw no change either way. She administered harmless, soothing herbs, which left the sick girl and the family with the illusion of some treatment. As on every such occasion she felt the same blind hatred against irreparable injuries, incurable diseases, death, the ridiculous torments that shake heart and mind, the revolting superstitions and the intolerant beliefs that destroy even the idea of any possible or accessible happiness on earth. Antonio, the fiancé, provoked those recurring, ravaging attacks of bitterness and horror. She departed well aware of having done very little for the sick girl, which was inevitable, and even less for the family—for which she reproached herself. Fernanda accompanied her to her house. Fernanda knew it all. There was no need for words. She embraced Clara before leaving her.

'Should they be prepared for it?' she murmured.

'I do not know,' said Clara.

'Antonio will accuse you. Be careful. He is crafty. Surprise would be preferable. Despair could brutalise him.'

'Does he love her so much?'

'No. Perhaps yes. But he is very proud of her. And of us. Think about it.'

'It would be better for me. But for your parents? I ought to speak to them.'

'I will do it,' said Fernanda.

Clara pushed the little door open, bolted it as was her habit, put down the medicine chest, then suddenly like the stab of a dagger she was struck by a memory: Kotor. Never before had she felt such anguish, such terror. Inexplicable. It was like waiting frozen in front of an abyss.

Chapter III

Upstream from Villafranca de Xira the Tagus stretches out into a plain furrowed by small canals, where the eye cannot distinguish between land and water. The horns of black bulls rise above the reeds. Horsemen, wearing red waistcoats and long white woollen stockings—riding boots are too expensive—pursue and marshal them together with small steel spears on the end of their ash-poles. The sails of the *fragatas*, gliding on the river or the canals, and charged with forage, vegetables and wine, do not attract their attention. The longer and more slender barques, the *saveiros*, reai river vessels, bring from Spain travellers who fear the bumpy roads, the bad springs of the coaches, or the bandits.

Dusk makes it even more difficult to find the frontier of grass and river. Navigation becomes rare, then ceases. One more sail. Then a very large yet empty ship appears. Only one man at the helm, dressed more like the lackey in a nobleman's household than a sailor. His is a real livery; on the ornate metal buttons if one looks carefully the lion of Bohemia can be distinguished. The barque slips along driven by the wind and the current past Villafranca, leaving the Ribatejo, to enter a vast stretch of water, the Sea of Straw, which is no longer the river and not yet the ocean. Night falls. One begins to see the lights of Lisbon scintillating at a distance. A strange vessel.

In the hold trunks are stacked, and under the hatchway six coffins in a row. Venus appears in the sky: the night is here.

The lid of one of the coffins, as if pushed by an invisible force, rises a little and drops slowly onto the floor boards. Almost simultaneously the other five lids open and fall in the same way. The movement is slow and continuous, like the daily habit of one who, having awoken, throws back the sheets and blankets of his bed in order to rise.

The vault of the hold, which resembled a crypt or an underground chapel like the Mithraeum, would have given a spectator, were there one, the impression of an almost religious scene.

Kotor was the first to appear on deck. Always that enormous fur collar. A giant in both height and girth. Laurent, then

Barbara, followed him. Kotor's black greatcoat reached to the floor. Brother and sister were slim and fragile, their eyes limpid and transparent, their sunken cheeks pale. The young girl's very light fair hair fell on her large, black cape. Behind them were three shapes.

The man at the helm did not even give a start, nor did he salute them. One saw only that the appearance and presence of his masters filled him with internal joy that lit up his face.

Kotor went forward to the bows of the ship. Laurent and Barbara, close to each other and joining hands, took their places behind him. The other three were slightly behind them. Kotor's almost phosphorescent eyes shone. He scrutinised with intensity the darkness that was now very opaque. The last quarter of the dying moon was reduced to a thin crescent. From the depth of the obscurity rose the throbbing lights of Lisbon.

Worried, Barbara looked at her father. Was he taking Lisbon for a haven, a refuge or a quarry? It was difficult to decide. He sensed her eyes on him, turned to her and smiled. She felt joy and relief. He could be terrible with his bouts of fury and rage, especially when contrary forces came to thwart his plans and projects. For example, the madness of leaving their castle in the Carpathians for the Jewish quarter of Prague, and again the escapades at night in Bohemia with the terrorised population that needed to be persuaded and seduced, yet which hid, scattered and ran away.

The family would have to support and restrain him. She put her tiny hand on the huge forearm. So much experience, grand dreams, titanic fights—immense generosity and immense kindness in conflict with a boundless rage. It was essential to soothe and calm him, for so much would depend on Clara and their first contact with her.

In the darkness they began to make out the quays and a pier, to which the shouts of the boatmen guided the vessel. Kotor, Laurent and Barbara moved back a little. A servant ran to the prow, and threw the rope to a man who stood like a sentry at the end of the pier. The vessel was brought alongside. The long and dangerous voyage was over.

Also enveloped in a long cloak Clara stood waiting. A heavy Berlin drawn by four black horses could be distinguished behind her. She advanced onto the pier with Ursula at her side carrying a lantern, quite unneccessary for the travellers, who, surely unable to see clearly except at night, had already left the vessel and were advancing like a flock of migrating birds, Kotor leading, the others one behind the other. Porters urged by Ursula ran to the ship. Their small lanterns disappeared from view as they jumped into the hold to fetch and bring along the pile of luggage. Kotor and Clara walked slowly towards each other. Clara could not control her persistent shudders. They were not caused by repulsion but by sheer fear.

They recognised each other instantaneously despite the weak light of the lanterns. Clara's premonitions were blown away in an instant.

'I am Count Kotor,' said Kotor. 'These are my son Laurent and my daughter Barbara.'

'I am Clara of Alfama,' said Clara.

She held out her hand. Kotor and Laurent bowed ceremoniously, neither of them touching with his lips the magician's hand; whereas Clara and Barbara half-curtseyed to each other.

Urged on by Ursula, Kotor's and Clara's servants put the luggage on top and in the back of the Berlin. There was nobody else on the quays. Policemen and customs officers never took the risk of going beyond the tacitly admitted frontiers of Alfama. The pier was neutral ground, a natural prolongation of the district.

'Count,' said Clara, 'I have a dwelling prepared for you, a small palace which does not look impressive from the outside.'

'The most modest retreat would have been sufficient for fugitives like us.'

'There is a large interior garden, courtyards and an old cloister. The monks' refectory can be used as library or laboratory, and there are stables, and a separate building for your servants.'

'They are not many, but their loyalty during the trials turned them into genuine friends to whom my heart is attached.'

There were with them two men, both giants, and a woman wearing the dress of a Carpathian peasant woman under her vast cloak. The man who had held the ship's rudder had for his three companions the sort of respect one hardly notices. One felt he belonged to a different kind. He went to look at the horses.

'Ivan,' said Kotor, 'my man of all works, groom, porter, messenger. We have strange habits. We never go out during the day. In day-time Ivan alone will be visible.'

Clara showed some surprise, but asked no question. She introduced Ursula more as her *alter ego* than her follower, and they all got into the Berlin. The servants went on foot beside the carriage, carrying lanterns. Kotor's two giants' open capes showed they were armed to the teeth. The lights of the lanterns were reflected on the grips of pistols, the hilts of daggers and the pommels of swords.

The cortège slowly advanced from the pier to the quay, then took the first very steep slopes of the alleys mounting to Alfama. The Berlin just managed to get through. The black horses, the dark carriage, the group covered in black cloaks gave shivers to the few passers-by who swiftly gave way to them. Not a murmur, not an observation. The unwritten yet respected law of Alfama was to be astonished by nothing, notice nothing, say nothing and comment on nothing.

Halfway up the hill, in the geometrical centre of the town within the town, there is a small triangular area. A gigantic palm tree, brought from Africa by some navigator lucky to return safely, had grown as if in its own country. The palm rose above the glazed façades of the houses round the precincts. At each point of the triangle a network of alleys and covered passages gave on to the mysterious streets of the district. One of the houses, the most modest of them, was actually the entrance to the secret palace. The Berlin disappeared through a gate that closed hermetically behind it, and after twenty yards or so under a vault it entered another world. A large courtyard, stables, outhouses, a few steps then a great sweeping staircase in front of an admirable Baroque façade which combined purity and delicacy with madly overladen ornamentation. Getting down from the Berlin, Kotor exclaimed loudly, and behind him Barbara cried out in admiration. Frankly, it was a miracle, a hidden pearl.

Trunks were opened, and everywhere garments were unfolded and shaken out. Kotor supervised the unpacking of paniers full of books and scientific instruments. He helped to stack them in the large room that would serve as his laboratory. The walls of the monks' refectory and of the adjacent, disused chapel had been knocked down, making one huge hall.

One had to go down a few steps to reach the lower level of the chapel which was placed at right angles. The general effect was an L-shape which permitted anyone at the bottom of the L to undertake activities that could not be seen from the refectory end. An earlier guest had already installed a laboratory-bench, a hand pump, two sinks, a laboratory hood, a system of multiple furnaces, and an oven, in brief a foundry on a reduced scale. Retorts, vast carboys full of liquids of every colour, crystals, powders, the whole arsenal of a chemist, a biologist, in short of a sorcerer.

Kotor smiled his satisfaction. Clara watched the unpacking, trying to guess from what she saw, mentally recording the exact line of her guest's researches. The settling-in ended at last. Kotor's giants and Clara's servants disappeared. Laurent and Barbara vanished to the rooms allotted to them. Left alone, Clara and Kotor stared at each other in complete silence for a long time.

'I can well see,' said Kotor at last, 'that you have a question to ask, and you are wondering whether I shall answer it . . .'

'Who are you?' asked Clara after brief reflection.

She played the game. If he wanted a question there was none as important as that one. She had found her composure again, but retained her irresistible curiosity.

'It is not my intention,' said Kotor, 'to hide the truth from you. When you have listened to me you will be entitled to get rid of us if you want to. We will continue on our wanderings. We are accustomed to it. It has lasted for two hundred and fifty years.'

He waited. Clara neither moved nor blinked. Curiously she was under the impression that it was she who was being examined in a way, and that Kotor was not afraid of being rejected, preferring that to being accepted for the wrong reasons.

She was determined to hold back all show of surprise, possible panic and her trembling.

'I was the first to die,' Kotor went on. 'That was two hundred and eighty-five years ago. I was fifty years old. Laurent and Barbara died very soon after, and we entered our second existence. For some time nobody noticed the difference, but after a few years the people around us began to be astonished. We departed. Since then we have never found true rest.'

Kotor stood up, and started pacing around the large room. Clara's eyes never left him. He admired her calm, yet feared she might lose it for the most difficult part was still to come.

'The oldest traces of our family go back as far as the reign of the Emperor Hadrian. My farthest ancestor in direct line was high priest of Mithras. It was he who conducted the emperor to the screen of the Bull, who anointed his body with the still warm blood of the Bull, and surveyed with him the construction of the great wall in Scotland. He increased the number of the shrines and the small communities of the initiated all over England, and we have gone on serving Mithras, from father to son, long after the god's death. My father was the last of the real high priests. I know that gods are born, live and die like men, but at their own rhythm. I never wanted to serve a god who was but a feeble echo of himself. I am the new John the Baptist of knowledge and faith reconciled. I do not even know whether I shall see the new era. I am in the darkness, and nothing has announced the dawn as yet. That is why we are creatures of the night.'

'I think I begin to understand better, but I won't try to hide my fear from you.'

'The terror and repulsion we inspire are centuries old. All should conspire in our favour since we bring life, another sort of life. But there are no creatures in the Universe more ill-treated, more calumniated.'

'There is some justification,' said Clara.

She got up, and went to stand in front of the large fireplace in which burned an entire tree trunk. She was frozen all over. Now she knew.

'For all, nearly all the religions,' continued Kotor, 'and for black magic of every sort the *vampires* are the spewers up of Hell. But there is no Hell. The Devil is just a disguise. The monk Luther needed him to massacre—in accordance with his worst enemy, the Bishop of Munster—the peasants in revolt.'

As if inadvertently Kotor had slipped the *Word* into one of his sentences. But the power of the *Word* was such that in spite of himself he had accentuated it, and could not help observing that Clara had imperceptibly stiffened. He continued pacing the floor.

'I have told you that we bring life, and are accused of giving death. For the first time in the history of all beliefs we incarnate the oldest dream of humanity, the oldest hope, the one which already before the far-away ages of warriors made our farthest ancestor tremble dimly beside the first fires lit by Prometheus: how to defeat death.'

'And have you defeated it?' Clara inquired.

'Not completely, not definitely. I shall die. We can die.'

'A second time?'

'The first time it is but a dark passage to a strange anti-chamber.

The second will be the real mystery. The aim of my life is to win the second battle.'

Clara took a step, and lifted from a shelf a large book, bound in cracked leather, now nearly in shreds.

'Here is the compilation of the Benedictine monk Dom Augustin Calmet. 1698. He was twenty-four years old, and it already is the opus of his life.'

'I met him years ago in Paris,' said Kotor. 'I did not dare to tell him who I was. His words are a horrible pile of ill-natured gossip and superstition. A mountain of ignorance and credulity.'

Clara turned a few pages. A book opens on the pages that have most been read. She spoke in the old tones of a scientific discussion so as to hide her confusion.

'He describes very well the methods of conjuring up and executing vampires.'

Abruptly Kotor burst into prodigiously alive, jovial laughter. The reflected light of the flames, his fur great-coat, even his corpulence, the gold necklace round his neck, the valuable rings on his fingers, gave his appearance a Barbaric truculence.

'Those tales about the crucifix and the sign of the Cross protecting one—how can you take them seriously? I am not a Christian. The Oupyrs of Poland are Hebrews by tradition. In Greece the Brucolacs are descendants like me of the followers of Mithras. The Ghouls of Moslem countries are all austere and orthodox Sunnites. Ten years ago in the heart of Africa I came across death-deniers who were the sons of Apollo of the Yorubas, the warrior god Xango, taken as slaves by your compatriots to Brazil.'

'Deniers of death,' said Clara dreamily. 'Is that what you call yourself?'

'Sometimes. Many of us do not know clearly who they are. Many cannot understand what has happened to them. They become beasts of prey, wolves. That happens to men too . . .'

'I have no respect either, for human nature as such.'

There was repeated knocking at the refectory door, and Clara reluctantly went to the other side of the large hall, while Kotor too stepped over to see what was taking place.

In a low voice Ursula was speaking to Clara. Behind her one could make out the shape of a young woman whom Clara recognised as Fernanda, a daughter of Alfama. Clara rushed back to Kotor.

'It concerns a young girl I am trying to cure. She is lost. Her sister has come to tell us that she is dying. Probably this very night. I am not as well armed against death as you.'

'One could perhaps . . .'

Clara, who had turned on her heel, stopped brusquely.

'You?'

'I do not know. What I mostly do not know is the reaction of her family. I can make her live differently—the real and only problem is whether she and her circle accept without horror that other kind of existence.'

'Come,' said Clara simply, taking Kotor's hand and leading him to the door. Ursula and Fernanda stepped back to let them through, then followed them as if driven by a violent gust of wind.

The Fonsecas, father and mother, stood close together at the head of the bed. The fiancé was telling the beads of his rosary in a corner, and did not even raise his head as the group entered. He just threw an oblique glance at Kotor, and made a swift sign of the Cross before returning to his prayers.

'She is lost,' said the mother, throwing herself into Clara's arms.

'Come with me,' said the young woman, pushing father and mother into the next room.

Kotor seemed far away; Fernanda and Ursula exchanged a few words in a low voice. Everybody held his breath. All one could hear was the death rattle of the sick girl. Long minutes went by before Clara and the two parents, who were very shaken, reappeared. The mother approached Kotor.

'Count,' she said, 'we are very frightened by Dona Clara's proposal. Nevertheless, we took the decision of doing everything possible to keep Lavinia with us. Can you promise us that her soul won't be damned? We make ourselves entirely responsible for the sin.'

'Her soul is in no danger. No sin is attached to it. Nature alone is the cause of it. I am no devil, but only a poor magician—I have access only to some simple marvels . . .'

'Count, I believe you,' said the father. 'I leave the fate of my family in your hands.'

The fiancé leapt from his chair, his face disfigured by rage, stupidity and fear.

'Sacrilege,' he shouted. 'You are risking the salvation of Lavinia's soul.'

'You prefer to see her dead, senhor?'

'Yes,' said the young man in a dull voice, 'rather dead than lost to the Holy Church.'

'Understand, my son,' said the father, approaching him.

'I am not your son,' shouted the fiancé. 'I will never be your son. I won't denounce you to the Holy Office because I loved your daughter—but you horrify me . . . you are not Christians.'

'In my Father's house are many mansions,' murmured Kotor.

'Heresy,' said the young man.

He stepped back, his eyes glittering, then taking a sudden decision he burst from the room.

'Imbecile,' said Fernanda.

'No,' said Clara. 'Unfortunate.'

'Hound of the Inquisition,' said Fernanda. 'Good riddance. If Lavinia escapes death it will be a blessing for her. He is jealous, and a hypocrite. He always peeps under my skirt on the stairs.'

'That is enough, Fernanda,' said the mother. 'Count, we entrust her to you.'

'Leave me alone with her,' said Kotor.

All of them hesitated, for the moment had come. Clara gave the signal and was the first to withdraw, hiding her panic under an assumed self-assurance.

One by one the others followed her, Fernanda last. She wanted to hold the door ajar so as to see everything. Her mother had to force her to draw away and close the door properly.

Kotor meditated. At every new initiation he felt the solemn exaltation of the priest at the moment of the sacrifice, or officiating at the threshold of the mystery, but also the excitement and rushing blood of the alchemist at the supreme moment of an experiment nearing success.

Never before had he gone to find a soul so near to the gates of death. Never before had he dared to fight his adversary at the absolute frontier of life.

He slowly bent down to Lavinia's frail neck, to the spot where the big artery throbbed almost imperceptibly. Life was still there. He acted like a priest taking the Host. His canines penetrated the fragile flesh. Blood gushed forth. He sucked it for a long while.

When he drew himself up Lavinia let out a long sigh, which was surely her last. She stopped breathing, her heart ceased beating, and hers was absolute majestic peace.

Kotor went to the door, opened it and gently called the family in. Clara and Ursula were as ones paralysed. The mother rushed to Lavinia.

'Oh my God!' she cried. 'She is dead . . .'

'No,' said Kotor, 'just in another world. She will return every evening at the very instant of the sun's setting and she will live among you throughout the night . . . In the morning she will return from whence she comes, a shadow among shadows. I am still unable to make her support the sun. I myself have not seen the light for several centuries. If she exposes herself to the light of day she will die, and it will be real death this time. The same would happen to me. But I will find the solution. You see the way I live. It will be her lot too from now on.' They were all sad at heart listening to him, unable to say a single word.

'Friends, do not let dread fill your hearts—I will tell you, your daughter will tell you, that there is another truth beside the truth you know . . . You have entered a mysterious brotherhood . . . be strong . . . we fight for life, for another sort of life, a centuries-old combat that will last for centuries more.'

The night was ending when the heavy Berlin returned from the port for a second time. Clara lifted her window curtain and looked out. She had not exchanged a word with Kotor since their journey back from Alfama. She had let him go alone to his laboratory. She saw the two giants unloading the six coffins that had been in the hold of the vessel. They must have made inquiries, for they already knew of the existence of the large cellar under the palace, and took the coffins down there. Clara trembled. It was essential for her to know. She knocked on the laboratory door, where Kotor with a chronometer near him was taking notes. A strange bronze-coloured mixture boiled in a water-caltrop.

'I will leave you very soon,' said Kotor. 'We must be in our place of rest before daybreak.'

'Just as the legends say,' said Clara.

'They cannot be altogether wrong. We are in a state of very fragile equilibrium. Daylight would reduce us to ashes without any doubt. The sun sends its rays in all directions, unknown rays that would be deadly for us.'

'Do you run any other risks?'

'I do not really believe in the stories about silver bullets,' smiled Kotor. 'But I am certain that if I were stabbed in the heart . . .'

'With a wooden spear?'

'I do not know exactly whether the wood plays a decisive part

—undoubtedly I lack experience—our hearts have remained undamaged—if they were pierced our blood and our life would flow away.'

'Do you sleep? Perhaps you dream?'

'I cannot remember any dream. My daughter believes she has had a few.'

'You bring back nothing from your daily journey to the kingdom of the dead?'

'In truth we do not ever enter death. We have access to another form of life, undoubtedly different but life even so. When we really die the journey will be without return.'

'But where have you found this new knowledge? You said a little while ago that Lavinia would reveal another truth.'

'I can give you no clear explanation. It is like that. I state a fact. I experience it every day, yet I cannot explain it. After our first new sleep a special understanding comes to us. Absolutely analogous with what your own senses give you. You see, you hear, yet can you explain to me what sight and hearing *are*? To describe to you what happens to us would be like describing images, every image, to a blind man.'

'But, in brief, do you transmit the powers you have?'

'The only thing I know is that our disciples, our accomplices, our foster-brothers, after what you call death, live again in the same shape as ourselves—like ourselves, as much as ourselves, prey to the same danger, and threatened in the same fashion with final death. I think it is a gift that is transmitted by the exchange of blood.'

'You could have preys or victims,' said Clara after a short silence, 'in lieu of disciples and accomplices.'

'Surely, but I do not want it. Some of us have done so, perhaps are still doing it. Do not look any further for the origin of the terror and the horror we inspire. I and mine seek only consent and conviction.'

'Conversion.'

'That is true. Those of my ancestors who practised the religion of Mithras, a religion of blood, left me this discipline of life.'

'Nevertheless, they died.'

'I am the first of my line to have won the first battle against death.'

'Why do you speak of the first battle and not of victory?'

'Victory,' said Kotor, 'will be brought about by my long

patience and my stubborn fight. I am still terribly vulnerable, terribly menaced. And I still deeply miss the light of day, and have deep nostalgia for the gentle heat of the sun.'

Fascinated, Clara slowly approached him. One step, then another. She threw herself into his arms.

'And the gentle heat of two arms,' she asked, 'do you still feel it?'

'Can you doubt it? We have retained every human sentiment: love, friendship, trust, the passion of knowledge. I love my children. I am devoted to shared friendship and loyalty.'

'I am your friend. Some day I shall be your disciple, or your accomplice as you put it. Right now if you want it . . .'

Audaciously, she unbuttoned the collar of her blouse, and offered her neck.

Kotor gently pressed her in his arms.

'I want you to decide on that with a cool mind, not in the heat of a privileged moment.'

She staggered. He kissed her long on her trembling lips. She returned the kiss.

'I have to leave you,' murmured Kotor. 'My place of rest would either cause you horror or give you a sense of pity.'

'No. I saw your servant at work. I accompany you. What better proof could I give?'

They went arm in arm down to the cellar. The other five vampires stetched out in their coffins had already pulled down the heavy wooden lids.

'Leave me,' said Kotor. 'You could not support it.'

'You do not know me well.'

They embraced again. Kotor climbed into his coffin, and lay down.

'Dear friend of my heart,' said Clara, 'when night comes back this evening you will find behind that statue of Hermes a large panel. It opens if you turn the hand of the god. A corridor takes you directly to my house. I will be waiting for you.'

With a firm hand Clara closed the coffin lid, and taking a few steps towards the wall she went behind the statue of Hermes standing among other gods. The panel opened, and she entered the darkness of the secret passage.

Chapter IV

The Marquis da Silva brusquely closed the heavy file. Most irritating. For the last three months reports had been piling up. A rivulet, a thin thread of information, inquiries and denunciations had little by little begun to show the outlines of a curious sect spread across Alfama, a network of complicity. It was almost impossible to find out what was really happening. Most unpleasant for a hitherto efficient chief of police. Not a single member of the sect had been captured, not one deserter. Darkness itself. Witchcraft, certainly criminal witchcraft, yet an impenetrable secret. On the lowest rung one distinguished a small group of the initiated; and on an even lower rung one guessed the presence of the accomplices. But no means were found to discover the secret leaders who ran the organisation. All that one knew came from the occasional reports through the contacts established with similar organisations such as the Freemasons and the Rosicrucians, who were patiently infiltrated by police agents. But as reciprocal mistrust between these small groups and the newcomers was very strong the police remained in complete ignorance. The same went for Ricardo's city police, the same too for the criminal class. Alarm signals were heard here and there, but that was all. His Eminence would have the last laugh—which would not suit the Marquis at all. Three months had gone by without his making any headway with Alexandra. He had thought at the end of spring that he had taken a positive step forward, yet the summer finished without any result. The Cardinal and his beautiful niece slipped through his fingers like eels. The King was mad about Dom Manuel. They played chess and hunted, and had been seen riding together with the squadron of musketeers half a mile behind them, throwing dried fish to the seagulls on the beach of Caparice, leaving at dawn, coming back at dusk, white with sea salt, damp with the foam of the ocean, a good excuse to rush to the baths.

Despite all this, Dom Manuel remained as virtuous as an anchorite. Frequent visits to His Eminence's laboratory were all he could be reproached with. He may have tried his hand at alchemy. Servants had overheard the Cardinal joking about black magic, accompanied by a gale of laughter. However, that did not take one far.

A secretary entered to tell the Marquis that the Cardinal summoned him into his presence. The world was topsy-turvy. And there was no way to right it. For obvious symmetrically opposite reasons João was in a delicious mood. Bernis had sent him from Paris the plates and volumes of the *Encyclopaedia*. He was lazily turning the pages when the Marquis arrived, and started squinting at the books.

'Strictly for private use,' said João. 'No question of letting this bomb leave the premises. A present from the French Minister of Foreign Affairs. Monsignor de Bernis pays a lot of attention to our little country.'

The Marquis nearly started. Bernis secretly supported everybody who worked against the Inquisition and the Jesuits. And French gold was worth something. Decidedly it was instigated by the Cardinal-Duke himself.

'If Monsignor de Bernis enjoys playing with fire it is his affair.'

'My dear Marquis, I did not ask you to come here to discuss the merits of the Comte de Bernis. I need you.'

The Marquis stiffened.

'His Majesty would like to try out one of your small fast boats. They are yours, are they not? Two at the tower of Belem, two at Villafranca. That is quite a lot, eh?'

'They are earmarked for the supervision of the Sea of Straw and the quays of Alfama. Your Eminence is well aware that I have no other use for them.'

'Alfama is very quiet. If it is your work, congratulations.'

'I should like it to be mine, but I have no share in it.'

'Your candour does you honour. What is going on?'

The Marquis pretended not to understand the double meaning of the sentence but to take it for a real question.

'Things are happening,' he said, 'as though a police force inside Alfama were slowly taking shape, like an alien body that is tolerated and even accepted by all and sundry.'

'And your agents?'

'As perplexed as yours, Your Eminence. And yet, generally and without wanting to criticise you, mine are more efficient. Which is normal since they *are* the real police.'

João remained like ice. To answer a provocation is to play into one's adversary's hands.

'Have you any ideas?' he asked after a brief silence.

'Four very mysterious and wealthy foreigners have established themselves in Alfama since the end of spring. Two are agents of the Sultan of Miquenez. They buy mostly orphan girls. Then a rabbi disguised as a Dominican. And a Bohemian Count. They should be looked at more closely.'

João searched among the papers scattered on his writing table. He found what he was looking for, and waved two sheets covered in cypher.

'Let us leave the rabbi, who is waiting for a cargo from Bahia. And I fear the Bohemian is also a false trail. Ladislas, fifth Count Kotor. What is so curious is that he seems unbelievably old. Or possibly the father is taken for the son. He is under the high protection of the Court of Vienna. He had trouble with the hierarchy in Prague, more to do with alchemy than politics.'

'A venal sin,' said the Marquis, smiling.

João laughed too. The hour of settling accounts had not yet chimed, and he could indulge in a joke.

'I have had him shadowed,' said the Marquis, 'but without any result. He never goes out. His family neither.'

'I am told the daughter is magnificent.'

'She has been seen in the town, now and then, buying knick-knacks from Paris. Pale, thin, and blond. She is not the type of beauty for our Latin countries. She is surely a widow, cold and distant. An iceberg in my opinion. I believe one should look elsewhere.'

The conversation was dying; the Marquis decided to leave. There was no great cordiality between them. Nevertheless, on the threshold he tried out his luck.

'Meninha your niece, would she grant me the favour of paying her a call?'

'Alexandra is in bad health these days . . . Have patience, my dear fellow. She will recover.'

'Bad health', you tell me. The Marquis was frothing with rage. She was bullfighting every day on a farm in Ribatejo, dressed as a boy, killing the bull like a Spaniard (which is strictly forbidden in Portugal). If he wanted to catch her out . . . But she was a sensible girl in matters of love. Every virile man in the Lisbon cavalry had tried his luck in vain. That was a compensation. The Marquis remained patient. Surely a virgin, incomprehensible in such a family, yet true all the same. The mother in her small German court had a symphonic orchestra entirely recruited among Apollos. And the stepfather busied himself with the singers, from sopranos to contraltos. A fine division of work. Regarding the uncle, the Marquis made three bows—the etiquette with a prime minister—and went out.

The moment the door closed João shook with unashamed laughter: then he straightened his face, and Manuel, who had been scratching on the wall behind the tapestry, opened the door and entered.

'What a trial,' he murmured, throwing himself on a seat.

'It is for a good cause,' said João, laughing. 'Do you want a glass of sherry?'

'I would prefer some of your port, the white and dry one.'

'Bravo! Will you accompany me? I am going home.'

'Certainly.'

'You will kill yourself.'

'One should not forget that the human species has two different sexes.'

They went out by the hidden staircase.

Clara emerged from the hidden passage behind the statue of Hermes, and closed the door carefully. Through the air-holes in front of every arch of the cellar one could see daylight still penetrating. The coffins seemed asleep. She went up quickly to the laboratory. There was not a soul in the long corridors. She went in. Night was on its way. After lighting the candelabra she stirred the fire in the enormous fireplace. A weak reddish glow came from the cauldrons, and there were still some embers alight under a crucible. She bustled about, for night had arrived.

Kotor appeared, and Clara threw herself at once into his arms. He led her to the cauldrons.

'We have been waiting for days,' she said, 'for the *coagula*, yet it always is a *solve*.'

'The wrong approach once more,' said Kotor. 'I must start all over again.'

'I shall have mercury and "royal water" tomorrow. We shan't be able to do anything tonight. I have not seen my patients for a week. I will profit by it, Ladislas, I have had a harpsichord brought in. You won't be able to work in any case. I received a book of sonatas from Italy. Would you care to hear them?'

Kotor sat down in a deep armchair. He felt strange anxiety, a vague, obscure and diffuse premonition. While Clara played Scarlatti he lost himself in a long reverie, and did not even notice when she stopped. She came and sat at his feet.

'I too am worried,' she said. 'I am certain that the Marquis' police are watching me. But you know that.'

'They cannot do us any harm. I am a stranger, so it is understandable that they should watch me. Anyhow, I do not see anybody.'

'Perhaps that is the cause of the danger. It must seem unnatural for a man of your rank.'

'I have received from Vienna a letter of introduction to the Cardinal. That was a fortnight ago.'

'It would be madness not to send it to him.'

'You know,' said Kotor, 'that daytime is forbidden me. Besides, the letter is a strictly private one.'

'In that case invite the Cardinal-Duke to come here incognito.'

'Under what pretext?'

'You could organise a night reception for the twenty people who matter in Lisbon, the polite gesture of a newly-arrived nobleman. A bit late but not too late. It will be taken for extravagance and exotic originality. There is nothing better.'

'You think so? I have a feeling of danger, or a hidden peril.'

'Precisely why that is the best way to react. You present your family to the grandest families of the town. Very simple.'

Kotor was only half-convinced. If one leads a hidden life, every careless move can help those who are in pursuit. Prudence. Withdrawal.

'I am also very worried,' Kotor said, 'about the big rise in the number of our disciples.'

'For a long time you deplored the halo of fear which accompanied even the mention of your name. For the first time you have met a group of people who love, admire and protect you. Since the reappearance of Lavinia, since her entry into a second existence as you put it, it is not infrequent to find other vampires in the bosom of their family.'

In fact, in ten homes, and that was precisely the cause of Kotor's fears. He felt, without being able to say anything, that the situation was running away from him. The lifting of the age-old malediction was a wonderful thing, even if raising the vampires' number was not the final aim, and it did tend to multiply the risks. Clara's zeal, and the zeal of some of the new disciples, were the inevitable price of his success. All religions, Kotor said to himself, must have known such a moment. The creation of a church and a clergy had been the answer to the problem of a small number becoming a large one. Nevertheless, he did not see himself as the head of a church creating bishops. It was becoming necessary to put a brake on that development and extension. But it was too early, the work was not yet accomplished. We are not a sect, I am not a Messiah, but only a stage on the road leading to another kind of man who will be immortal and the master of his destiny. Rather the successor of man in a sense. I must make Clara see that she has to moderate her zeal. The energy women have. A secret tradition, Semiramis, Messalina, Joan of Arc. Will-power, the shape of her chin, the beauty of her perhaps already too heavy breasts, her ripeness which I like most in a woman, the time of decision and boldness in carrying out the decision. He got up, touched and caressed her. Some day we shall live in the sunlight again.

In a sense Fernanda envied Lavinia. She was her sister-accomplice in that she was aware that some day she too would lead that nocturnal life. She questioned Lavinia unceasingly, and was exasperated by the little she gathered. To be able to touch with her finger the secret of the mystery, while not understanding that there *was* a secret and mystery . . . Lavinia found her new condition completely normal. And in a fashion she *was* normal. The family, and a small circle of friends, once surprise and marvelling had been overcome, settled down to the new rhythm of life, without asking themselves any questions. Lavinia's reappearance at every nightfall, her departure at each dawn, and the coffin in the cellar had simply become another rule of conduct, Fernanda the only one to appreciate that it was a kind of miracle. Kotor intimidated her too much. He could have answered or tried to answer her questions better than that simpleton Lavinia who spent the nights with her embroidery, and then went down to the cellar to draw wine for her father, finding it natural to have her coffin next to the wine barrel on the cellar floor. The people in the district and the neighbours did not seem to have noticed anything. The law of Alfama was the law of silence. Everybody minded his own business, nobody poked his nose into other people's affairs. Ever since her childhood Fernanda was, for example, aware of the next-door neighbour earning his living by stealing the money in the collection boxes of the churches in the centre of the town, and that her father printed rather curious books. The engravings dried in the attic, and the little girls giggled their heads off trying to imitate the contortions represented by somewhat naïve engravers. Some day she would have to speak to the Count.

Clara arrived at the house. Day was breaking, and Lavinia had already vanished to the cellar. The parents had gone upstairs to lie down. Thus Fernanda was alone.

'I want to ask you a favour,' Clara said.

'Anything you want,' said Fernanda.

Clara showed her a fat pile of letters which she threw on the table, large envelopes with red seals bearing the coat of arms—a winged dragon—of the House of Kotor. Clara explained that all should be delivered during the course of the day.

'Do you know anyone to help you?'

'Gianvittorio, the son of our neighbour,' said Fernanda.

'The Italian? The King of the pickpockets?'

'The son is marvellous. He is a musician, plays the violin, and is a composer.'

'And you love music,' said Clara, smiling. 'Is it not unwise? Is he one of us?'

'He will be on the day I want it,' answered Fernanda, sure of herself for reasons she knew.

Through the association of ideas Clara suddenly remembered Lavinia's fiancé. What had become of him?

'I always took him for an imbecile,' said Fernanda. 'He is in the service of monks somewhere near Sesimbra. I do not know exactly where the monastery is. No one sees him any more. I hope I shan't ever see him again.'

'As a matter of fact, do you know all our friends?'

'Nearly all of them.'

'You will help me in something else too. The Count wants all of them warned to be careful, to hide themselves, and not talk too much to their neighbours.'

'We have all noticed the policemen. Everybody understands, nobody will breathe a word. Neither those in the know nor the others. There is a synagogue in the rua do Bicho. Father has told me that it has existed for more than a hundred years. Upon my soul, the Marquis knows nothing about it. It is the same with us. I know everything. You too, I believe, Dona Clara.'

Clara scrutinised Fernanda. A scarcely visible, fresh scar showed beneath the light lace scarf. Fernanda understood what she was looking at. She glanced at Clara's neck: the same scar. Clara embraced her.

'For a long time, you know,' said Fernanda, 'I have wanted to ask you . . .'

'Yes.'

'If I could help you. Dona Ursula has too much to do. I could classify the plants. I am acquainted with them.'

'I have said yes, no need for you to insist.'

After quickly reading through the invitation João played with the envelope. Though he had broken the seal a little fast, one could still see the coat of arms. He rose and took from a shelf a thick volume of heraldry. He swiftly found what he was looking for. The coat of arms was absolutely authentic, a princely house, almost royal. Nevertheless, the name of Kotor reminded him of something else, and a little irritated he searched for it in his memory, which had been a magnificent tool, but nowadays let him down more and more frequently. Yet fifty-five years was not such a great age. If I start to watch myself, and take precautions, I am lost. At the same time it is an easy excuse for surrender. He sighed. Thirty years ago I wanted to make war, twenty years ago I wanted to write books, five years ago to change this country, to change man himself. He lifted a letter off the table. What did Bernis write to him? 'I am the minister of Limbo.' A good definition of his own role, yet he had to carry on. He knew that in a month, in a year the fragile balance of his power would break. The King's death, a wrong step would make the Marquis the victor. In any case time was meanly measured. The heir to the throne was in the hands of the Jesuits. If he survived his father the Marquis would throw him into the arms of the Holy Office. What then? Continue to preserve that tiny island of reason, so fragile, so menaced? What else? Bernis too was on a dangerous slope.

He was searching for an escape hatch through which to disappear. It was enough to read his allusions to the biretta. Gondi also received the scarlet hat. And then? In any case Bernis would make an excellent cardinal. He should think of writing to the Pope who would not last much longer either. At his death the assembly would be amusing. It would be his first, and João adored Rome.

Eussa looked in, mischievous, full of curiosity, like a spring. No, he was not working. She made herself comfortable. Never in her short life had she worn a chemise before. He burst into laughter. Worried, the little girl jumped to the floor. They wanted to dress her up like a lady. She clapped her hands, for the garter and the stocking madly amused her. The corset suffocated her. A real doll. João lifted the heavy brocade dress. She let him do so, delighted by the novelty. She was compact and hard like ebony, and would remain so all her life. Oh, the off-white obesity of fat duchesses! Suddenly he stopped, and ran to the bookcase. Memory was an engine that functioned all alone and without control at the back of the head. He found it at once, a long work on geomancy, but not the one he normally used.

'Geomancy has the same relations with the science of astrology as algebra with geometry, which explains why the Arab seers were its trustees for centuries. Master Roger Bacon succeeded in opening those obscure doors that had for so long been kept obstinately closed after the Chaldean sages.'

Not bad. Printed in Prague in 1650, *Brief Observations on the Ancient Traditions of the Sages of Geomancy*, written by Count Kotor. Only five hundred pages! Oh well. I wonder whether it is his father or grandfather. Anyhow, I am going. It will be amusing to talk to him. Surprised, Eussa watched him hurrying to the bookcase. She was not certain whether to readjust her dress. She was a little shy. Gay and reassured because the engine was still functioning, João returned to her, and told her what to do. Purring like a kitten she immediately took the posture he wanted.

Chapter V

Extra servants were hired, athletes who could be recognised as belonging to the best teams of *furtados* of the bullring. Lined up in two rows they held torches made of pine soaked in a tub filled with resin. These crackled and smoked, giving an exquisite smell. The servants were dressed in gorgeous liveries, and from the corner of their eyes the guests tried to make out the coat of arms on the brass buttons: a winged dragon.

Standing in the doorway, Kotor seemed to come straight out of a portrait by Holbein or Dürer. His vast fur coat, and the heavy gold chain hanging to his chest, were from an earlier century. He looked like one of the Magi. The large interior court, full of orange trees in boxes decorated with tiny multi-coloured lanterns, was filled with guests. On two large tables stood a fantastic array of extravagant dishes and drinks: caviare from the Volga, Scandinavian smoked eels next to exotic fruits from Brazil and the West Indies. An orchestra was installed on a balcony. Two sumptuous waiting rooms were lit by immense candelabra, and beyond them were drawing rooms for those in need of sentimental or worldly or private conversation. The luxury and taste of their host dazzled the guests, and the Count rose in their esteem far above the petty tittle-tattle of the little kingdom.

As it was known that the Cardinal-Duke had agreed to come incognito, and that the Marquis immediately followed suit, nobody refused the invitation even though it had been sent out by complete strangers. There was talk of an Italian entertainment, and indeed a small stage was set up in the of corner the court, the performance awaiting the Cardinal's arrival.

João arrived with the beautiful Alexandra on his arm. Kotor went up, gave his name, bowed, and spoke of the honour they paid him by their presence. At once the two men took to each other, feeling strong mutual sympathy. Kotor introduced Laurent to them. Entirely dressed in black silk, barely accentuated by gold braid, his pallor was so conspicuous that all eyes were on him, as if moon-beams surrounded him. Alexandra's eyes never left him. A Nordic prince of the night, in short the dream of her childhood. She had to turn away for a moment to hide her feelings. As pale as her brother, haloed with the aureole of flaxen, unpowdered hair, Barbara approached, dressed in white. João was bowled over, Alexandra was fascinated. When she rose after curtseying she saw that Laurent had disappeared. Perhaps he was frightened. On the small stage Captain Swashbuckler appeared, hailed with general laughter, and many were amused by the coincidence of the Marquis making his entry almost simultaneously. He should have been interested in the Kotors, but he had eyes only for Alexandra. Meeting her after many days of trying in vain to see her made him lose his composure. While the entertainment lasted, he pursued her from one group to the other. When the play was over the audience broke up. A collation was brought, and the orchestra began playing again. Exasperated by the Marquis' constant attentions, Alexandra took advantage of the ensuing confusion, hurried through the waiting room, pushed open a door purely by accident and found herself in a small drawing room, Barbara's usual retreat. It was a quiet, simple room made for relaxation and containing a guitar, a harpsichord, books, collections of prints and engravings, comfortable sofas, a chaise-longue, veiled lights and a fire to fight the already noticeable chill of the night. She made herself at home, coolly drew the bolt, and felt safe at last.

When the entertainment was over, Kotor left the party to run its own course, and took João to his laboratory. A tapestry had been hung to hide the lower part of the huge L-shaped room, so that it could be taken just for a library. The two men seated themselves.

Barbara joined them almost at once, and had liqueurs and cakes brought in. The conversation revolved around literature at first. From Italian comedy and improvisation they moved to a more general discussion of the theatre and the role of tragedy. They quoted from Sophocles, then Shakespeare, who was still little known outside England. They were pleased with each other. They knew and loved the same books, the same scores. João's free and easy manner and swiftness of brain enchanted Kotor. Kotor's hazy background filled with tragedy, mystery and universal culture fascinated João.

All would have stopped there had Barbara not seated herself in a tenderly familiar fashion on the arm of her father's chair. João was one of those men who the presence of a pretty and attractive young woman, as a third party to a conversation, spurs on to shine without any reserve or limits with brilliant paradoxes and rapidity of ideas. Having acquired the art of seduction from long experience João had built up his own techniques to amuse, excite and then confound the listener's mind by undermining the foundations of all reasoning and moral sense, thus appealing to the unformulated desire for freedom, that is to say sacrilege.

As the lover of young and docile girls, he not only taught them the practice of postures chosen by him, but also the quest for their own pleasure. He enjoyed breaking down the barriers put up by prudery, prejudice and obscure taboos. Many of his young mistresses subsequently made great careers in the art of love. But he also loved mature and energetic female partners who knew how to pass from passivity to action. Nothing gave him more pleasure than the, alas too rare, results of the blending of these two types.

Perched on the arm of her father's chair Barbara could not help revealing her delightfully slim ankle from under the slightly raised white silk skirt, betraying with anatomical precision the shape of the leg, the narrowness of the knee, and the elegance of a long thigh. He lost all self-control, and was ready to give himself with frankness and sincerity, even with the warmth he would never have given his intimate friends—if he had any. With Kotor and the young woman, whom he saw for the first time, and against whom more or less explicit secret reports had warned him, he reached a familiarity that would have been surprising even had he known them all his life.

Kotor and Barbara, reserved at the start, slowly succumbed to João's charm. Quite unconsciously, they were flattered by the confidence amounting to a confession that emerged from the Prime Minister's conversation. Amused, Barbara had watched the red-faced corpulent man with protruding blue eyes, his skin riddled with the marks of abuse, going out of his way to please her. Everything about him indicated the man living only for his pleasure. From the lace cravat held together by a Roman cameo, the head of Caligua, burst a neck as large as a bull's. All the signs of a taste for vice were there. He was surely born under Scorpio. She had seen the way he had looked at her ankle. He undoubtedly longed to take possession of her with brutal rapidity. Never would he stroll in the labyrinth that preceded her pleasure. *Gradus ad Parnassum*. She remembered with hidden laughter her music teacher, a genius for labyrinths, who was the first to teach her that strange solfeggio. João, who was speaking about astronomy, wondered what caused her sudden and upsetting mirth, promising himself to find out the reason once he was better acquainted with those graceful shoulders.

'I should like you to taste,' said João, 'an exotic liqueur which comes from my Brazilian plantations. I have some in my carriage. Allow me.' He rose, and crossing the courtyard he sent for a stone demijohn which he took back, closing the door carefully behind him. He filled three glasses.

'Eau-de-vie of sugar cane,' he said, 'and the essence of a little medicinal fruit, the *maracuja*. Drink it. It will make the blood throb faster in your veins and bring an enveloping heat.'

Kotor and Barbara emptied their glasses more from politeness than enjoyment while João, without bothering too much about politeness, felt his verve increase.

'The history of religions,' he said, 'is an endless nightmare.'

'Your Eminence could merely say history,' said Barbara, smiling.

'My Eminence feels safe with you. My dear Count, it is unnecessary to emphasise that for me to speak of those things and for you just to listen to them makes us perfectly worthy of the stake.'

'I think I am beginning to know you, Your Eminence,' said Kotor cautiously.

'A pack of heresies co-exist with the same aggressive intolerance, the same belief in rigid certainty.'

'Calvin had Michel Servet burned,' said Kotor.

'Do not be mistaken. I am in my fashion a good Catholic,' said João.

'So I was not mistaken,' said Barbara. 'You must adore the facilities of confession. "How many times, my son?" could be the answer to everything.'

'It is for me,' said João. 'Nevertheless, I am always surprised by the fantastic and permanent construction of paper cathedrals. Arius fights a lifelong battle, just misses rocking the world, battles tooth and nail against the consubstantiation of the Father and the Son. Stakes throw up their flames, the blood of the victims runs for two doubtful lines, probably tampered with by some ignorant and imbecile clerks.'

'Kings, princes and dukes have fairly similar habits,' said Kotor.

'One can see quite clearly what they want,' said João, throwing all caution to the wind.

'And what they expect from their priests,' said Barbara.

'Most certainly,' said João. 'The divine approbation of the upholding of the established order.'

'It seems to me, Your Eminence . . .' began Kotor, who wanted to call a halt to the dangerous self-revelation.

'Call me João.'

'Duke, I like you,' said Barbara.

'I am doing what I can,' said João, uncertain whether to put his arm round her waist, and at the same time furious with himself for not daring to. He stood up, his attention caught by a chart of the firmament on a bookshelf, a simple one, illustrated with the signs of the Zodiac and the constellations.

'*Terrae incognitae*,' he said. 'When one thinks of the image of the universe they once had, those men and civilisations of yore, whom we consider even today to have been leading lights of mankind, well, I feel quite dizzy.'

'Plato certainly was ignorant of the circulation of blood,' said Kotor. 'But does that diminish the importance of his ideas?'

'For me yes,' said João. 'I do not trust the moral and metaphysical theories of men whose knowledge was so fragmentary. They interest me as a historian for their place in the evolution of thought. But I do not see them as teachers.'

'An interesting outlook on Genesis,' said Barbara.

'I won't contradict you. In private, of course. As Prince of the Catholic, Apostolic and Roman Church, I defend the literal truth of the Scriptures.'

The three of them laughed. João was electrified.

There is something in the solitude of a public figure, he thought. I have protégés, temporary allies, mortal enemies, pleasing weaknesses, yet I have nobody, not even Alexandra, to whom I could put one of my thousand questions. How can I explain this confidence, this surrender to people I do not even know? It is true that I could be more dangerous to them than they to me. I can be the attacker, they only the attacked, an easy position in a discussion. They are surely on their guard, like me with Manuel. Never mind; I am going on.

'I often ask myself whether man, as we know him and as he is, is not but a stage on the road to something different.'

'A different man?' Kotor asked.

'Not exactly. Imagine an inhabitant of the moon visiting us: he would need a fabulous imagination, the intuition of a genius to understand that the larva, the caterpillar and the butterfly are the same insect but at three different stages of its life. And if we, without knowing it, were the caterpillars of a future butterfly?'

Kotor was shaken. Take care, for this is a man of power who jokes among friends, but the shadow of the prison is never far. He must watch his step. A provocation, whether malicious or unconscious, was always possible. I can see he wants to meet me halfway, but I must know the reason first.

João looked at Barbara. He must concentrate on her. For many months he had not had a similar sensation. He approached her as if by accident. I do not know how to court a girl any more. The habit of getting what you want is the worst one of all. The thought of the effort he would need to make excited him profoundly, as did the ironic light in Barbara's eyes, as though she could see his private reflections. He thought at once of all he would love to do with her. And would do with her.

After the building at the edge of the royal courtyard came a warren of corridors, a labyrinth in which Alexandra lost her way. I wonder if there is a Minotaur inside it. Virgin at the age of twenty, daughter of the brightest queen in Europe and niece of the patron saint of libertines, it is high time to take a decision. Perhaps I am frigid. That is not true: bathing with Kristel in the young, ice-cold Danube, then drying ourselves in the sun of the Black Forest, frightening each other with stories about the little dwarfs who haunt the undergrowth, and then madly kissing each other. My Germany . . . Afterwards all Kristel's little girl friends followed. However, technically I am still a virgin, good enough for the Minotaur.

She shivered. Really and truly she had lost her way. After taking her bearings from a fountain with hunting scenes in glazed tiles she noticed a groove between the tiles, and guessed there must be a secret passage, which she certainly would not have noticed if she had not been attracted by the beauty of the horses on the tiles. Looking more carefully she made out a small hidden door. Her curiosity aroused, Alexandra attentively inspected each drawing, looking for the concealed spring. Under the principal scene which made a complete picture was a geometrical frieze, then some panels, each representing scenes from Portuguese bull-fighting on horseback. Suddenly the solution burst upon her: the button of the spring must be the rosette on the bull's forehead. She pressed it without the slightest hesitation. The whole panel turned and a passage appeared, giving on to a garden brilliantly lit by the moon. Enchanted, Alexandra advanced towards it.

A courtyard, a French garden, trimmed yew trees lined up like sentries. But there was no fourth wall to the inner courtyard, only a secret terrace looking out over the Tagus, with covered roofs like a staircase as far down as the river. It was like an immense window, invisible from the outside except maybe from the hinged skylights of a distant house.

The moonbeams lit up the Sea of Straw, stressing the geometrical precision of the sweep of the river. A distant dark mass was the Mountain of Arrabida. The bottom of the garden seemed somewhat complicated. One could make out an avenue of black fir trees, which filled Alexandra with sentimental longing.

Suddenly she jumped: a fir tree—or was it a yew tree?—began to move, and advanced in her direction. She nearly shouted, wanting to escape. The tree continued approaching, but when it was twenty feet from her she recognised Laurent wearing a long black cloak that reached to the ground. Of the same height as a fir tree, he must have remained perfectly motionless while she had made her entrance, and the light from behind did the rest. In a second she went from fear and panic to absolute happiness. A wave of burning, almost insupportable heat ran through her. I like him, she said to herself. This is the first time I have liked a young man so much.

When he had seen her entering the garden, the moonbeams playing on her golden hair, Laurent had remained still. The memory of the looks she had given him before, and which had made him rush from her presence, now made him walk towards her. As always, his features were drawn. Before his death he had already been unfriendly to girls. Since then . . .

Curiously enough it all began well. Alexandra's favourite place was not Bohemia but the Black Forest, a good beginning for their talk. They discovered they were mutual admirers of the musicians of Mannheim, they spoke of obscure violinists, discussed the advantages and the novelty of the pianoforte. In a few seconds Alexandra guessed that there was a strange, shadowy side to Laurent. He wanted, he should have liked, to speak to her open-heartedly, but something held him back. If he preferred boys he would have shown it. I would have felt it. He surely understands that such considerations do not put me off. It is more complicated. Were he a Jew it would take him another three minutes to tell me.

Yet he cannot often meet girls like me. Remain modest or you will frighten him away. It is like riding a horse for the first time. I must accustom him to it.

While they strolled under the firs Alexandra, for whom time had ceased to exist, took his arm just to see his reaction. He trembled like a leaf. I am far stronger than he. I am moved by him and am mad about him. If he feels it or if he doubts it why must he go on talking about popular poetry?

As though a curtain were being pulled a little daylight began to appear. Laurent stiffened, then suddenly took his distance.

'You will excuse me,' he said, 'but I must withdraw. Duty calls. Believe me, if you want to, I have never been so happy in my life.'

Astounded she saw him penetrate a wall, as if swallowed up by the stones. She could not get over her simultaneous victory and defeat. Deep in thought she retraced her steps.

João felt truly drunk. I could, whenever I want to, write a methodic essay on the influence of drink on the soul, the spirit and the body. Classify the drunks in groups and smaller groups like Buffon, that young botanist, whom I met in Paris. All science begins with an effort at classification, but temporary changes should be added. When I am in a good mood drink ennobles me because I am sociably drunk. Acceleration of glibness of tongue, lightness of the spirit and of words, a sense for nuances, though illusory perhaps. Am I drunk or brilliant? When I am sad drink adds to my sadness. With two glassfuls I am dead, a sot, mournful and silent. However, when I am hunting I can drink gallons. For now I hunt. Take her aside, suggest the house in Cascais since it is empty. I must be careful, circumspect and discreet at the start.

Barbara was the first to see the weak rays that precede dawn. Not dangerous; there was half an hour at least. With a quick glance she indicated to her father the window and the light beyond it. Kotor rose, regretting the interruption of a conversation that amused him, impregnated with Latin wit, superficial charm and jests. He was also amused by the fact that his partner in the conversation was the Prime Minister himself. But no illusion could be attached to that. João, Cardinal-Duke of Queluz, former Vice-Roy of Brazil, would never jeopardise his comfort and interest by defending a protégé or a friend, however dear a friend he was. A strong, critical, irreverent mind, sacrilegious too in private, that would make common cause in public with the throne and the altar. If I were King, to ensure my security I would choose ministers of this kind who act and mime intelligence, benevolence and tolerance, and could make me accepted and justify the very foundations of my throne. Moreover, I should have a police force. That reminds me, I ought to interest myself in the head of police. I saw him at the beginning, perhaps he is still here. It is urgent to get everybody to leave.

The guests, who had appreciated the quality of the entertainment, the collations and the sumptuous hospitality, did not understand why they were hurried off the premises. It seemed to them that their host, obeying a sudden whim, had but one desire, namely to get rid of them. At the front door there was great confusion with the carriages. Owing to the sudden end of the party, the guests left in high dudgeon, blaming Germanic rudeness and the heavy-handedness of the people from the North. The Marquis, after Alexandra had disappeared, fretted the whole night, furious with João for having monopolised their host. On top of it he detested Italian music, and when the entertainment was over he was practically assaulted by the audience, he who never received anybody. One more reason for his awful mood.

As if from nowhere Alexandra suddenly appeared. She was looking for her uncle, and sent the Marquis packing without the slightest compunction. While Kotor was dismissing his guests with the same mechanical movement, João could not tear himself away from Barbara. Although aware of her haste he saw he was not the cause of it, and taking advantage of this offered her his house in Cascais. Barbara promised to visit it some time. João swore that she would be awaited permanently, and he would appear only when formally invited by her. The light was getting strong, the hosts disappeared, and the last guests were literally thrown out by the two giants. The front door closed. In the square some small groups remained, shortly to be swallowed up in the alleys of Alfama.

In his carriage João was relaxed. Alexandra immediately understood the reason.

'You, my uncle, are planning some adventure, thinking that you won't find such a good occasion for a clandestine escapade in a long time. Go on. I will busy myself with getting rid of the Marquis who is watching us from under that porch over there, down below to the right.'

João embraced her.

Alexandra pushed her head through the carriage door, and signalled to the coachman, who was ready to start, to wait. A saddle horse, ridden by a young groom, was standing by the two leading carriage horses. It was her mare.

'Lucas,' called Alexandra, 'bring me Penelope. I will ride her home.'

The groom turned the mare round, and as it recognised Alexandra it danced with joy. With a rustle of skirts, Alexandra flung herself from carriage into saddle. The mare trembled with pleasure. The wonderful legs revealed by the lifted skirt made the Marquis lose his reason. He called one of his policemen.

'A horse, Antonio!' he shouted. 'A horse!'

Forcing Penelope to turn in small circles, maliciously Alexandra let the pleasure last.

When she saw the Marquis being painfully hoisted onto a police horse they had brought for him, she gave Penelope the reins. The mare had wings. The Marquis dashed after her, and the servants had a good laugh.

Alexandra let him catch up with her, then she flew away like a bullet. The unfortunate Marquis, haggard and sweating on his police horse, was living in a nightmare, his hatred of riding an added injury. At last Alexandra was past the aqueduct, and charging along the road to Cintra. After a turning she jumped a stream, and plunged into a copse. When the Marquis arrived some seconds later he wanted to do the same, but his horse refused. The Marquis was thrown over his head and ended up in the stream. He heard Alexandra laugh.

'When I catch you,' he murmured, 'there will be prison, chains, whips, padlocks, hot irons, an iron collar and cages.'

Alexandra exulted, her face swished by small branches pushed aside by Penelope's speed.

Like everybody else João had seen the start of the chase. He knocked on the window, the carriage moved, but at the first corner he opened the door and jumped from the moving carriage. Ten seconds later he was in the first alley to be found, and began to run. Though he knew only vaguely where he was, he knew exactly where he wanted to go. It was years since he had been to Lucinha. According to latest reports she continued to receive little girls from Macao, thin, lithe and slim like tropical creepers, without counting the poppy seed one could find there. He increased his speed. It was daylight now. His thoughts were of a pyramid of shaven private parts and tight openings.

In the cellar of the palace complete silence enveloped the lined-up coffins. After a general tour of inspection Clara appeared on the threshold. From the pantry she had run the whole show. Now that the extra helpers had been sent off, and the large reception rooms handed over to the cleaners, she had come to see that all was well with the Kotors. Yes, they had left for the frontier between two different worlds.

Chapter VI

Alexandra could not bear to sleep with closed windows. This pleased many a footman, and moved more than one chambermaid, for she slept naked with no blanket, her arms and legs wide open. The sun entered the bedroom, moved along the bed, turning it into a sundial, and shone a yellow light on the sleeping girl's belly. She had not yet opened her eyes. Her expert fingers slid into the pleasant warmth, a habit she had taken to when still a small child. She would have hated to start a new day without giving herself a pleasure that was a slow, skilful ritual with carefully studied details. How it amused her when she was asked whether she had said her morning prayers! Then she took her decision, and jumped out of bed. It must not be deferred. If I wait until I hear from him I shall have to wait for a long time. It is said that men detest women who take the initiative. But if I do not take it nobody else will.

'Saddle Penelope,' she called to a groom through the window.

She threw a morning wrapper over her shoulders, but then took her time in getting dressed: grey riding dress, grey buckskin boots. She chased down the stairs, Penelope pranced, and they flew off together. The people of the neighbourhood knew them both, and prudently got out of their way. It was more complicated once they reached the town. A sedan chair lurched across the road. A merchant got out, his wig askew, and ready to swear. Alexandra was already far away, yet he still could not believe his eyes. On reaching Alfama, she slowed Penelope down. Faces appeared in windows to have a look at them. Alexandra craned her neck, trying to see into the more famous brothels. Respectable elderly men swiftly hid behind doorways so that she could not see them. She laughed silently as she recognised the Count of Araujo, respected grandfather, and the Viscount of Piraja, severe patriarch. At last she reached Kotor's mansion, and knocked on the door. Silence. Her impatient banging was echoed by the empty vaults.

She dismounted, tied Penelope to a post, and simply pushed the door open. The courtyard was empty, not a soul was about.

Everything had been cleaned and washed down, without a trace of last night's confusion.

A horse pawed the ground. Alexandra went straight to the stable. A stable boy was grooming one of the four black carriage horses, a spendid mare. Alexandra expertly approached her, and patted her neck. Friendship between me and horses is instantaneous, the same with dogs. A superb turn-out, one of the finest in Lisbon. One rarely sees such diabolically black horses. I say, what makes me think of Hell and old Faustus? The devil as a black dog, or something like that. The stable boy took off his cap.

'Where is the Count?' Alexandra asked.

'Meninha, the masters are never here during the day.'

'Where are they?'

'I do not know, Meninha.'

'Who are you?'

'Thirty years in the Count's employment.'

'And you do not know where he is?'

'Alas, I do not, Meninha.'

Alexandra turned on her heel, trying to hide her disappointment. She walked about filled with curiosity, watched surreptitiously by the stable boy. He made a sudden movement when she approached the cellar door, but she only gave it a brief glance. Silent tombs and antique statues. Bizarre, as if the mansion were abandoned. She shivered. A climate for legends. Yet I am not too impressed by fairy tales. Princes turned into toads mean very little to me. In the meantime the prince has vanished. Little Alexandra is defeated, a good lesson in not taking the first step.

She returned home dreamily. Her uncle was getting ready to go to Cascais.

For once he was very avuncular. Where are we going if my breasts do not attract him any more. He had the gay look of a schoolboy in luck, his smile somewhat malicious.

'Where have you been?'

'My dear Uncle, this is a question I am not accustomed to answering. Surveillance? Jealousy?'

'Not at all, my silly one. I put the question because I know the answer already. Otherwise I would not have permitted myself to put it.'

'I failed. I hope Venus will be more favourable to you.'

'What do you mean by failed?' asked João. 'Does that imbecile dare to scorn you?'

'It is not that. Simply their mansion is the castle of Sleeping Beauty. Not a living soul. Surely they have not left?'

'Certainly not. I should have known at once.'

'It is convenient to be in with the police.'

'I am not *in* with the police. I have my own police which is not the same thing.'

'Yours is a disgusting profession.'

'If it was not me someone else would do it in my place, and in a dirtier manner, believe me.'

'A weak excuse, the same as every executioner's.'

'Enough. I will get angry.'

'I know only too well,' Alexandra said, 'that you will never speak seriously to me.'

'You are mad.'

'No. I should like to frighten you. And I hardly appeal to you.'

'There you are mistaken.'

He wanted to touch her as was his habit, and his hand received a whiplash.

'Oh! Oh! Upon my word you do love him.'

'Maybe. In any case you will never have me. Too late.'

'How angry you are!'

Alexandra's anger suddenly evaporated. She embraced him tenderly, and he left laughing. She rushed to throw herself on her bed, to daydream. A little maidservant pushed her head in with a questioning look and ready for her. Alexandra threw a slipper at her. She disappeared: Alexandra whistled: she came back.

'Help me to undress,' said Alexandra.

The little girl knew the ritual. She started to unlace Meninha, to unhook the garters. She did it expertly. Alexandra threw herself on her back, and with both hands grabbed the little neck to guide it. Her pleasure came unbelievably quickly. Alexandra fell asleep almost at once.

João reached Cascais shortly before dusk. He had had the little house built in imitation of the *casino* he had rented in Venice, and which he had dearly loved. When he left he made it over to a funny young chap called Giacomo Casanova who pretended to have just arrived back from Constantinople, and told breathtaking stories about the seraglios. João made fun of him, finding him conceited and a chatterbox, but exceptionally well-disposed and healthy. João had his own ideas about harems and Islam. Puritan, sectarian and scornful, they did their little business in three minutes, evidently ten times a day, but in silence without bothering about the unfortunate creature under them, always in the same posture, convenient for going from one orifice to the other. In their case one could hardly see why they needed one hundred and fifty posteriors at their beck and call. It would have been sufficient to use the same one a hundred and fifty times.

Casanova did not appreciate that description of Moslem joys—so different from his own tales. João had a good laugh: he had spent several months in Algiers and Tunis, spoke Arabic, wrote like a *hadji* and had been entrusted by the Knights of Malta with negotiating the ransoms for Christian slaves. The confidences of the little marchesine captured in the Gulf of Genoa made one die with laughter: a penis like a donkey's in permanent erection, but incapable of pleasuring the partner. In short, defeated Casanova was forced to laugh with him. And João celebrated the reconciliation in a fitting manner: three young sisters, one of them a certified virgin whom they played for at faro. Casanova cheated to win her, João cheated to lose because he loathed virgins which was the reason why he held himself back with Alexandra. Anyhow, the *casino* was ravishing. An octagonal drawing room, the walls covered with mirrors decorated with figures from Jules Romain for the sonnets of Aretino. He had had it all reproduced in one of the main buildings. The octagonal room was flanked outside by eight small porches. An eye unaccustomed to architecture would not have believed that there was a room inside. Two colonnades led to two symmetrical pavilions, one for the host, the other for the hostess. The bottom of the park sheltered the cells of the novices and the rooms of the two severe guardians who maintained order.

It had been emptied when João learned that the Marquis knew about his retreat. João had transformed one of the pavilions for Barbara's use, and replaced the guardians with maidservants, two daughters of Sesimbra fishermen, both muscular and devoted. One of them came to meet him.

'Has the lady arrived?' he asked.

'No,' said the girl, 'but Your Eminence should be reassured. She has sent an enormous amount of luggage. Suitcases and a chest larger than a coffin. She sent word through the messenger, asking that all of it be put into the cellar, or into a dark room if there was not one.'

'And then?'

'Your Eminence is aware that there is a cellar under the pavilion.'

'So you know about it?'

The girl blushed. She had probably explored the entire premises without quite comprehending. Night suddenly set in, and just as suddenly a light appeared in the pavilion's window. João and the girl started.

'Is that your cousin?'

'No, Your Eminence. She has gone into the town with the coachman.'

Puzzled, João went to the pavilion. In front of a dressing table sat Barbara, wearing a splendid muslin dressing gown, combing her flaxen hair. She smiled at João, stood up and came to him. He took her into his arms. She let him embrace her, and her lips parted for his kiss.

'Come,' said João at length, 'a supper has been prepared.'

He took her to the octagonal room. She cried out with delight as she entered it. The lights of Venetian chandeliers shone, and were reflected *ad infinitum* in the mirrors. A table was laid, the sofa looked inviting, the champagne cooled in a bucket filled with ice, and there were roses everywhere. Supper or sofa, that was the question. Barbara let the dressing gown fall to the ground. Her pale body was also reflected *ad infinitum* in the looking glasses.

'Supper can wait a little,' she said.

Already João was on his knees. He had guessed perfectly what she liked most. A silky thigh rubbed his cheek as it was lifted over his shoulder. The other leg stretched out, then bent to maintain the balance. Barbara's nails scratched the nape of his neck. His hands grasped two small, hard and round buttocks before one hand got down to work. Barbara, who had to hold herself back from shouting and throwing herself on the sofa behind her knee, let the waiting last for a considerable time. She wanted to prove her gratitude but, laughing, João stopped her, and pushed her into a chair in front of the small table. The champagne sparkled. He cut into slices a pâté of goose-liver from Périgord. Only much later did he succeed in getting her agreement to the position he preferred to all others. Bruised all over she let out a sigh. She received his pleasure, and to her surprise felt her own sudden climax, unexpected after all the pain.

The chill of the night awoke Alexandra. With one jump she flew out of bed. Her sole domestic requirement was always to have hot water at hand. She was a maniac for lustral water. Next to her bedroom she had had a room built that was walled with alternate marble plaques and Venetian mirrors. Three steps led down to a large basin, a miniature swimming pool beside the unheard-of luxury of an earthenware night-commode in place of the filthy privies of the preceding century. Ever since her childhood Alexandra had pissed standing, like a man. She poured scented water on her body. She was mad about perfumes. In a small crystal bottle was an essence of roses made in the Versailles laboratory of Louis XV, himself a notable chemist, given to the Pompadour by him, by the Pompadour to Bernis, and by him to João, a very private present on the occasion of his receiving his cardinal's hat. The French Minister had for his friend the Cardinal-Duke of Queluz the regard of a brother or an accomplice. They told each other everything—or nearly everything. Alexandra's bathroom had belonged to the beautiful Venetian mistress of Comte de Bernis, the divine M. M. who had also been the mistress of Casanova, the Venetian adventurer whom João had met on the Laguna, the subject of his only quarrel with Pierre de Bernis. João, who was something of an expert in such matters, believed that Casanova was the spy of the Holy Office in Venice. He had escaped from the prison of the Piombi, and with an astonishing journalistic flair had published the story of his flight in a small leaflet which enjoyed great success.

Bernis rocked with laughter while João remained convinced that the escape had been a clever trick to cover up for Casanova, and lull suspicion. Anyhow, Alexandra's bath had been designed by Casanova for the dissolute nun. Alexandra whistled, the little servant girl appeared, astonished at not being called before, as there was a ritual in the bath too. But Alexandra was in a hurry.

'Have Penelope saddled. The English saddle.'

'Meninha is going out alone? At such a late hour?'

Alexandra made a haughty movement. The young girl could not hold back a cry of admiration, and came to plant a light kiss on Alexandra's flat belly. Diana the huntress. Alexandra smiled and gave permission, uttering precise indications at the same time in a dry voice: she would dress as a boy. It was done, and Alexandra looked like the handsomest young man in the world. The young girl melted again. 'If I were your lover,' said Alexandra, 'I would do this to you.' She threw her on a divan near the bath, lifted her skirt, and returned her kisses.

'Hurry up. I will finish dressing alone.'

The little girl vanished. Alexandra put on light boots, a cape, and on her head a three-cornered hat with black plumes. All the rest was as white as kid gloves. She put a small, polished steel pistol in her pocket. Sword and dagger followed. She was ready.

The mare too. One could guess that those night-time escapades were not unusual, especially when His Eminence was absent.

The streets were full of life. Old Pombal, João's immediate predecessor, had admirably rebuilt the town after the earthquake, and simultaneously made an immense fortune. João never tried to confiscate it, which was the Marquis de Silva's great political idea.

Demagogic, said João. The Marquis had a fairly strong idea about pure and tough dictatorship, whereas João found that corruption inevitably created a certain amount of freedom.

There were still building sites everywhere, but the public lighting was already working and was the best in Europe; that is apart from Alfama, where one plunged straight back into the middle ages. Alexandra advanced rapidly without heeding the passers-by. I am getting madder and madder. I am in love. Is it the first time? Like this certainly. He will be left breathless by my audacity. Timid and romantic without a doubt. A male virgin? That would be the crowning misfortune. Luckily I know the theory. She shook with unbecoming laughter, remembering surprising her uncle with the two little girls from Bahia—a marvel of balance. The whole group threw itself carefully on the floor when Alexandra made her appearance. Laurent would not care for that sort of sight. Deplorable, the lack of a sense of humour, but—curse God! as the porter of the convent says—I love him, because of those very things, most likely. Two kicks of her heels gave Penelope wings. She entered the courtyard of Kotor's palace. The sparks escaping from a chimney gave a vague light. They rose towards the clear sky, and turned into stars. So he is an alchemist too. If he is a freemason like uncle it will be an amusing encounter. She tied Penelope to a post, and through the dark passages rushed to the garden.

The moon shone as though it were daylight, and lay reflected in the Tagus, and with its light picked out from profound darkness the chain of the Arrabida on the other bank. A few small lights in the town, a light tower, a manœuvring ship with all her lights on. The trees were lined up as if on parade; in the midst of them was Laurent, the same black immobile figure.

Alexandra slowly approached, Laurent's eyes shone, her heart was bursting inside her.

'I have come,' she said.

He studied her gravely, which she found inexplicably moving. She clearly saw there was no timidity in his reserve, only an inexplicable and firm determination. Will pitted against will, the victory would be hers. She put her arms round the young man's neck, drew him to her, and gave him a long kiss. He let her do as she wanted; he gave in. His ardour even astonished Alexandra.

For a few minutes he seemed to have lost his head. He was like a river that an invisible dam had held back, but having burst it, it rushed now free and fast. The reserved, thoughtful young man, who appeared to consider every step he took, said meaningless sentences, sentimental and naïve clichés followed one another, and precisely those clichés seduced her most, sending her into rapture. Detached lewdness and the coolness of witty minds she was acquainted with, including their roundabout way and limitations. The unexpected heat of that torrent of sentiments, which would have repulsed her on the lips of anyone else, coming from that young prince of darkness (as she had rightly guessed) delighted her. They strolled for a long time, embracing madly every few seconds. She let herself go in the same manner as he. Alexandra thought it heavenly, and for once did not ask which was the shortest way back to earth. The urge of her soul that already in Germany and Bohemia had made her feel the tremor of the undercurrents of music, and made her understand in the midst of the intrigues of her stepfather's small, provincial court the lyrical side of some young poets, mad about Nature, mad about Jean-Jacques Rousseau—that same urge pushed her with all its strength towards Laurent.

The halo of mystery that surrounded him, his unknown origin, his sudden appearance in Lisbon, the smell of sulphur that floated all over the house added to the urge instead of holding her back. Her energetic nature, the as yet unspent strength of her ardent temperament, her audacity, her taste for acting the second she had to take a decision, the decision usually taken on the spur of the moment: it all combined to give her the sensation of an exceptional adventure, an occasion that should not be missed.

Her power over men had amused her as much as the light in their eyes when she uncovered a breast or a thigh, or threw herself naked into the river. The stepfather first, the uncle afterwards, circled warily around her aggressively proclaimed virginity, the more perturbing because she used, as in a Shakespearean comedy, foul language that was innocent of prejudice and moral values. I have morals, namely the legitimacy of my pleasure, but no moral sense. The company of girls had taught her sexual pleasure and to practise it calmly without worry or remorse. Solitary pleasure had become as natural to her as food, bathing, moving her bowels or riding on horseback. A frank animal, vigorous and powerful, she watched from the height of her physical, intellectual and moral superiority the vices, the complaisance and hypocrisy of her stepfather, and the pretended blindness of her uncle. The only man she had ever known was the ivory penis of the prima donna of the Italian troupe of her stepfather's who had initiated her into the games of Sappho. Laurent's pallor, perhaps even his lassitude, had moved and touched her body. In his arms, in that garden, in the light of the full moon for the first time in her life she had no desire to sneer at the ecstasy of love.

A long time went by. The kisses became chaste towards the end, their mutual rapture desperately innocent. Laurent maintained his reserve. Perhaps it was getting even stronger. A clock struck ten, and Laurent shuddered. True the night was still young, but it was necessary to take the decision and speak to her, cynicism not being his way. He had to put his conscience at rest. He decided to rush into it. He stepped back.

'Alexandra,' he said with a solemnity to which the young girl immediately responded. 'Alexandra, I must take the terrible risk of telling you something that will turn me into an object of horror in your eyes.'

'Whatever you say you will never be an object of horror in my eyes—even if you decide to confess to the most awful crimes.'

'Not crimes, but dreadful all the same . . . I am a monster.'

'So am I. A monster of egoism with a taste for enjoyment and violence—' She suddenly realised that she mustn't interrupt him, not create a diversion with wit and jokes. His solemnity was profound, and deserved to be answered with equally profound solemnity. She nestled in his arms, and raised her eyes to his.

'Go on . . . speak. You can tell me *everything*.'

She discreetly noticed his trembling and his heart beating faster. Laurent held his breath like a diver before diving. The *word*, the *name* he would have to pronounce. His father was engaged in inventing a new science to study the meaning of words, the magical qualities of names, the confusion into which most minds fall between the word and the object, which he calls between the label and the contents of the bottle. He says that all the interior conflicts of the soul, all the confusion of reasoning, are on the level of the word and not of the object, on the level of the confusion between a sentiment and the name one gives it, jealousy, possession, even love, between a form of reasoning and formal logic. He who hears the word 'vampire' uttered looks at the label and not at the reality hidden by the label that pretends to define it. Father has made Aristotle, his principle of identity, and his philosophy and logic, into his mortal enemies in the name of what he calls (in the fashion of Heraclitus) the dialectic of drift-sand. One has to *be* a vampire to be able to measure the ravages a name can give, a name loaded with horror. In a second I am going to pronounce that name, and this sublime creature made of fire, a miracle of strength and energy, will be horrified. Once again.

'Is that all?' said Alexandra. 'Is that all your secret, all the mystery?'

'But you must surely know the abominable stories that are told.'

'If I had to listen to all the abominable stories . . . Look, my uncle is reputed to be a sorcerer.'

'But,' went on Laurent, 'we are considered monsters, creatures of Hell, the children of the Prince of Darkness.'

'What would be the value of having been educated as a strong-minded person if I listened to old wives' tales? Explain everything to me.' Laurent could not help being astonished. Calm once more, he gave vent to a lyrical passion. He spoke with growing enthusiasm. He told her about the defeat of death in the first skirmish, which was, however, not the whole war. He talked about the immense hope and immense task that awaited the faithful, brothers joined together in a mad gamble. He spoke of his father's efforts and researches to win the second stage that will turn man into a new man to whom the Universe will be promised, who will master Nature, who will fulfil the old and fabulous dreams of Prometheus, the old and fabulous promises he had made to mankind; the inheritance of the old Titans defeated first by the Olympians, then by the Cross, the inheritance of old Mithras. He spoke of his own share in that fight. The Count was the engineer, the magician, the chief of the armies, and the *Pontifex Maximus* at the same time. He, Laurent, was the bard and the poet who would give the new believers their canticles, their war songs, the words to incarnate their hopes. He had picked up the lyre fallen from the hands of Apollo and Orpheus. He would sing of the bubbling of generous blood, the triumph of life, the conquest of the stars and the Universe, the adult age of man, abandoning like childhood toys the successive dynasties of imbecile gods, savages and criminals in whose name the Christians were thrown to the lions, the heretics by the thousand on the stake, the unbelievers to the sword.

He spoke of the universal horror that got Spartacus crucified by Crassus, Christ by the Sanhedrin, the Albigensians burned by Simon de Montfort, the Protestants massacred by the members of the League on the night of St Bartholomew, the Jews burnt by Torquemada, the sorcerers drowned by bishops and German clergymen, the Anabaptists beheaded by Luther and his Catholic enemies united in defending the sacred treasures of wealth.

Above the words Alexandra heard their music, and let her soul be charmed by them and her spirit take wing. She was far from the petty intrigues of men of her class to fatten their purses and invest their funds. Little men with meanness and precaution, little men full of hypocrisy, spite, avarice and cruelty. The she-centaur had found her centaur.

He told her about the most hidden mysteries, the strangest pleasures, how to drink deep the rich blood of one's brother, how to give and transmit life. He was at the heart of the horror, on the threshold of the unspeakable, the crucial moment for her not only to consent but to adhere to the faith and share the zeal of the battle that had already begun. He stopped, but the dark music of his words continued in the silence like the chords of the organ long after the organist has ceased playing.

Alexandra remained in his arms, and her luminous eyes did not leave the almost phosphorescent eyes of the young man. She saw the passionate and silent questions in them.

As if in answer she stepped aside. He trembled. She planted herself in front of him, and her eyes bored into his. With a very slow movement she unhooked her lace collar, and offered him her neck with the throbbing jugular vein.

Transfigured, Laurent bent over her. She waited, anxious and trembling with a little fear still left in the dark shades of her soul.

It was like the kick of a splendid drug, like finding access to unimaginable and never described happiness, a happiness that Laurent shared, drinking deep draughts of life itself, sacrificing to the most secret mysteries of the cult of Mithras, becoming the officiating priest reaching to the very roots of sanctity.

Then arm in arm, the two becoming one after their communion under the sign of love that had exalted them to the highest level, they went determinedly to Laurent's room to sacrifice to other mysteries, to follow the design of another ritual.

Dazzled, Laurent undressed Alexandra. Taking off the man's shirt she wore, her admirable breasts appeared, small and tense, and the almost colourless nipples hardened as he kissed them. The black silk drawers joined the boots and stockings on the carpet. The vulva was covered in thick, shining fair hairs. Laurent's hands opened the softly consenting thighs. His mouth followed the curve of her belly, reaching her firmly erect clitoris. Alexandra cried out. His lips moved up, and his tongue met hers while he gently penetrated her. She felt her pleasure rising. He took his time in finding his, thus forcing her to climax twice. He turned round tenderly, obliging her to get on all fours, and his clever fingers prepared the road he would take. The buttocks stretched, then opened to the fingers that would help the hard member to find its place. She shrieked in acute pain, which slowly and patiently turned into pleasure. It was Laurent's turn to shout. They collapsed worn out, but in a close embrace and mad with joy. They forgot time. Alexandra had never been so happy before, and nor had Laurent.

A faint light appeared in the window announcing dawn. Laurent pulled Alexandra out of her contented torpor, made her get up, and dressed her ceremoniously, watching with passionate attention the lovely body disappearing under the clothes.

Long kisses on her belly and backside punctuated his farewell. Dressed, she did the same for him with similar kisses. She felt desire returning, her pleasure too with the same serene joy that had been hers the whole night. He was dressed. Suddenly he hesitated, shaken by a new fear. She smiled, for she had understood.

'Show me where you rest. I must not remain ignorant of anything about you.' He led her to the cellar. The three servants were already in their coffins. The Count was in his. His eyes were already losing their light, but on catching sight of Alexandra and Laurent arm in arm he gave them a smile which was a blessing. One could see that he was pleased in his grave manner. He disappeared in his coffin. Laurent slid into his, and courageously, mastering with all her strength the remnants of her horror, she helped him to lie down. She gave him a long kiss, and closed the sculpted, heavy coffin lid.

She came out, untied Penelope, opened the front door, let the mare through, then closed the heavy door behind her. She jumped on Penelope, and tired, bruised, aching all over but triumphant she galloped in the young light of the sun.

For João and Barbara time was measureless too. Yet João was the first to start worrying. He had been surprised by the knowledge, movements and inventions of his partner, but he soon turned into her equal. The two peasant maidservants, who silently struggled with each other to look through the keyhole, were flabbergasted by the sight. But Barbara had not Laurent's reasons to speak. She searched in João for the same pleasures and the resourcefulness which he had given her. Without being aware of it he had fallen seriously for her. She did not think he had touched her heart or soul. Nevertheless, real friendship and complicity were already born.

They rested half-dead after a fresh skirmish, a new exploration of their resources and mutual techniques. João jumped.

'Four o'clock. I must go back.'

'Your Eminence works too much.'

'Apparently. You cannot suspect me now of wanting to attend to anything else than government business. I give the whole world an example in early work. It is at dawn with a cool head that real political courage manifests itself.'

'Are you trying to tell me that you have a cool head now? It would not be flattering.'

'Certainly not today,' said João, 'but generally yes. I wake up in a second, and I sleep only three hours at night—or in daytime.'

'But drink . . .'

'I practise moderation in my excesses.'

'That is the sort of moderation I prefer.'

'I have noticed it.'

He got up. He had the body of an athlete, and his weight was most reasonable for the century. A reddish complexion, a hardly noticeable baldness that necessitated the wearing of a wig—but he preferred not to, an evident sign of vanity. Around fifty, thought Barbara. Not bad considering the life he leads. João dressed quickly yet carefully. He bent over Barbara.

'I am coming back tonight.'

'Your Eminence is in his own house.'

He disappeared. She heard the noise of the carriage on its way to Lisbon in the dying night. Tired and happy, Barbara sighed her contentment. One of the young maidservants entered, dying of curiosity to have a closer look at the new mistress of the premises who had appeared so mysteriously out of nowhere.

God! how beautiful she was, how literally fascinating her eyes. Barbara looked at that healthy creature, that palpitating bosom approaching her. Her special gift, which she had received as her share, was the strength of magnetic and hypnotic suggestion, a subject of endless discussions with her father. He accepted only the absolutely conscious, determined and convinced participation of disciples. On several occasions Barbara used her power to suck the blood of boys and girls who were more victims than accomplices. When Kotor found out he went mad with rage. In vain she mocked his moral values. He kept to them; severity marked all his actions. And Barbara's behaviour, although he found it immoral above everything else, was also the source of a grave peril, linked with the source of the age-old terror inspired by the vampires.

But Kotor was not present. In the little house in Cascais Barbara was at last in her own domain in complete freedom. Her eyes subdued the young peasant girl who slowly approached, already unhooking her blouse, already consenting to all that would follow. Barbara drew the girl to her, then threw her on the bed. She smelt of straw, milk and washing. The shirt was stiff with starch. The girl was in ecstasy, letting Barbara do as she wanted. With deep gulps Barbara drank avidly the strength of that young life.

Alexandra and João arrived almost simultaneously in the ducal palace. She was unsaddling Penelope when the carriage arrived in the yard. Her face shone with happiness. Jumping out of the carriage like a young man, João saw it at one glance. He too was radiant. He embraced his niece.

At last he said, 'Do I know him?'

'You do. You will like him.'

'It is the brother.'

'And you, was it the sister?'

They laughed. They certainly knew each other well.

'I will speak to you after dinner,' said Alexandra. 'I have a plan.'

João threw her a quick glance. He did not care for that kind of decision, but Alexandra had unrestrained energy. A lioness as always, sighed João. The day would be a hard one.

Chapter VII

Though as strong as a horse, Clara felt a sudden fatigue towards the end of the afternoon, which nailed her to her armchair. She was short of breath, her veins throbbed, she was overwhelmed. She was unwilling to abandon her patients, and now the whole organisation rested on her shoulders. Kotor had said, 'It is better to remain few in number, at least in the beginning. The more we become the more difficult it will be to trust our brethren, the easier for the enemy to introduce spies or informers into our midst.' Easier said than done. Since Lavinia's transformation a powerful reaction to the previous sense of horror had set in. First one family followed her example, then ten. There would soon be a hundred. Round each new vampire a small core gathered of faithful friends and accomplices. Each follower who took the step knew that he might survive in a different manner after his first death, and could wait until Kotor succeeded in winning his second, decisive battle against final death. New morals, metaphysics and a new way of living in a community took shape like an aura around every new vampire and the little group that surrounded and nourished him. These small groups instinctively rediscovered the life style of the more or less secret cells of the heretics in the time of the Cathars, the Vaudois, the Alains, and the early Christians organised by Paul of Tarsus, one of the first great organisers of clandestine networks. Following his example Kotor and Clara took to visiting each of the little groups almost every day. But Kotor had also to fight against time, eagerly pursuing his researches and experiments each night. Other means had to be found, the more so since the movement, once launched, could not now be stopped. The small groups tended to meet and mix, and commune in the new faith: the mad hope of defeating death, which was an irresistible lure to people who had from time immemorial been accustomed to the omnipresent fear of death.

Properly speaking it was not a new religion; in theory the old religions were untouched. In fact, they had exploded. Those little groups, though that had not been Kotor's original intention, began to question the social structures. They practised a communal spirit where their fortunes were concerned, without any social or racial discrimination. The absolute equality of all persons, which was a direct consequence of the way of life of the little groups, became a new aim, a new reason for hope. Charity was advanced. Freedom of thought and beliefs, even of morals, was total. A new system of moral values was born from the movement itself, and became a new means to the end. Thus not only the fight against death and its possible victory began to attract and draw people, but it also offered a refuge to the oppressed.

Alfama was a hotbed of such people. All those that society treated as marginal elements, that were more or less persecuted, gathered there. Thieves, galley slaves, escaped convicts, ponces, whores, smugglers, receivers of stolen goods, heretics and madcaps of every sort were thick on the ground, all of them leading a precarious existence in that warren. All the houses were connected through their caves, terraces, gardens and the vaulted passages between the alleys and the streets: a labyrinth, a thieves' kitchen, which no-one, except two or three secret leaders, Clara for one, could boast of knowing inside out. Alfama was the century-old despair of the police, who for decades had not dared to enter it. The Marquis da Silva was powerless there, and had to be content with keeping Alfama segregated from the city. Every entry to the town was guarded by police stations full of policemen both in uniform and in plain clothes, watching the comings and goings of the inmates, and grabbing anyone imprudent enough to try to escape. Some twenty of those nostalgic folk who dared to leave their shelter were hanged each year. After several months of effort, means were found to close the barriers. A few spies tried and succeeded on rare occasions in making reconnaissance raids into Alfama.

In his office the Marquis, instead of the traditional Gobelin tapestry generously offered by the King of France, had a large map on the wall, a bird's-eye view of Alfama. Small marks in different colours indicated the various hidden spots, here an alchemist, there a synagogue, yonder a smuggler's store. If he could not destroy them, at least he knew where they were. Every night the Marquis had the same beautiful dream: the King gave him troops to take Alfama by assault. It would be treated like a conquered town, and at least part of it would be razed to the ground. However, when he awoke in the morning he remembered that the regiments, paid six months in arrears, were unreliable, and were usually defending the frontiers of Spain, which was always hungry for conquest. Admittedly there was the *corps d'élite* of the Marines, who supplied the men for the King's guard; but the Navy Minister who was the King's brother—a firm tradition since the time of Henry the Navigator—had his own ideas about the use to which the Marines should be put. Half of them patrolled between Goa, Macao and Timor, and the other half hunted slaves in what is now Dahomey and Angola to the great satisfaction of the planters of Bahia and the mine owners of Ouro Preto. The family of the Prime Minister, the Duke of Queluz, had its own large slice of that enormous cake. And the Marquis, mad with rage, knew he could do nothing against such a coalition.

There was thus no question of touching Alfama, which lived in freedom on the steps leading from Graca and the Castle of São-Jorge down to the Tagus.

Clara's real problem was how to safeguard for as long as possible the anonymity of the groups of vampires. Here and there alarm bells were rung. Other groups, other secret cells, had put out feelers, and discovered the existence of the new and strange group, and tried to approach it to find out what it was about.

Because Clara was considered a saint and a healer, whose moral authority was recognised and admired by all, the corporation of beggars, the network of brothels with their owners and inmates, the syndicates of receivers and counterfeiters were reassured. They would keep aloof and neutral, restraining their curiosity. The same went for the clandestine printers, the smugglers, and the brotherhoods of thieves and escaped convicts. With the religious sects it was not so easy. The secret Jewish community smelt some nameless sacrilege. None the less they would not budge, aware that they could at once be involved in a persecution. It was far more difficult to deal with the two or three Protestant groups who spoke of the Devil with the vehemence of Luther, and were in touch with some powerful, rich and well-protected foreign embassies, the English, Germans and Swedes. One had to be careful with them. There remained sorcerers of all kinds, astrologers, geomancers, Arab or Chinese, brought by ship from Macao, for whom the new groups might mean dangerous competition. Appropriate threats linked with assorted explanations might perhaps calm them down. They had great respect for Clara.

No, the real problem was the Freemasons. Clara knew through

different channels that the Freemasons were strongly implanted in Lisbon. She had never found a genuine one or met someone who admitted to being one. She had only a vague idea about their organisation. She had discovered some vague approaches to the circle of the initiated through people who held her in high esteem, especially a Swedish friend who had made many allusions to an ever-present secret force that was the enemy of thrones and altars —all of which was attractive to her. But she was less attracted by the apparatus of Deism and the diffuse religious sense. She had spoken about them to Kotor who seemed to know them better. It was not impossible that some time or other Kotor had been received as a brother, which would be understandable. In the situation the Count found himself in no protector, no ally could be overlooked. She would speak to him after dark.

Fernanda arrived with a radiant smile. Clara was thinking of making her her lieutenant in military parlance. Ursula would slowly take over the work in the house and the visits to the sick, while Fernanda would be the liaison officer between all the groups, passing on Kotor's instructions and collecting information. Thus Clara could concentrate on Kotor's great work. She liked Fernanda: her vitality which was so similar to Clara's own, the liveliness with which she communicated to others, her love of life without calculation or hypocrisy. The two young women embraced each other. Clara noticed a little flame dancing in Fernanda's eyes.

'Some great happiness has come your way,' said Clara.

'Yes, Dona Clara,' said Fernanda, holding back her laughter.

'What is the name of that happiness? Let me guess. What is the name of the Italians' son? Gianbattista?'

'Gianvittorio.'

'Tell me about them,' said Clara, suddenly serious.

A curious idea had come to her that instant. Throughout the night of the feast she had searched the crowd and the excited groups for a trail, a sign that could have led her to one of the top brothers. She was acquainted with some modest adherents in general, members of corporations, even masters of them, who were usually hard-working and active people, oppressed by the bankers, the police and the customs, anxious to create defence and mutual help organisations. They escaped to Alfama for shelter and from there they weaved their spider's webs. The dock hands, for instance, formed a solid group like the jewellers, the printers and the carpenters. Now and then ethnic or national groups held sway over a whole profession. The house painters were either from Genoa or Lombardy. Fernanda's Italians certainly had their organisation too.

'Have you ever made love with him?' Clara asked.

'Naturally,' said Fernanda, still amused.

'You love him? Does he love you?'

'Yes to both questions.'

'You know him well?'

Clara's intensely serious voice caught Fernanda's attention at last. She understood that all these questions had a reason.

'Have you spoken to him?'

'Not yet,' said Fernanda, blushing.

'So you have no confidence in him.'

'It is not that, but it is not easy to explain it.'

'And he? Has he spoken to you about what he does?'

'No,' said Fernanda, who had grasped what Clara was aiming at. 'But if you think there is the slightest risk of his being a policeman you are very mistaken.'

'It is not what I fear. I am searching.'

'For what? I will do all you want.'

'You must find out whether he is a Freemason. I will explain to you what it is.'

'That's unnecessary. I know. They have already come to talk to my father.'

'Who were they?'

'Gianvittorio's parents.'

'You must bring him here,' exclaimed Clara triumphantly.

João felt weary and undecided, even though the memory of his ardour and success the previous night should have raised him to the heights of exaltation. Surrendering to the bitter pleasure of reflecting about himself, and his gentle complaisance, he merely felt uncertainty. I have more intelligence than character. I have a very clear idea about what I wish for myself: the use of absolute power in moderation, and the prudent satisfaction of my caprices. I would have made one of the few good Roman emperors. Tiberius is my model. Cruelty that is not self-destructive, that does not destroy in proportion to its exercise the possibilities of existence. But Tiberius was a great general too. He knew the hard physical suffering that went with travelling and making war in that age. Why not the austere Hadrian? I should never have had his strength and courage. I am on the point of sliding down a fatal slope. The activities of a juggler and a conjurer are my lot, at the mercy of an easy-going, capricious, nervous, changeable and inconsistent king. I protect him from all troubles, but I have to leave him with a few toys to serve his vanity; yet a kick from him could be mortal for me. Would he ever know how to apply it? He must be dying to do so. On whom can I count? A party chief with no party; my tolerance is almost amusing. At least in the short term it allows my enemies to organise themselves in peace. My well-known lack of convictions is my real chance of survival.

He sighed. A man of action who does not care for action, a man who works but hates work, a hedonist who has not discovered how to live only through, by, from and for his pleasures. A failed life full of dangers: the Jesuits, the Inquisition, the Marquis. If they join up together, I am lost. Luckily they all pull in different directions. The Marquis would support the Inquisition, but he continues to offend the Jesuits. I must find allies. I will never become the General of the Jesuits, which is a pity. I must find other means. Bernis urges me to join the Freemasons. Already Casanova has sounded me out twice on his behalf. But it is impossible for me to consent to permanent contacts, let alone official ones, with that Venetian debaucher who has no honour, but is vain and over-sensitive. Ah, well. What does Kotor represent? An exile, almost certainly a fugitive. All he has is his money. But at least I have money too.

The memory of his tobacco, sugar and cacao plantations in Bahia made him shiver. How foolish to have come back. Viceroy at the other end of the earth with the joys of Salvador, the town of all saints and all sins. He saw himself back in the steep alleys of the Pelurinho, eating an *acaraje* bought for two tostos, on his way to one of his hidden retreats, where he could do absolutely what he wanted. In a boat on the Reconcavo wearing only a pair of linen trunks, two lovely girls rowing for his pleasure and eight men for the speed. The shift of wind bends the mast. The smells of the market, and those of the slave market on the little triangular area with shining cobbles. The four years he had spent in Bahia had marked him for life. Two journeys to inspect his plantations and mines—his trading interests too—had strengthened his real passion for the tropical way of life. On the last voyage he brought back about twenty negroes, men and women, whom he installed on his estate on the other side of the Tagus, near the beach of Caparica that reminded the slaves of the beach of Itapoa. He did not go there often, one or two nights a month at the most. In his honour drums were beaten. Thus the old, black African gods, transposed to Brazil, had found a bridgehead in Europe. Full of curiosity in such matters João let himself be initiated. He was made an *obas* on the right of Xango, and was entitled to an armchair in the *Barracão*. As son of Ogun, the god of iron and war, he had a small altar built in his palace. But running the affairs of state turned him away from that road. Nevertheless, now and then he was driven by nostalgia to see the dancing women from Bahia, as one might get drunk at night. He kept the place as a secret refuge, a last resort. The African gods who had made the voyage with the slaves in the holds of slave ships had first fascinated him. In his bedroom there was still a statue of Iemanja, the goddess of the sea. Besides, they looked too much like local gods. It seemed to him that the notion of turning a heap of stones, a *herma*, on the edge of a field in Attica, into a god who would become Hermes, the essence of Greek polytheism, in fact masked an atheist pantheism, closer to his own approach to the divine and the sacred. He thought he could recognise the Greek Olympus in the black gods: Oxala was Zeus, Iemanja Aphrodite, Ogun Ares and Xango surely Apollo. The survival of the Greek gods was his dream. He had danced with his slaves, and seen the *iaos*, the initiated, each turning in the haunting hell of the drums and the *agogos* into the horse of his god. But to his estate in Caparica the gods came no more, or if they did he was not told of it. He now preferred to believe that the religion imported from Bahia by the Nagos of Katu represented no more than a simple collection of medical herbs, hallucination, and over-simplified divination. Geomancy he considered far above the *jogo* of *buzios*, its cousin. In brief, his feeble effort to build a bridge to the mental, spiritual and religious universe of his slaves had failed, without his being really conscious of it. He attributed that to spiritual motives, although it was only the outcome of his own state of mind.

He emerged from his short meditation to find himself in front of the chessboard with very little room to manœuvre. How could he eliminate the Marquis, who could become the queen in the subtle game he was playing against an unknown and invisible enemy, namely destiny. A castle, at least, and it had two rows: one vertical, which was politics and corruption, and the other horizontal, which was religion. Sacrifice a piece, but which one? The answer came at once: Alexandra, who as the wife of the Marquis would push him into his camp. He would give her to him only against solid guarantees, such as the restitution of incriminating documents, disbanding the secret police or giving up his position as their chief. Then only could he turn against the Inquisition or become their ally to expel the Jesuits, take in hand the governing of the King, on which Manuel was not firm enough. After the King's death—he was eaten up with venereal disease caught from contaminated sailors—he would attack the queen, who would succeed as regent. To give pleasure to that old, devout woman would be a pleasure in itself. I am Picchrocole, he said to himself. I draw my new frontiers, yet I have not reached the first hurdle: how to persuade Alexandra.

She appeared, dressed convincingly as a cavalier. Narrow hips, the buttocks of a boy. She will never be mine. The young man seems to have shown her a different world.

'Uncle,' said Alexandra. 'I have taken a decision.'

'I have also, a decision that concerns you.'

'Do not make me laugh. I know what you are going to say, but you lack the energy.'

'You don't.'

'Frankly no,' said Alexandra simply. 'You indulge in illusions. You are about to ask me to marry the Marquis, even try to force me to. And in your weakness and love of compromise you will lose everything. Listen carefully to me . . .'

She sat down. João admired her, for most of his women lacked energy. He listened. What else could he do?

'You will announce to the Marquis that you succeeded in persuading me to marry him.'

'How is that?'

'Do not interrupt me. You will ask him to return to you the moment the contract of marriage is signed, the documents he holds against you and you will destroy them in his presence. The wedding will take place eight days later. I will sign the contract too, and on the following night you will organise with the Marquis one of your little feasts . . .'

'With the Marquis? You must be mad!'

'Not at all. You will enjoy learning about his habits. Thus you will have him in your power, with no weapons left against you.'

'And you?'

'I,' said Alexandra coldly, 'will let myself be accompanied as far as the threshold of my bedroom. And during the night while you are both busy I will escape. You will not be implicated.'

'And what will become of you?'

'Don't worry about me. I know where I am going, I know what I am going to do.'

'In short, I lose you.'

'If you put me into the bed of the Marquis in the palace of the Marquis and into the life of the Marquis do you not also lose me? Where is your logic?'

'But,' said João, disconcerted, 'you could lead a normal life with him. He would give you all you want.'

'What you call a normal life is sheer hell for me. Life for the wife of the Marquis is inevitably hell. I am not even speaking of the need to allow a truly stinking creature to climb on top of me every night, no doubt several times, but of the social and worldly duties of that frightful person.'

'In any event you will lead a worldly life. Even your mother . . .'

'All my mother thinks about is making love as often as possible. To get her ration she is ready to do anything, even to live with a ruling Prince-Elector who, if one may say so, is nothing but a wretched, tiny, German rag. I always knew that I would never accept that sort of life. Now I know what I want. I am fond of you, you amuse me, your weakness moves me, everything interests you—but you are fickle, an egoist, and unfaithful. I leave you and the likes of you.'

João looked at her in alarm. Recently, in an unpleasant legal examination, he had encountered a young fanatic who had chased off peasants, burnt down a castle and hanged its owner with equal gusto. From time to time, in some village or university, rabid creatures who preached revolution and vengeance were arrested. They were broken on the wheel, after their flesh had been torn with red-hot pincers; and then they were skinned alive. João did not care for these methods, but order had to be maintained. Alexandra's tone of voice reminded him of the tone of voice of these young men to whom he happened to speak before they were taken to the scaffold.

Having said what she had to say, Alexandra got ready to leave. João tried again.

'All the information I have about Count Kotor and his family suggests that they are gallows-birds. Heretics, magicians, felons.'

'Uncle, instead of thinking of a trial of strength, do listen to reason.'

'But it is you who want a trial of strength. You force on me *your* solution. You insult me and let me neither understand nor argue.'

Alexandra laughed aloud. João relaxed. Her laughter meant that there was still a bridge left between her old world and the new. Perhaps a tenuous one, but even so; Alexandra embraced him.

'You are right, my cherished uncle. I treated you like a little boy. Admit that you rather like it.'

'I do. But strictly speaking, I prefer choosing my own time.'

'We shall talk about your vices some other time. What do you think of my plan?'

'Excellent, but completely impracticable.'

'That's my business.'

Kotor raised his head from the manuscript he was studying. Laurent and Alexandra had just come in. Father and son looked at each other, and Alexandra, who watched them, was aware of their power of instantaneous communication.

She envied them for it. She decided to question Laurent. With one glance Kotor had perceived the whole story of Laurent meeting Alexandra and their new situation. He received the young girl with paternal warmth. I wonder how they communicate with each other. She added, how *we* communicate. Kotor started to speak about his work. Alexandra understood that what belonged to the realm of words, the passing on of ideas and notions, was discussed with spoken or written words; but matters of daily life and sentiments were transmitted in one lump with specially rapid signals. She also understood the sharing of tasks between father and son. Kotor was in charge of research, the exploration of the inexplorable, of experiments and theories. Laurent meditated, trying to map the dark roads, the metaphysical implications of their existence and condition. Kotor, in a sense the high priest, watched over the organisation of his church which he had largely entrusted to Dona Clara. Laurent would celebrate that great dream, the battles, victories and defeats. Clara entered at that moment. She too had begun to learn the method of instantaneous communication. Within a second she perceived both Alexandra's presence and the meaning of it.

She approached and embraced her. Viscerally, with all her being, Alexandra felt that she had found *her* family.

Clara brought important news: the arrival of a visitor. Alexandra had no idea what it was about, yet felt immense interest. Clara and Kotor spoke to each other with fast concentrated sentences which had no meaning to her who knew nothing whatever about freemasonry.

Gianvittorio entered the hall. Kotor took his hand, and made in the young man's palm the classical signs with which brethren recognised one another. Gianvittorio stepped back, electrified.

'You, Count?'

Kotor made a quick sign on his chest resembling the sign of the Cross.

'A master,' murmured Gianvittorio. 'I am at your service.'

He also made the same quick sign.

'I was wondering who it was who runs the movement of the brethren in Lisbon,' said Kotor. 'Now I know.'

It took Gianvittorio some time to recover from his astonishment.

'I am known here,' he said, 'as the son of a family of Italian artisans.'

'I would not have looked for you here.'

'Were you looking for me?'

'Since my arrival in Lisbon.'

The two men studied each other with friendship and interest. I would not have believed it, thought Gianvittorio. I do not believe it yet. It is clear that he has a sort of network, a group, but is it a group of brethren? I must be on my guard, and make him do the talking.

Kotor caught that quick thought as clearly as if he had read it in a book.

'I will speak to you very frankly,' he said.

'Lies always begin with that,' answered Gianvittorio, smiling.

Alexandra heard as clearly as if they were exchanging words the warnings that Kotor and Laurent were frantically transmitting to each other. She was acquiring the *gift*. Kotor's calm prevailed. He knew where he was going and where he wanted to be.

'The masters consider me as one of them,' said Kotor. 'At home in Bohemia . . .'

'The legendary meeting in Dobris,' murmured Gianvittorio.

'That is it. I harboured the young Balsamo for months.'

'So you are the mysterious great-uncle,' said Gianvittorio, kissing Kotor's hand.

'Yes,' said Kotor, 'but I am not exactly one of you. And I never shall be.'

'None the less, we are at your service.'

It all became easier. They both knew now that each had to find and discover *who* was *who*. Alexandra, who understood nothing, sent a telepathic question—her first—to Laurent. She sensed his amusement. Use your head, little idiot. He felt deep tenderness rising in him.

Candour, thought Kotor, can be the worst form of hypocrisy. Since I perceive half of his thoughts at least, those which are in the clear zone of his conscience, the dice are loaded in my favour. In the dark zone there is almost nothing. No fire in that abandoned part.

Gianvittorio looked at the family with avid curiosity. His memory worked at full speed. Scraps of stories, fragments of legends came back. The old man from Bohemia, simultaneously the oldest friend of the Order and the heir to a strange mistrust and reticence, was an ally who should be treated gently and within limits assisted. However, the Order was not as powerful in Lisbon.

'As you can see, I was working,' said Kotor, 'but I will leave it for a while.'

Everybody began to move, sensing a potential confrontation, the preliminary to a battle which would not take place but for which something else would be substituted. It had been a dress rehearsal.

Brusquely, Kotor attacked.

'You ask yourself what separates me from the brothers, and why they accept me as one of them.'

'The Order is very rigorous,' said Gianvittorio, smiling. 'It recognises neither the lukewarm nor the middle way. One is friend or enemy—as a rule no compromise is possible. You live on a strange border line of the Order. I wonder *who* you are, for the brothers neither to accept nor to reject you.'

'As a matter of fact I never really wished to enter the Order. I saw it born, I knew of the heavy steps that preceded it—the groups of the initiated, the Rosicrucians, my fellow alchemists. Years do not count for me any more.'

Gianvittorio gave a start. It was not yet clear to him, but part of his mind *knew* and slowly prepared for the arrival in his consciousness of a revelation that could be insupportable in its brutality. He also felt a kind of sadness and melancholia, unaware of their coming from the other side of the gates of death.

Gianvittorio suddenly sensed that death would be the centre of the question.

'In the first period of my life,' said Kotor, 'I had the irresistible tendency to consider man a brutish animal. Besides, I was the perfect example, having in ten years become a complete monster.'

He found himself centuries back in the past, as if it were yesterday. In the clearing the fifteen horsemen galloped, shouting. Kotor looked back to see whether the others followed. Alongside the three halted carriages footmen and guards took to their heels. The petrified passengers pushed their heads through the windows; in a split-second they realised the fate that awaited them, on seeing Kotor severing a head with one movement of his wrist. He wheeled his horse round, and returned to the first carriage, where three little girls were trussed and turned on their backs under the weight of the riders who had jumped on them from their horses. The travel bags burst with precious cloth. Kotor tore the door open. And there were those blue eyes. Two hundred and fifty years later, Kotor still felt their impact with the same violence. He groaned. Gianvittorio looked at him in amazement.

Months or perhaps years had gone by without Kotor reliving with such intensity his youth as a bird of prey, as the most aggressive of the young bandits of the Carpathians. He went on expeditions as far as the road to Vienna, selling the loot at Temesvar and the women to the agents of the Sultan.

The mobile groups consisted of fifteen horsemen each, every one independent, living like wolves off the land. Kotor had a gift for map-making. He drew with thorough precision the itinerary of each group with time-table and meeting places. Ten times the Emperor's troops had tried to catch him, but he always managed to escape, leaving no traces. Until he saw the blue eyes. Thus Dina entered his life. The head he had hewn off with his sword was her father's, a singular way of opening a relationship. But Dina did not think of that. As the carriage door was torn off, she was his even before she had seen the fiery lion that he was. Their love story lasted for ten years. She died giving birth to Laurent, ten years after the birth of little Barbara, fruit of their first meeting. Before he met her, Kotor had considered himself immune to passion. There followed ten years of total bliss during which he discovered first with bewilderment then with utter delight the existence of woman as a person, and of the couple. Dina's death changed everything again, as if a series of changes were needed to turn the young pirate through successive stages into an adult person.

Dina. She was vividly present in Kotor's mind, and he realised that he had not thought distinctly of her for a long time. He had an attack of tender melancholia. Memory is unsure. The father had been a physician, and Dina a goddess of the Renaissance who recited Sappho, Anacreon and Pindar by heart, who could argue like François Rabelais about the relative merits of the Mechanists of Cnidos compared with the Psychosomatists of Cos. A flash of lightning for Dina accompanied by a flash of lightning for medicine and divination. When they got out of bed they would throw themselves, drunk with words, confidences and discussions, on the archives of Kotor's grandfather, who had been burnt as a sorcerer, and whose papers had never left the loft. In fact, everything had begun there, the unbelievable wager lost by Dina and half-won by Kotor.

The chests contained innumerable treasures. Some of Roger Bacon's manuscripts; copies of treatises by Democritus, lost forever in the burning of the library of Alexandria; Hebrew and Chaldean texts. In the centre of all that was to follow, in the feverish whirlwind of research and sleepless nights, Dina did not even notice the birth of little Barbara. At the end appeared the unmasked face of the enemy—death.

Mechanically, Kotor uttered those last words aloud. Gianvittorio was dazzled. The *Word*, the keystone, had fallen into place. He suddenly *knew* who Kotor was and the secret of those disciples who were beginning to populate Alfama. Surprised, he noticed that he was less frightened than he should have been. He was in fact, rather satisfied and relieved at having pierced the obstinate secret.

Kotor looked at Gianvittorio, disentangling in a second the knot of reticence, secret questions and intense curiosity. Again candour, or a pretence at it, would be the best course. He related frankly and drily the different stages of his life.

As a young giant, the heir to a small estate and a little market town on a peak of the Carpathians, and free to use his strength as he wanted at the age of sixteen, he became within a few weeks a ferocious bird of prey. Years followed, of extortions, rape and orgies, with at the same time a frenzy of study and reading. Besides five or six European languages, young Kotor spoke Arabic, Greek, Hebrew and Sanscrit. His idols were Maimonides, Avicenna, Roger Bacon, Arab geomancy and the cabala, a theory of complete man which was perhaps only a purely verbal pretext. He was indeed a wild beast, but able to indulge all his whims like a Roman emperor. His immense curiosity gave him his chance. During the worst criminal orgies, without being quite aware of it, but due to another moral conception, he was building up a new way of life. While in the stables the lackeys disembowelled the already half-dead, wretched women his curiosity would drive him at dawn to the laboratory, an inheritance from his grandfather, where the furnaces had never been extinguished because he would not allow it.

Immersed in a pile of hurriedly written and practically incomprehensible notes he pursued the secret, as on the shaking bodies of tortured girls he pursued another elusive secret. It was a strange time, to which Dina's blue eyes put an end.

There followed ten years of a different frenzy, the pursuit in common of a chimera in the lurid glow of the castle's cellars, or in the lofts among the heaped-up papers, manuscripts and wizards' books accumulated by his grandfather. Three or four years later Kotor and Dina began the experiments. Now an even greater terror surrounded the castle, which became truly an accursed place. Kotor and Dina systematically explored every channel, all the magics, all the alchemies, literally tracking down death, making an inventory of last convulsions, last breaths. Kotor, who had never had any respect for the lives of human larvae, tested out some ideas, collecting quantities of blood in vast basins which were kept at the temperature of the human body, and which he furiously saw coagulating at one moment or another. His discovery of a Chaldean book (translated into Old German by Paracelsus, then transcribed into French, changed and altered), and named the *Book of the Oupyra*, meaning vampires, was *the* great revelation. After a few years the couple reached their target, the first step of a gigantic staircase. Drunk with delirious dreams, Kotor and Dina threw themselves exhausted one night in three on their enormous bed to sleep for a few hours. They made love in a similar state of exaltation, crossing the road of Pietro Aretino as they had before crossed the road of Maître Albert.

The birth of little Laurent and the death of Dina came with

dreadful rapidity at the very moment they thought they had found *the* solution. Too soon, and with rage in his heart, Kotor saw Dina dying in his arms. An instant more and he might have saved her for ever. His rage cruelly justified all he thought about mankind. Consciousness and the Ego, from the moment they exist, consider themselves entitled to immortality. Cheated of immortality, brought back to the last gasp, to a flutter of the eyelids of the Earth, man turns into a wild beast, a wolf for other men. Kotor searched here for the roots of cruelty rather than in some obscure instinct or in some compensation for some secret lack. Studious nights with the medical manuscripts of the schools of Cnidos and Cos brought him near the seat of the soul in the network of nerves and arteries. He believed he was on the eve of success in that mad endeavour when Dina's fragile soul was taken away.

For an instant he gave up and summoned his men at arms, but ten years of inaction had softened and fattened them. They could no longer get into their chainmail. Red, and short of breath, they were like too well fed dogs, no longer the pack of thin wolves of the old days. He cursed them and dismissed them to their feather beds and harlots. Frankly, the temptation had not lasted long. He went back to work with renewed vigour, pursuing his target without the old pleasure or joy. Mournful, frozen, he wandered all alone in the Carpathians in search of the lair of the last Oupyr, an unspeakably foul thing, neither a human being nor a beast, unaware of the value of the secret of which it was the chief trustee. The thing was dying of hunger. He gave it his blood, offering the jugular vein with cold detachment. The Oupyr's eyes shone with covetous desire which left him indifferent. He hardly reacted to the quick and intense orgasm of the beast, and was repelled by its wild gratitude.

He left its lair, and with his dagger he carved a boar-spear from the branch of an oak. The Oupyr was sleeping happily. Without awaking, it was hurled into the void when Kotor pierced its heart. The old texts were right, he said to himself with evil joy and a scientist's detachment. Death had lost a battle but not the war. It retreated but had not given in. The next task was to verify the second part of his hypothesis: without any further hesitation Kotor swallowed the contents of a small phial made of rock crystal which he always carried on him. Immediately he died his first death. That night he awoke. He never saw daylight again. Dead as a man, he was reborn as vampire. The centuries opened up before him. He went back to his castle, running for entire nights, hiding at dawn to sleep his new slumber as deep as the grave. He needed contact with Mother Earth. He comprehended the traditional reason for the coffin. On his arrival he followed the tradition scrupulously.

Prudently he began to explore the limits of his new condition. Henceforward he was a creature of the night and nearly eternal, and time had ceased to have any importance for him. He quickly converted little Barbara and little Laurent, who on their death joined him in the dark kingdom. A chosen few among friends and faithful servants gradually joined them. The castle became the eyrie of eagles of the night.

Fanatically, Kotor thought only of the second step of the staircase, the second battle against death. The enemy seemed to have stolen away. He had advanced to terrain on which no man had yet walked. There was no precedent, no prior experience. Yet there should have been. There must be traces somewhere, perhaps survivors. Barbarossa for example, the emperor who disappeared without trace; or Rabbi Loew, who evaporated (it was said) after the catastrophe of his golem. He must get to a town to be near libraries and the laboratories of alchemists. The capital city of alchemy was Prague. A line of carriages left the castle for a small and apparently modest house, in a loop of the Vlatva near the Jewish cemetery.

Under the house were immense cellars, and a warren of unexplored underground passages. Kotor started work again with renewed ardour, and the decades went by like hours. Succeeding generations of sorcerers, alchemists, initiates of all kinds, scarcely had time to be astonished by the astonishing longevity of their new colleague before they died. For the young Kotor quickly became the senior member, the prodigious old man in his mysterious cavern, more a legend than a reality. Those who had not met him, the majority, did not believe he existed. Not only years but centuries went by. The world changed. The old tradition of the materialistic Greek philosophers had loomed up again after miraculously surviving all the repressions, the systematic destruction of their writings and testimony: Empedocles, Democritus, Heraclitus, Kotor's old companions. The century of the Enlightenment passed in neither peace nor harmony, but seemed a fantastic intellectual hotchpotch, revealing a more subtle, a larger and more agile truth than that of Reason and the Spirit. Kotor received a visit from Swedenborg. They were as distant from each other as two stars, yet corresponded and communicated occasionally about Swedenborg's strange instruments. For the time being these were merely rough designs for machines that at some distant future date would harness and use vast invisible forces—a feat from which even the most audacious imaginations of the time would shrink.

The old Holy Roman Empire awoke, and began a systematic harassment of sorcerers, alchemists, astrologers, men of science, researchers, the initiates and members of secret societies. Persecutions and investigations recommenced, and the bonfires were relit. Despite his discreet life and the complex precautions with which he defended himself, and despite his clever social tricks (saying, for example, that he was his own great-grandchild), Kotor felt himself threatened. He knew that he had to run, find a new refuge, and leave no trace behind. The meeting with Clara had been a miracle.

A long silence followed Kotor's story. Gianvittorio now felt that all the pieces of a complicated puzzle had fallen into place. There had been many rumours, echoes of internal rows, strange informal alliances with sects or individuals by the Bohemian brothers. All was now explained, all could be understood.

'Why did you not become one of our brothers?' he asked.

Kotor looked at him strangely. Was it naïvety, machiavellism or ignorance? For the moment he could not decide. If Gianvittorio really had the rank and functions he claimed, his question was inexplicable. Provisionally, he chose naïvety.

'A few differences concerning metaphysics,' he said.

'They are the most important,' replied Gianvittorio gravely. 'Immediate political questions can always be settled.'

'I have an irresistible tendency to say the contrary. A cynicism inherited from the Renaissance.'

'The only part I have of that inheritance is an irresistible tendency to say no,' said Gianvittorio. 'I do not believe, or I believe no longer, in the future of cynicism in politics. Bernis is cynical. I sincerely believe that he wishes humanity well, and thinks he can achieve his aims through repugnant manœuvres. There is a lot of naïvety in that sort of cynicism. If he succeeds in putting through some minor reforms they will be sufficient to turn his masters against him, and he will be taken for a dangerous ideologist. And the moment he wants to touch the essential, namely the privileges of the nobility, the clergy and the army, he will be thrown out. I believe in the political future of generosity, madness, illusions, imagination . . .'

'And you find that among your brethren?'

'Frankly no. But I am not certain. There is everything in freemasonry. Even a weapon of war.'

'War, certainly. But against whom?'

'Against the roots of the ancient social order. I believe, though I know it to be a chimera, in a different social order, fraternal, humane, without classes and castes.'

'And to achieve that you make yourself the instrument of another class,' said Kotor. 'You will never make me believe that Paralis, alias Casanova, agent of the Lyons lodge, sincerely wants the abolition of privilege. He lives too well in the midst of the contradictions of this age, from which he gets all his manifold fun.'

'You cannot take Casanova as an example. He does live gloriously and pleasantly on his dungheap. But we have two lodges in Lyons. Freemasonry is divided into different factions.'

'I should say split.'

'Society will collapse,' said Gianvittorio. 'It depends on us whether it then gives birth to a monster or to a vigorous child.'

'It won't collapse on its own.'

'Certainly, it has to be pushed. You are approaching my ground.'

'It threatens to be a very bloody ground.'

'That is what bringing forth a child, and a massacre, have in common.'

'We do not have the same aim. My enemy, the enemy of mankind, is death.'

'Oppressors do not deserve to live. Having said that, I find your fight admirable, but illusory. You touch mysteries which the human mind cannot understand.'

'In the present state of our knowledge that is certain. The same goes for you. From your revolution, despite yourself, a new oppressor could be born.'

'We will fight him. We shall show less mercy to the traitors who slip into our ranks than to our enemies.'

'That would be fine if you were not already involved in compromises and understandings.'

'I do not follow you,' said Gianvittorio, taken aback.

'You merely re-establish God, who is the cement of your adversaries' coalition, upon a new throne. The God of the Catholics is the chief instrument for maintaining order, and the Church is the police force.'

'We fight the Church.'

'No. At best you will help it to reform itself. Truly, a good priest, who has compassion for the misery of the poor, always appeals to the charity of the rich; but he never incites men to revolt or to the destruction of the social order. In this case a cardinal like Borgia is a better proposition. That is clear, I know your lodges at least. They celebrate absurd masses. Be atheists, honestly, and I would join you. You think atheism as dangerous as the papacy. Your Supreme Being will either become a new Jehovah, cruel and intolerant, or he is just a useless fiction. The Great Architect of the Universe will inevitably be a great policeman. Your mummery, your leather aprons, your rites of initiation, your secret hierarchy are an obstacle to man's liberty.'

'And you? Will you bring it to him?'

'Yes,' said Kotor. 'Death frustrates man's elemental right to life. As a mortal, man is but a wolf, a beast of prey, limited in his spiritual, moral and mental development, slave to superstitions, fallacious promises about an illusory beyond, a play-thing of magicians, a miserable child.'

'Prometheus,' murmured Gianvittorio.

'An absolute blasphemy of course,' said Kotor. 'Zeus is just one of the facets of oppression. He punishes Prometheus and mankind. He wishes to maintain his rule, and counts on the slavery and blindness of men in order to reign. You ought to have the courage to espouse blasphemy. Having said that, you can see that in the short term I am fully with you. Your enemies are the same as mine. If we were caught, we would both perish at the stake. I can die: the light of the sun would reduce me to ash; if a boar-spear were to pierce my heart, the precarious equilibrium that allows me to survive would break. That is why I am also the ally and friend of astrologers, alchemists and every sort of sorcerer. Our persecutors are the same. Yours too. But reason alone is not enough. When I was denounced to the Inquisition by a necromancer mad with hate, the Inquisition had him burned as a coward. This was moral and edifying. He who works with the police finds sooner or later the police turning against him. That is the way with all police.'

'We are for the federation of the oppressed.'

'On condition that you control it.'

'But no. Why that distrust, why that suspicion?'

'It is nothing against you.'

'I do not matter. I have no private life, I account for all my acts. But let us stop, Count. You know too many of our secrets, which leaves me only the choice of killing you before I go, or making a good treaty of alliance with you.'

'Are you the master of your choice, without taking orders?'

'You are being offensive.'

'That is true,' Kotor admitted. 'I lost my temper. If you wish let us be friends. But bear in mind that it is dangerous for you.'

'I have no intention of permitting myself to be converted.'

'I was not speaking about taking you as a disciple, but of the extra risks you will run. The Marquis' police seem to be efficient.'

Suddenly the tension ceased. Laurent, Alexandra and Clara had followed, not without some anguish, the confrontation of the two men. Clara and Alexandra left the room, and came back with drinks, an emergency supply. Gianvittorio felt at home.

'If you will allow me to say so,' he said, 'I find that you recruit too many disciples—and without enough discernment. You reproach me for our taste for secrecy. May it please destiny that you do not have to regret your unlimited trust.'

Kotor sighed. He was of the same opinion; but how does one hold people back?

Chapter VIII

The night was already pitch-dark, as João jolted rapidly along on the tortuous road from Queluz to Cascais. Being late exasperated him. Alexandra's plan had succeeded beyond expectation. Mad with rapture, the Marquis had destroyed under his eyes a whole case of documents, promissory notes, and memoranda concerning the slave and tobacco trades, and he watched the whole procession of the dregs of his vice-royalty in Bahia. After that, the marriage contract was gloriously signed by him, the Marquis and Alexandra with a valid power of attorney from her mother and stepfather. Alexandra had been irresistible. She let the Marquis, who was on the verge of apoplexy, kiss her cheek. Then in the evening she escaped after hurling a quick insult at João and the Marquis. The police lost trace of her after a cunning false trail in Cintra. João should have felt liberated. However, having overcome one peril he immediately met another: Manuel had completely betrayed him. He was tolerated at the head of the ministry, but with reduced power. Manuel did not want power, not for the moment at least, but only a frenzy of pleasures organized by a master hand.

A private guard was carefully selected, supposedly at the King's service but in fact devoted to Manuel, twelve poor cadets replacing each other four by four every eight hours. The husbands of the ladies-in-waiting were paralysed with astonishment, but he knew perfectly well that the edifice could crumble at any minute.

Every night he joined Barbara in the house at Cascais. She seemed to have no desire to leave, and appeared to have forgotten her family altogether. She slept the whole day long, and lived only at night. The servants, especially the women, were under her spell.

João did not quite know what she did with them. One day he would ask to see. On the surface he was the fulfilled lover, his nights with Barbara a permanent feast. Her inventiveness and ardour both enchanted and frustrated him, denying him the role of the master or the male. The choice, the decision and the running of the performance were in Barbara's hands. He saw that she took her pleasure with enchanting savagery. She knew everything, he could ask for anything he wanted. Despite that, he exhausted himself trying in vain to possess her: she escaped him, using him as an instrument, an accessory, a purveyor of her pleasures. That slender insatiable body, always willing, always at his disposal, always ready to do or try out anything, in fact slipped through his fingers like sand. Her spirit escaped him even more. At the end of the most frantic orgies Barbara was as fresh and willing as if she had drunk a glass of iced water, the most secretive, the most stand-offish and the most inaccessible creature João had ever met.

The manservant on duty, a giant of a man and probably a Slav, who was a nightbird like his mistress, opened the gate for him. He had seen him arrive. The carriage entered under a vault. Volodia had already opened the carriage door. Youthfully João took the steps four by four. Barbara appeared, naked except for white stockings held by sumptuous garters with diamond buckles. Her pyramidal headdress contained powder, pearls, white feathers, jewels, emeralds and rubies from Minas Gerais. Two black girls holding torches wore turbans from Bahia and heavy necklaces. They too were naked. In a small drawing-room supper was laid, but João forgot everything, even his secret anger. In the centre of the cyclone they found a miraculously still patch of unruffled calm water. The two young black girls, hidden behind a tapestry, had seen all, whispering and tittering. They appeared with a collation, wines of Champagne and some fruit which, apart from the champagne, Barbara hardly touched.

One of the two peasant girls also came into the room. Moving his fingers lightly on Barbara's cheeks João looked absent-mindedly at all the activity. Real beauty is based on the cheek-bones, the framework, perhaps its architecture, the contrary of that flabbiness which is known as beauty at Court.

A little beast, a little sphinx, incomprehensible, elusive. The young peasant girl took a snow-white table-cloth and laid the table. She bent down, her backside was strong and firm, her garters came into view. As quick as lightning the hand of one of the black girls disappeared under the petticoat. It was not fast enough to go unnoticed by João. His erection was of such suddenness that he himself was surprised by it. The other black girl saw it, and burst into laughter. She had to explain why she laughed, and they all found themselves on the suitably enormous bed. The peasant girl's ingenuity could be explained only by Barbara's teachings. The two black girls had been taught enough by João to know the ropes by heart. When the first stage had ended for all of them—like a country dance full of invention and spirit—João asked for the other peasant girl to prove his assumption: Barbara was systematically educating the whole little group. Eussa came back, laughing her head off. She put a finger to her lips, took João by the hand, and pulled him away. Barbara, who surely had guessed what it was about, did not budge. The house having been built as a monastery had two cloisters, one above the other, the first the real one, the second a sort of gallery from which the rooms opened up, and jutted out over an inside garden. In the garden feebly lit by the moon, the young peasant girl was making love simultaneously with the two watchmen, one in front, one behind. Eussa tested João's reaction and then she attended to assuaging him.

A little later, coldly lucid once again, João noticed that the trio had vanished from the garden, and the little black girl, taking advantage of his brief slumber, had evaporated too. Stealthily he returned to Barbara's room. A faint light on the edge of the horizon announced the approaching dawn. He would soon have to go back to Lisbon. He brusquely opened a heavy door that gave access to her room, and stopped petrified by what he saw, or rather what he caught sight of. The two peasant girls and the two negresses were spread out naked on the bed. Enveloped in a heavy, sumptuous black silk cape Barbara had her back to him. As she bent over one of the peasant girls, the top of her cape covered the upper half of her body like two wings. The head of the black girl was between the thighs of the victim, thus she was taken twice. The head of the other, presumably Eussa, had disappeared inside Barbara's cape at a convenient height, and the second peasant girl, strangely bent, served the black girls with her tongue and hands. A curious quintet, said João to himself. His approach disturbed the group, and it broke up immediately. Barbara hid her face inside her cape, and the peasant girl whom she had embraced held her neck, hiding with both hands the marks of the bite. The two black girls dashed up to João. Eussa immediately dropped on her knees, and her mouth was even more agile than normally; and Leia, the other black girl, had already guided João's hands to the inside of her thighs, which were as smooth as a gazelle's. João was moved, and the thought that the two girls wanted to protect the trio on the bed and give them time to get themselves smoothed out as it were, came to him only much later: he thought of it in his carriage on the drive back, but absentmindedly and with ironical indulgence. It was not logical to enjoy the competence and experience of women, and yet refuse them the means to acquire that experience. There remained but a vain regret and a hint of jealousy for having been deliberately excluded from the five young women's private feast. Still, there had been compensations. Eussa was just finishing when a messenger arrived at a fast gallop: the King wanted to see him.

He hardly had time to take leave of Barbara, who was herself in a strange hurry to shorten the farewells, as always towards dawn. He was unaware of it, but the scattered pieces of the puzzle were falling into place in the depths of his subconscious, ready to rise some day in complete order.

The exalting images of the night's joys in the little house in Cascais abruptly disappeared. What could the King want from him so early? The sun had now risen, lighting up the water of the Tagus. Rowing to the rhythm of their vigorous singing the fishermen made for the sea. *Post coitum triste* was sheer idiocy. João felt wildly gay and madly tender, full of strength and enthusiasm. Debauch exalts me, and I love life and action only in extreme excess—even more, then. This morning, power is within my reach again.

His humour, his verve, his contagious liveliness did not fail to get the better of the King's moroseness. Manuel swiftly understood that he would wear himself out in trying to destroy João. He could do it, but at what a price. A treaty of alliance was preferable. João enjoyed himself greatly, and left the castle confirmed as prime minister. The doffing of hats as he left delighted him. I am still very young. So much the better.

Part Two

Some months later

Chapter I

Nobody knew his real name. He himself had probably forgotten it. Ten years ago when he arrived in Lisbon he perhaps knew it still, but now . . . He played five musical instruments, and spoke four languages fluently enough to give the impression that he knew five more. In the first year he had been the terror of the librarians with his immense form. More secret were his visits to the brothels of Bairo Alto, where at first he was only a customer. He had a prodigious memory fed by unequalled curiosity. Very quickly he became a partner, a ponce, one of the bosses, then the boss himself, his Achilles heel being self-complacency and touchiness. He was called Luciano Illyrico or just the Dalmatian. In spite of all the recommendations, in spite of all his connections and ramifications, the freemasons refused to receive him. He spoke about his resistance to the Turks, his ties with the exiles and his wars. Some were tempted, some seduced, but mistrust won the day. Gianvittorio had made inquiries, but never divulged the information he received. He gave but one instruction, akin to an order: no ties whatever with that man.

Luciano knew about it, nursed his anger, and thought up dark acts of vengeance. He was banished from Alfama for ever. Bairo Alto having become too small for him he had tried to weave a sombre spider's web round Alfama. In ten years he achieved practically nothing, a few informers at the most. He had sold all that at a high price to the Marquis, who was so satisfied that now it was Luciano who ran the police, in fact, another police, one more police force. With the police of Ricardo, the police of the Marquis, and the police of João that made four in all. Luciano had become the most secretive and the most powerful policeman in Lisbon. In the beginning he thought that it was not known, but nothing can be hidden in Alfama. Eventually he found out that it was known, swallowed his anger, and stopped the flow of information to protect his legend. The *éminence grise* of the Minister—and seeing himself as the future *éminence grise* of the whole kingdom, a ferociously fought-for position—he prepared himself for the joys of being a king in his own right. However, things always happen the same way: as his goal approached he found his ambition had evaporated. The contempt of others, justified by ten years of secret moves, ended in his despising himself, a disenchantment amounting almost to sloth. Fortunately the affair of the vampires had given him fresh youth.

He looked at the file he would show to the Minister. He pursed his lips; for it was not much. He would show it but not leave it with the Marquis. One more secret religion, some initiates, clandestine black masses, real enough but which nobody had succeeded in seeing. The vampire network protected itself fiercely, and the Dalmatian had failed to place a single agent among them. One could, of course, invent them even if only to impress the Marquis.

He had tried it too with Ricardo the chief of the municipal police, who in theory was the Marquis' man. The Marquis, however, was delighted by the enmity of these two guardians of the peace. He made Luciano the chief of the state police, with vague powers. His department and Ricardo's were amusingly at loggerheads, competing against each other. Now and then Luciano the Illyrian took to reflection. He made light of liberty, sovereignty, rationality; hence his hatred for João. His presence in the police force, practically at the head of it, seemed astonishing to him. He no longer knew what he wanted. In his village in Montenegro he had always been with the brigands, never with the Turkish gendarmes. Correspondent of the Encyclopedists, founder of the lodges of Ragusa, tireless traveller, he had changed allegiance at the age of twenty-five for simple reasons: more money, power and rewards, the hope of a protective kingdom, all perhaps a mirage. In the long run nobody accepted the Turks' valets. Having failed he ran to the other end of Europe in fear of his masters' vengeance. Unluckily for him the lodges already knew about it. There remained the police, but Luciano expected nothing any more. The amusement of employing torture in the back cellars gave rise the next morning to as bad a hangover as the abuse of drink. And now this business of the vampires had come up. As a matter of personal pride Luciano was ready to bluff the Marquis while waiting to find out more. For a time he was amused. Alexandra had got the better of him, and he had lost her trail. She had entered Alfama, and that was the end. Evaporated. It had made the Marquis with his courtship ridiculous. This sort of girl was good only for rape or capture. You take her, you let the coachmen take her, then you throw her out. That's life. The Marquis wanted to marry her, wanted perhaps even to be loved. Luciano laughed like a hyena.

He collected together the different sheets of his file, and went to the Marquis. The map of Alfama still hung there, the few sure landmarks marked with red. Yet they were now not so sure. Luciano was convinced that the vampires' network covered the whole neighbourhood, but he could not prove it. For a moment he was amused by the Marquis turning the pages, shamming interest while searching for an opportunity to ask for news of Alexandra without too much loss of face. Luciano had none. The Marquis was in a bind. He could make no move since he had no weapons left against João. He would, even so, remain Minister of Police. He could not attack but he was unassailable. The trouble was that every new day strengthened Luciano at his expense. The Marquis wanted to use him, not be the prisoner of his zeal and efficiency. Throughout his career he had the constant fear of an indispensable associate becoming independent. And now it had happened. But Luciano, who had understood that, behaved with discretion. The bird was in the trap.

They looked at each other, and at that instant they both experienced an attack of unadulterated hatred for each other.

'Let us get down to work,' said the Marquis after a silence.

He will see through me, he thought. Let him.

The next file concerned the freemasons. About them, the police knew everything, or nearly everything. Luciano showed the Marquis a long letter from Casanova. The Venetian was carefully obliterating his traces so that no one should be able to get at him. Trusted by many of the brothers—all of them in high positions in society if not in the organisation—he chased without apparent reason all over Europe. Luciano was one of his most secret links with the different police forces. No one would have suspected that wary connection. Casanova hoped to contrive a return to Venice, perhaps even to find employment.

He had met Luciano years ago in Dalmatia. The dark aura of terror that surrounded Luciano already fascinated the Venetian. He thought that through him he would always find access to the darkest rings of the police underworld. Casanova was for Luciano the image of what he should like to be, but knew he could never achieve. He was ready to hate the tumultuous Giacomo for life, had not Casanova's grace and flattery disarmed him for ever. They wrote to each other twice a year, informing each other in detail about their respective ups and downs. Casanova advanced with extreme caution. Even apart, they continued to understand each other. During the last few years, Luciano's escudos had got Casanova out of many embarrassing situations. (An investment of his father's, the only one he possessed.) Casanova's notes, classified and endorsed by Luciano, circulated *via* the Marquis among the heads of police of five or six large and small monarchies. A spider's web in the labyrinth of freemasonry.

Luciano held back his sudden suspicion. Casanova might be under surveillance by some sort of internal police. His information seemed curiously manipulated, and was too coherent. Somebody or other must be providing him with these pieces of information, to send them on with the sole aim of verifying the existence of a channel of communication. For example, he denounced with much circumstantial detail a wine merchant from Madeira. The Marquis wanted to have him arrested at once, or to exile him at least. Being too rich he had lent money to too many noblemen. But fifteen dukes would invade police headquarters to get him out of jail, and Luciano had to work hard to persuade the Marquis to do nothing, not even put him under surveillance for fear of showing up Casanova. The thick-headed Marquis demanded all Luciano's patience. Luckily there was something less weighty: two little novices, accused by their Mother Superior of circulating forbidden books, had been handed over to the secular arm. They were in the cellar of the ministry. Luciano and the Marquis went down there.

The two little girls were on their knees, trembling like leaves. They had been brought there half an hour before, and they could not keep their eyes off the instruments of torture, evidently prepared for them, or off the gigantic executioner with icy eyes under the red cowl who was heating his pliers and iron rods in a brazier. The trestles left no doubt about the girls' fate. On the appearance of Luciano and the Marquis in the cellar, the executioner undressed the two girls more quickly and more expertly than the best lady's maid. They were slender, their breasts hardly developed, but already dark between their legs. Luciano found his own ritual more subtle than that of the Marquis who, as the executioner, began the torture of his victim, had his fun immediately; Luciano followed a more sophisticated method—at least that was what he said. The Marquis' victim deafened them with her shrieks.

Luciano's girl was prevented. She would, however, find her fate less enviable than that of her companion. It would take longer, that was all.

At the end of the performance the girls were in a very bad state, and Luciano wondered whether he should have them killed or kept for another occasion. Coming out of his trance the Marquis' face looked livid and ugly. He was the slave of his desires, not their master. Luciano was healthy enough to contemplate his pleasures and their consequences coolly. He let the executioner deal with what was left of the two girls.

Gianvittorio had posted two of his men in front of the house of Guilherme, the wine merchant from Madeira. Their instructions were not to watch Guilherme but those who might eventually come to watch him. Gianvittorio came for news. Nothing. None the less, he thought his trap perfect. An ingenious idea, he believed, giving information to someone one suspected of being an informer to verify the consequences and unmask the double agent. Casanova, warned through him of the supposed importance of Guilherme, should have squealed on him, and the Marquis should have had him watched. But something must have happened. Gianvittorio never thought of Luciano's role, unable to imagine even for a second that such a subtle brain was at the head of the police. He calculated quickly. Casanova had had ample time to inform the Marquis' police. If the police did not move that meant that Casanova had said nothing. Gianvittorio's whole theory collapsed.

He returned home bitter and worried. It was not easy to give up an assumption he had cherished for so long. Fernanda was waiting for him. He made love to her with added fervour because he felt unhappy and depressed. But as always the familiar feeling of plenitude and serenity followed. They chatted naturally; for his body and the young girl's body the exercise they had just taken was the source of unmixed pleasure. He enthusiastically decided that there was nothing finer than shared love. Mistrust and caution, which had always been the rules of his life, simply disappeared. But immediately he realised that he had used her like a utensil, almost like a medicine, a means to get the better of his own problems, but not for her pleasure. Abruptly he looked at her as if he had never seen her before, and found her more beautiful. He had an *élan* that surprised even him. She too was surprised, having found him a little distant before. He discussed with her his tactics, sometimes even his strategy, without revealing to her the profound reasons that pushed him to action. They lay naked and stretched out on the large bed in her small, hidden house in the centre of Alfama. If freemasonry, he said, was only a revival of Rosicrucianism, it would not interest him. Since his talk with Kotor he had felt strangely ill-at-ease while presiding over the ceremonies. The rites and appurtenances irritated his sense of the ridiculous. One could not leave the Church for that. It was true enough that many brothers—a certain number of them anyhow—accepted the double allegiance, and played complacently with the saints and Christ. Compared with them Gianvittorio felt like an atheist. It was no coincidence that they were the most ferocious in defending order on earth, as an expression of divine order, and that they sanctified the hierarchy as it stood. One cannot liberate oneself of the idea of sin, slavery and the limitations of religion without deciding to destroy the existing order at the same time. The throne and the altar were so interlinked that building a new altar implied a new throne. There was no means of getting away from that. Gianvittorio clearly saw that constituting a secret society within the secret society had become inevitable. There were brother and brother. Casanova for example. Gianvittorio trembled with fury whenever he thought of it. He would have given anything to catch him with his hand in the bag. Admittedly he did them favours, running around tirelessly, transmitting messages, tying the knots of the cobwebs woven by the Order. Gianvittorio did not consider himself a puritan; Fernanda proved this. But Casanova acted without principles, or rather with the sole principle of preparing a happy return to Venice. Gianvittorio knew without being able to prove it that he worked for Master Grande. Every time he spoke about it to his superiors the answer was 'Not important'; but one distrusted him at the very least. Gianvittorio, his thoughts distracted for a moment by Casanova, continued his reverie aloud, feeling lyrical for the first time. The grand dream of liberty fired him. Fernanda was fascinated. He clearly saw all the absurdity of the hierarchy and the initiations. It had frequently been difficult for him to hide his smile, the smile of soothsayers who meet in the streets of Rome. An organised party was necessary, he said to himself. One cannot lift a rock without a lever. Besides, the Catholic church was not ashamed of it. The ceremonies perhaps helped the party. He dreamed of a party that would not have one type of reasoning for the masses and another for the chiefs. Having himself become a sort of chief he fundamentally desired the abolition of the idea of chiefs. A fine perspective for a settlement of accounts if he came to power. Which power? In a kingdom which one would seize by intrigue and conspiracy? And what would become of an isle of liberty in an ocean of servitude? His spirit fought with itself.

In conclusion he tried out some new postures with Fernanda which her love accepted but her prudishness refused. And if one started the revolution by freeing women from their scruples? He meditated about that with some satisfaction and complacency.

Kotor pushed away the sheet on which he had drawn the geomantic shield. As usual the answer remained ambiguous, disappointing and extremely open. Burning to reassure him Clara had already suggested ten interpretations. Kotor sighed. He clearly saw a heavy wall rising in front of him at the very moment he thought he had succeeded. A dream-like organisation, numerous acolytes, dozens of homes with their own vampires spending long and cosy nights with their families, sleeping in the daytime in home-made coffins. In the streets the landlords of the vampires recognised one another by the scarves they wore round their necks, and by their quiet self-assurance. For all of them death had been defeated. Only Kotor knew to what extent the victory was precarious.

All had a sense of security, the profound conviction that a refuge had been found, so they surrendered to real comfort. Kotor questioned the stars, multiplying the geomantic computations. He knew how to recognise behind those amiable façades the dark faces of the worst premonitions. As the shepherd of a contented little flock, he forced himself to cut a reassuring figure. But his studies were not progressing, not at all. As commander-in-chief he had to pretend he believed in victory. With its warriors very quiet and well sheltered, the war took a curious shape. Yet it was hard to wish for a return of the persecutions to put them on their mettle. He could say nothing even to Clara. In Barbara's absence, and with Laurent's mind full of romance, he felt alone and depressed. The time which should have been given to the serious consideration of the validity of his work was spent in fabricating a sort of sham government of the sham, a clandestine state, yet without which the group could not survive.

He felt himself to be at the limit of the possibilities his knowledge had given him, perhaps of his entire logical system. Some centuries later airmen would thus try to fly over mountains higher than the highest altitude their aircraft could reach. His spirit searched for passages between steep rocks to improbable passes. He knew what he had to find, but knew too that he could not do so without a mutation beyond his reach. He overcame the tension caused by that sharp realisation of the contradiction facing him by falling asleep, which apart from his daily hibernations never happened to him.

Clara looked at him in amazement, and had to take him to his coffin in case he woke up after dawn.

Barbara sighed. Dawn was already lighting up the horizon behind the hills. There was no escape, she would have to go down. At night it was simpler, for the prolonged life was more like normal existence. João turned on his side in the bed and groaned. Barbara held back her laughter. She wore him out, he said. For some time his failures had been more frequent. João blamed his excesses of eating and drinking for it. Or perhaps the effect of excessive doses of aphrodisiacs.

His head ached. In the last resort what he enjoyed about women was novelty. At the beginning Barbara was novel every night. Now, although he did not admit it, she had become a habit. Since she did not give herself in that way she could not yet turn into a ritual. Headache and head full of schemes. An erection or the pursuit of power. João had the government but not the power. He applied naïvely enough to his case the rules of superstitious asceticism observed by some athletes during competitions. Then two days later he took larger doses of medicine.

To Barbara, these stories of derisory struggles for influence in a derisory kingdom made no sense whatever. Erotic contortions amused her more. Yet not much. Passion, sometimes ten orgasms in a row, then always that feeling of emptiness and futility. Any hefty groom, dazed, delighted, understanding nothing, could give her sufficient blood and spunk. After the excitement of their meeting she had vaguely expected something, something frantic. But in his way João was very reasonable. She lost all desire to initiate him, even if she had ever thought of it.

The light was getting stronger. She crossed the little fragile and elegant house, nearly running. In a boudoir she pushed a panel:

beyond it was a spiral staircase, and at the bottom of this a secret cellar, where on two trestles stood the coffin, her bed. She got into it very depressed, and fell into that strange slumber from which she emerged asking herself every time what sort of dreams there were that left no memory. When she had asked her father whether vampires dreamed he scolded her. She burst out laughing. 'When you give us true immortality, allow us to dream—and above all leave us with the memory of our dreams. Otherwise it is such a bore.' He immersed himself in his pots and pans again.

Alexandra awoke at noon. Not a sound in the mansion. Hers was now an easy, familiar rhythm: feverish nights, mad at times, then heavy sleep from dawn on, after Laurent's return to his daily death. She emerged at midday. The hardest thing was giving up all the dawns at dawn. But what could it matter in a love life at such a high level of fulfilment, to exchange it for the loss of dawn? It was not as bad as that. She would have taken it better in his company. But those long hours of inaction from noon to dusk! There was the library, but it was largely Kotor's, the books beyond her comprehension. And like physical exercise, it could not compare with their dream.

In the deserted mansion, around which she still did not really know her way, she went on a tour of discovery. Laurent lived in one wing, three immense rooms which he practically never left. And of course the cellar. What a profession to be a vampire's woman, she thought. She ventured into the next wing, went beyond the central building, the drawing rooms and Kotor's laboratory. Since their arrival in Alfama no member of the Kotor family had entered the other wing, which was left completely unused. It had the airiness, the silence and the smell of rooms which nobody ever entered. There was a music room turned store-room, where fruit, plants and herbs were dried; and next to it an enormous fencing room with targets for firearms and sidearms, swords, pistols, rifles, and even decorated blunderbusses, powder barrels, balls of all calibres, a little transportable oven, and moulds in which to forge one's own bullets.

Alexandra laughed happily. For some time she had been dressed as a man during the day for her own pleasure. In the evening she wore a dress, petticoat and stockings again. Laurent liked to lift dresses and petticoats up to the navel or up at the back. Or he asked her to lift them herself while he contemplated her—but with the stockings on. At the beginning she could not quite understand why he loved that. Women do not use their eyes for their orgasm, said Laurent, laughing. It was absurd to deny oneself one of the senses when one had so few. He expatiated upon the subject. Alexandra would have preferred to make love, but she adored listening to him. He spoke about the stars where men would live and enjoy more senses than the five classical ones. Already he was searching for instruments that could reproduce artificially those unknown senses about which he was so ignorant. He was like that. Words gave him sexual pleasure, seeing and contemplating.

She took off her waistcoat and jabot, and took up a sword to attack a quintain equipped with a wooden sword. The dummy turned on its own, and she nearly received a slash across her face. It annoyed her. Suddenly it was hot, she took off her shirt and continued. There was a large mirror at the end of the room, no doubt for learners to be able to see themselves and correct their stances. When she entered she had scarcely noticed it. All of a sudden she saw herself: a big girl with tousled hair, panting, naked to the waist, and a battle sword in her hand. She was struck by the sight, and within a second was as excited as she had ever been: like a man who has an erection in the street on seeing the knee of a girl getting into a carriage, she said to herself. Almost in a trance, she threw herself on a nearby divan. Afterwards she asked herself sneeringly whether it had been put there for that purpose, and whether other fencers had been as moved as she for the same reason. She pulled down her breeches, tearing the buttons open; then rapidly in full passion for the first, and slower and more subtly for the second, she made herself come twice. She dropped into a deep sleep which lasted for hours. When she came to her senses, night was falling.

Alexandra did not hesitate for an instant. She ran just as she was instinctively to the other wing with sword in hand. Laurent had just woken up and appeared at the top of the staircase as she entered the room. He stared in astonishment. She was naked to the waist, her pubic hairs were revealed in the opening of the unbuttoned breeches, her hair was like a bacchante's, and she held a sword in her hand. His surprise, she appreciated, was understandable. Laughing, she took his hand and pulled him to the fencing room. Panting with excitement she explained about the mirror, the divan and her pleasure. He had no time to be astonshed by her frankness: already he was looking at her in the glass.

She took off everything in a second, and attacked the dummy. Laurent could not resist it. Though nearly slashed by her sword he caught her in flight and dragged her to the divan. He was inside her already.

A little later she felt terrible hunger. Laurent had already had his essential nourishment. But he too liked the food of the living for his own pleasure. Alexandra got up, and hurried to the kitchen. She realised that she was naked only when she saw the surprised looks of the serving men and women. Yet none of them stared. Some were brothers, the others disciples. Nothing astonished them in Kotor's household, yet some of them could not help admiring the shape of the young mistress's back. Alexandra prepared the tray: a pie, wines and fruit. She carried it with great dignity.

Nobody uttered a word. In the corridor a pin pricked her foot. She swore, put down the tray, and pulled on the first footwear she found, light short boots, beautiful. When she entered the fencing room Laurent, who had calmed down, lost control again at the sight of her. The divan was used once more.

They ate, and Laurent pondered. She had told him everything, which was certainly desirable. But at the same time he had seen the danger of the long, idle afternoons, the danger of that accumulated, unemployed vitality. She interrupted him. She now wanted a pistol-shooting competition. Laurent gave in. They lined up. Alexandra was an excellent shot, yet could not match Laurent's perfect precision. They were engrossed.

The noise of the pistol shots reached the laboratory where Kotor was working. He straightened himself, and leaving a water-caltrop in which two liquids of different colours and density were mixing, he followed the noise like a dog on a trail. He could not believe his eyes.

Alexandra and Laurent, naked and as keyed-up as fleas, and unaware of the essentially erotic state of the situation, were arguing about fuses and the weight of the gunpowder charge. The scene amused Kotor, and then he became strangely excited. In a daze he returned to the laboratory. Clara appeared. She came at the right moment, but understood only a few minutes later what he wanted.

Chapter II

Dusk came at last—dawn for him. Laurent surfaced from his heavy, dreamless sleep. He should have liked to dream of the sun. Now and then in front of a fire he remembered the light and heat of the sun with awful regret. On rare occasions he had caught his father with the same poignant sensation. On those days Kotor worked even harder, or indulged with his son in endless speculations about what the world would be like without death, but with normal daily life, without the curse of the world of shadows: the hope of immortality; an endless life not confined to the night, cellars and coffins.

Laurent heard Alexandra moving about in the house. As always he was impatient to join her. That urge for life and heat, and for blood too. Although it was vital it was not essential. He felt restrained. Although this sensation might last for decades or centuries, it would end if Kotor's researches failed. The trials and the shock of his first death had given him a foretaste of what the second would be like. Understandably that twilight world in which he lived was preferable to the total night that awaited them. At times Kotor said: 'Imagine a planet turning round its sun, showing it always the same side because of some mathematical whim of the spheres, one side perpetually in daylight, the other in darkness. There surely would be a zone of penumbra. The frontier would not be a rigid demarcation line between shadow and light. We are in that penumbra between life and death.'

Laurent had never before understood the religions of Father Sun so well. He went on listening. Alexandra must have gone down to the stables to look after the black mare who was her consolation in Penelope's absence. Shortly, when he would roll her over on the sofa, she would laugh, smelling of the horse. She would cry for form's sake, 'So what? For you vampires, it is like a quick one in the morning, a reflex, an automatic gesture. Why don't you screw the maidservants who want nothing better, being vampires too.' He would laugh and roll her on her other side.

He smiled to himself, and went in search of her. She was

grooming the mare. She gave him a sidelong glance. 'You can't even wait for the sofa. You need the hay now.' Already she had unbuckled her belt. He did not have to pull down the army breeches she had taken to wearing: she had done so under the belly of the mare who was watching her mistress's contortions with indulgence.

They went upstairs, as pleased as peasants on a Sunday evening on their way home from the fields, where they had spent the day climbing on each other.

This time it was she who wanted it. She took herself to the bathroom, a replica built to her orders of her luxurious bathroom in the ducal palace, and undressed. She kept on only her stockings. The diamond studded garters came from João *via* Barbara, from one sister-in-law to the other. Laurent was reading. Her scent made him lift his head. 'The one,' said Alexandra, 'was as the hussars do it. Now it will be a long and complicated ritual, a climb to a peak that will appear at the turn of the road.' It was what she called the big one. It was like a staircase too. She had invented a new ending. One by one she opened all the doors of her body for him. She let him come a last time, having held herself back until then. Now she let herself go, and at that exact moment she stretched her neck so that the bite and the flowing blood she was giving him should immediately follow the apogee of her orgasm. She knew she could never make love with a non-vampire again.

So it was. Afterwards in each other's arms they told each other what their mental eyes saw, letting their spirits glide from image to image, from vision to vision, as on a stretch of sand from which the tide of slumber had withdrawn. Often they were shreds of the future, portraits which they knew to be exact, of several possible futures. Or phantoms of the past whose clarity equally impressed them. In Alexandra's case the strange biological and chemical process that would turn her into a vampire after her first death was not yet accomplished. Thus she remained more conventionally human. She still had dreams, and compared the visions they had together with the messages she received from the depths of her soul. They chatted and discussed endlessly. She was enthusiastic about those advantages her situation gave her as wife, sister and perhaps mother of a vampire, finding her destiny unique. She now remembered her old disgust for all men, and the change she had deliberately provoked, deliberately accepted and then taken the responsibility for upon herself, and which now appeared to her as the fulfilment of her need always to fight against and deny the bondage of her womanhood. She was happy, and said so to Laurent.

He did not altogether believe her. It seemed incredible to him that she did not suffer from her confinement, even if it was voluntary. He put questions to her, trying not to show his anxiety too much. Forests, rivers to bathe in, beaches to gallop along, she must surely miss these things. For him she was the picture of strength and good health and the joy of being and living. Yet that athletic creature was for the whole day locked in the palace-prison alone with those vampires in the cellar (the only exception being the grooms, who were not). Every day he felt the narrowness of his coffin, and longed to feel the sweet heat of grass in the sunshine, the harshness of an overheated wall; and when the sun had hardly vanished he ran to feel its last traces. He could not understand how she could sneer at this, or do without it. She reassured him. No, she regretted nothing. Not in the least. Her days went by quickly. She had jumps built in an unused courtyard and tired the mare out taking her over them. She read in the sunshine. Yes, in the sunshine, she said with laughing eyes. She was all right. She never gave a thought to the outside world, as though it did not exist. A desert island would not seem any farther. Above it all were the nights. That was life, her life.

Right. They had loved enough, talked enough. It was time to work, to help Kotor find the way. Laurent got up, left the room, and his footsteps died away. Alexandra stretched herself like a cat. She rose and went to the window to see what Laurent was up to. The yard, illuminated by the moon as if it were daylight, was deserted. She put on a dressing-gown and started out for Kotor's domain. They adored each other.

On reaching the laboratory she looked round maliciously, searching for the woman. She hoped that Kotor like Laurent . . . In brief she would have tried it out with him happily. There was nobody there, neither Laurent nor Clara. He was working alone, and received her with frank but paternal admiration, without glancing too long at the leg she was showing or at the bosom which was in evidence in the opening of the sumptuous dressing-gown.

She seated herself on the arm of his chair, and he was obliged to put his arm round her waist, her favourite posture for a truly serious conversation. It was surely so for Kotor too. She came to him like that on certain evenings to rekindle his eloquence. Clara was an assistant, a fellow researcher, and occasionally a rival. They now no longer spoke of the goal, but only of the means, the cooking utensils. But from time to time he could not resist the desire to speak about the aims he pursued.

Kotor was boiling over. Old treatises about alchemy were piled on his table. Old theological and historical works too. Absent-mindedly and respectfully Alexandra turned the pages with one finger. Christian belief, Kotor grumbled in a low voice. The massacres of Arians; Charlemagne's conversion by the sword of the robbing, murderous hordes; the armies of the Crusades, the Cathars, the Albigensians, the Vaudois, Cortez, Pizarro, the Inquisition, the stake for Jews and witches—and in opposition to all that the aura of terror that the Church, that all Churches, had created around the idea of the vampires. Here in Alfama, for the first time and because of the health of that little community, the word vampire had slowly turned from negative into positive. Kotor badly needed to lean on somebody. He spoke about the massacre of the Red Indians, the Pueblos, the Incas, those who peacefully dreamed of the Sun their father, and were dragged from their peace by fire, the sword, torture and Christianity. Even with Clara, Kotor had never dared before to formulate the words he began to say to the dazed Alexandra.

'The eagles,' he said, 'those rapacious birds of heraldry that adorn the shields and helmets of the Teutonic knights, the banners of the military orders, and the flags of the emperors, are the appropriate image of the nature of the Christians; yet they only have to say we drink blood to terrify feeble souls.'

Until then Alexandra had always found Kotor to be admirably calm and serene. She gently stroked the old man's white hair, a bush of swan's wings, astonished as with Laurent by the marble-cold skin, yet retaining like a memory or an echo the warmth of the skin of mortals.

Kotor continued a little more calmly. He had forgotten the Church of Christ and the massacres. He called himself the heir of Empedocles, Prometheus, Æsculapius, Hippocrates, physician and cook at the same time. As always he spoke of the school of Cnidos and the school of Cos, and the terrible backward jump of humanity, the systematic destruction of the works of Democritus. He got up, took a large volume of Pindar, and read aloud the third pythic: *dear soul, place not your hopes in an illusory immortality, throw yourself into action.* Then he spoke of the story of Castor and Pollux, one mortal, the other immortal, who finally left for the stars outside time and space.

Alexandra strongly felt that he was indecisively turning in circles round a revelation, an essential secret. Finally he spoke about Mithras, the Roman armies infiltrated since Hadrian's time by secret societies ready to make Mithras the heir of all the ancient gods; but then came Constantine's counter-move. He related Hadrian's sacrifice of a bull in Egypt, sprinkled with the bull's blood . . . Yes, he was close to Mithras, if not Mithras himself.

Alexandra offered him her neck on which the traces of Laurent's teeth were still visible. Kotor could not decline her offer. He took her in his arms, and for some time he bit the neck on the other side. The blood and life of Alexandra entered him. Then he straightened himself, appeased and as happy as she was.

From the yard came the sound of horseshoes on the cobbles. Alexandra ran to the window. Laurent was looking up at her, holding by the bridle a shining, white stallion, the finest horse Alexandra had ever seen in her life.

She raced down like a madcap, and threw herself into his arms.

'The best present that was ever received,' she said into his ear. She stroked the magnificent coat of the horse. He quivered. She was overcome with joy. It was like a halo round her.

'Has he a name?' she asked.

'I do not know,' said Laurent. 'I went to the stable of the Peralta brothers. They were surprised to see me coming to them at this hour to buy a horse. I saw him, took him, and rode him away in less than two minutes. They could not even count the money twice. Here he is.'

'I will call him Mithras.'

She jumped into the saddle. Mithras started prancing on the spot. Laurent ran to the stable, and brought out Lili, the mare, as black as Mithras was white.

Ceremoniously the horses made each other's acquaintance.

'One cannot be content with turning round in circles in the yard with these beasts,' said Laurent.

'It is imprudent to go outside,' said Alexandra. 'I am quoting you. It's *verboten*.'

'Never mind. It is nearly midnight. There is nobody in the streets.'

'Go where?'

'To the lanes of the park beneath the Rossio. We shan't see a soul, and not a soul will see us.'

Already Alexandra had the permanently closed front gate opened. They galloped out through it.

If anybody had walked every night that week through the wide lanes of the park, which was deserted even in daytime, he would have seen a strange spectacle: a black mare and a white stallion at full gallop, and Laurent at Alexandra's side, their hair floating in the wind, and their faces aglow with happiness.

The horses went like lightning, as happy as their riders. Every night they got bolder, both riders and horses. Alexandra waited more anxiously than Laurent for the first signs of dawn. For her sake, because of the pleasure she took in those outings, he might have forgotten to take care. She was mad with joy, and even pretended they were leading the normal life of normal lovers. They made rapid love in the stable like fugitives at a frontier. Then they woke up, and decided to be careful, be more moderate, to ride out only every second day, and perhaps that was what lost them, or was the first step in their undoing.

One night one of Ricardo's policemen, staggering drunk among the bushes, could not believe his eyes. He returned the next night and saw nothing. He was ready to give up but obstinacy got the better of him. He came back the third night, and saw the black mare and the white stallion, Alexandra recognisable anywhere. The policeman observed the rhythm of their motion, and was amused by its precision.

Then he tried to follow them, but that was difficult. He was afraid to expose himself, yet took the risk of losing them on entering Alfama. But he waited next night for them at the spot where he had lost sight of them. They did not come. He persisted the following night, and he was right. They rode past him like lightning. He followed them to São Miguel, where he stopped. He came back the next two nights. Of course, they came past the second night. Thus habits are established. It was easy to track them as far as Kotor's palace, their nest.

Somebody must be told. But who? Ricardo, Luciano, the Marquis or, the very top, João? He hesitated, aware that his career depended on his choice. He chose the Marquis. Luciano would not forgive him. But if all went well the Marquis would become prime minister.

The first thing the Marquis did the moment he knew about Alexandra's lair and the nightly follies was to tell Luciano, who almost immediately found the ill-advised policeman at police headquarters, dragged him to the back-yard and beat him into a pulp. He would have killed him if he had not wanted information. When he knew, he killed him. He could not tolerate even the slightest attempt upon his aura of terror.

What now? He wanted to get Alexandra out, and thought of organising a police raid. Ten to twenty men coming down from the Castello, others from Graca would meet up in Alfama. But Luciano stopped that. By the time they reached the tenth house they would be noticed, counted and killed, and their prey would be warned.

The Marquis fumed, but he would not give up. His eyes narrowed. Luciano could guess his rage as he imagined Alexandra in ecstasy, lying bloodless under her vampire. He announced a plan, though he did not yet have one. He raised the bonuses of the police spies. In his office the reports accumulated in the files. Luciano felt shivers running down his neck. The vampire heresy gripped Alfama body and soul, a vampire in the family circle in many homes. They were known as the Pure. Their families spent the whole night with them, and put them into their coffins at dawn. The more timid among the initiates wore scarves, cravats or shawls. The others could not care less, and showed their scars, talking freely among themselves, as happy as conquerors. The worst of all was the air of happiness and hope. The priests understood nothing, dropped their arms, and went furtively to the deserted churches to say Mass. Even confessions were much fewer. A dark curtain of silence had come down. Provocation brought no result.

Luciano found himself confronted by a problem: a general massacre was the only solution. He had nothing against massacres, but in this precise case he did not consider it an efficacious procedure. The arch-priest of Alfama raised his arms. He would not even dare to entrust his priests with obtaining information. If that were known, and it would be known, they would be swept away.

Because of its shape the district was a natural fortress. The points of entry being few, they were easily barricaded and defended. Luciano too had known the legendary Casbah in Algiers. The Bey's police stopped at the invisible frontier of the Casbah, which had become a free city, an autonomous and inaccessible territory.

Yet the answer had to be found. There is always a means. The Marquis was unconvinced, but did not dare to do anything.

João felt he had won, but he did not understand how or why. The Marquis kept silent in the Council. Ricardo had become a hard worker, keeping himself busy with the highways and the drainage; and without making any secret of it he had made a lot of money, as if wanting to show that he was corrupt but not ambitious. Luciano moved in the shadows, and was seen no longer. He let João know that he was not watching him any more. João did not care for these gifts but had to accept them. Even the stars interfered. The horoscopes and the geomantic compositions were exceptionally favourable. Only the obstinate presence of *Cauda Draconis* in all of them indicated a permanent, obscure danger.

So João decided to hold feasts. Unable really to overcome Manuel, the King took to sharing his pleasures. He went with girls without giving up young boys completely. João met Manuel. His heart was not in it. João clearly saw Manuel's long-term strategy, his gambler's patience where his downfall was concerned. He made him friendly offers, and Manuel did not even blink. He accepted everything, promised nothing, nor even hinted at it. The day he took over, João would be fortunate to escape with his life. He gave Manuel limitless credit for the department of pleasures. The Prime Minister, Duke, Cardinal and Archbishop became the producer and organiser of feasts for his future successor and executioner, and for the King.

The canal on the estate in Queluz was ravishing. João had the glazed tiles of the little bridge changed for lewder scenes of a mythological character. An engineer from the naval dockyards built a genuine frigate with three ivory masts and silk ropes on a scale ten times smaller than life. She had room for twelve sailors, who were naked and booted, and disguised as buccaneers. None was older than fourteen. They were whipped with the cat-o'-nine tails bending over canons made of jacaranda wood. Then the pages took them; and all the King had to do was to take the well-disposed pages.

The ladies of the Court installed themselves on the banks and the bridge, their skirts lifted, front or back. Manuel had a look, then disappeared. Worn out and sad after the voyage in the frigate, the King gave himself over to the pages in his bedroom. Despite the cordials and medicines he remained dazed on the sofa for hours, and signed whatever João wanted him to. Manuel did not even bother to distrust him.

As a matter of prudence João had left Cascais. No one knew that on the other bank of the Tagus he owned a small mansion, built by an Italian architect, pure *seicento*, a square building with a pointed tower at each corner, a vast interior garden, and colonnades. It was known as the Quinta das Torres, and stood among olive trees at Azeitão, far from anywhere and near everywhere. Barbara had moved there at night. It was a mere whim, she said. It had been a strange convoy in almost total darkness. The olive groves round the vineyards and the cellars had been in the possession of João's family for centuries. Even a dog could not change his bitch without everybody knowing and keeping silent about it. The change rekindled João's and Barbara's passion.

João left Lisbon at dusk. From the quay at Sodré, in the confusion of the traffic, a boat with six oarsmen, all natives of Bahia and darker than the night, took him across the river. An hour later he was at the Quinta. Barbara encouraged his tastes. Shortly before dawn he had a meal, and chatted about the government. As the sky turned pale a stable boy saddled João's and his bodyguard's horses, and they left before the sun rose, which suited Barbara. She saw him leave, then after taking a little blood from the peasant girls and the black girls she went down to the cave. João suspected absolutely nothing about the vampires.

The Marquis and Luciano examined all his papers. All the information brought by João's police remained with them. Apart from having wisely expressed his disapproval of the vampires, João remained almost entirely ignorant about the whole business. On certain evenings their Brazilian slaves admitted João and Barbara to their ceremonies. João had given permission to an old woman, 'Mae' Meniniuha, to build a hut in a hidden vale under the olive trees. She made for him a *jogo dos buzios*, and he acquainted her with geomancy. They respected each other. João and Barbara, pressed against each other, watched the old gods of Africa, who after their singular detour through Bahia had come to lay hands on the Daughters of the Saints. Drums were beaten, the dances of possession lasting for hours. They were received among the initiates. Barbara was the daughter of Iansa, goddess of lewdness, and João the son of Ogun, god of iron and war. When consulted, Oxala, father of all the gods, gave his approval. Barbara fully understood that 'Mae' Meniniuha knew everything about her, but that embarrassed neither of them. Rather, it amused them. One night João had to leave earlier, and they chatted until sunrise. 'Mae' told Barbara that she believed she was in touch with the Eguns, the god-spirits of the dead, and was perhaps an Egun herself. Barbara smiled, Mae trembled. Barbara thought of bringing Kotor to see her some day. Since then ten pairs of eyes had never failed to watch her, whatever she did. She realised she would be protected for ever. Among them was a superb, strapping fellow. She made him possess her, and she took blood from him. Thus she became a goddess.

Chapter III

Very slowly, things began to move. The Marquis had a plan; so had Luciano. They were different, but they could coincide. Luciano was anxious for the Marquis to show his hand, but all soon became clear. The Marquis wanted to force an order out of the King to attack Alfama. Assuming he could obtain it, there remained the problem of how to set about it. That was where Luciano came in. He was unwilling to make a free gift to the Marquis of his own plan of attack—which seemed to him a work of sheer genius. They would have to meet to talk it over.

The Marquis, who hated Luciano as much as João, took some time to make up his mind. Ideally, he sought a way to set them against each other. Besides, he wanted Alexandra alive and at his mercy. But avarice triumphed over sheer hatred and lust. He was not prepared to pay the price. He first unburdened himself to Ricardo who remained imperturbable, appearing to understand nothing, resolved to remain neutral as long as possible since he had not yet unravelled the knot of each one's intention. But suddenly, he saw light which put him in the right position as if by chance, and was even astonished at his own astuteness. There must always be someone who knows how to make a mayonnaise even if he has no oil and no eggs. Neither Luciano nor the Marquis wanted to take the first step to speak to each other: they would have to be brought together and forced to specify their policies, projects, ambitions and demands.

Ricardo had a *quinta* in the forest of Cintra near the Franciscan monastery. Since the monastery was much visited, any coming and going in the vicinity would go unnoticed. He had a simple family feast prepared: no wine, no girls, the guests willing to forgo the gratification of their vices and tastes. Only one dish was served, the very popular *cozido*. They lunched like peasants, and then moved to the veranda with sober heads. The three men were left alone. They had not yet spoken. Smiling, looking like a typical cotton-merchant, Ricardo took a sheet of paper, and after a silence began to speak:

'It's very simple,' he said. 'Every one of us wants something definite. Who wants what? And who gives what to have it? Together we have only to hold out our hands to have it. Afterwards we will see. Each will make his arrangements.'

The other two were taken aback by this frankness, which was no part of their own natures; they could not believe that it could be part of Ricardo's.

'It's like a puzzle,' continued Ricardo. 'Each of us has only a limited number of pieces. If we put them together a complete picture will appear.'

The other two still held back.

'Our Marquis knows how to force the King's hand when there is a crisis. But he does not know how to provoke the crisis, nor how to attack old Kotor. Senhor Luciano has up his sleeve a magical plan to seize Kotor, but knows nothing about the King's entourage. I know how to precipitate the King into total melancholia, which would give the Marquis the chance to act. You see, gentlemen, that we are forced to work together despite the hatred and disgust we have for each other.'

Nobody protested. Only Luciano smiled briefly.

'Go on,' he said. 'Let us hear your conditions.'

'I want Senhor Luciano to hand over to me the general direction of the police,' said Ricardo. 'I will leave him the secret services which are his life-blood and his vocation. And I desire that His Excellency the Marquis surrender his properties in Alemtejo to me with the title of baron. Also one hundredth of your fortune, Your Excellency, which you can recover in ten days. In return I will give you a trap for the King to fall into.'

At last the party began.

'I follow you,' said Luciano. 'His Excellency will give me the fruits of the operation which I plan, and which can only be implemented with the King's agreement. You, Ricardo, leave me control of all the dregs of Lisbon. I am listening.'

'What do you offer?' asked the Marquis.

'An infallible method of turning Alfama inside out.'

'What proof can you give?' asked the Marquis.

'If I give it now,' said Ricardo, 'you will get on with it alone. You must be satisfied with my word. I need absolute secrecy.'

'I agree,' said the Marquis.

'Your Excellency has not said what his price is,' said Ricardo.

'That is unnecessary,' said Luciano. 'We all know it: freedom to dispose of Dona Alexandra.'

The Marquis did not even have to agree.

'There remain your ways and means, my dear Ricardo, of reassuring His Majesty's state of mind,' said Luciano. 'Our Majesty is happier and more tired than ever. Everything goes through His Eminence or Dom Manuel, which for the time being amounts to the same thing.'

'My secret in exchange for yours,' said Ricardo.

'Let us leave it at that,' said Luciano. 'And let us judge ourselves by our acts.'

The Marquis stood up. Already his accomplices were irritating him.

'Wait, Your Excellency,' said Ricardo. 'I appreciate your haste, but we must fix the timetable.'

The Marquis was forced to remain.

'Ricardo should start, I think.'

'Certainly,' said Ricardo. 'But all will have to be done in a few hours. If the King pulls himself together João will intervene. I will arrange to keep His Eminence out of the way for a few hours. It is necessary to choose the right moment very carefully.'

'Perfect,' said Luciano. 'I think I can guess: the King gives in towards the evening. I need one night. Next day we attack at noon.'

'Good,' said Ricardo. 'Next Monday. That leaves us five days. Be ready. Gentlemen—sorry, Your Excellency: we won't meet before. My signal will be plain. Let us leave our options open.'

The Marquis departed. Luciano remained, and Ricardo was silent, wanting him to speak.

'Lisbon is pretty far,' Luciano murmured. 'I should like . . . '

'Choose,' said Ricardo. 'My house is yours.'

'You still have that little maidservant?'

'She is waiting for you.'

He let Luciano go upstairs, then went to the stable and saddled a horse. At last he was enjoying himself. He had been waiting for it for months. It was hard to recall that victory should only be celebrated when it has been won.

Manuel had had a plan, and above all the necessary will, assisted by great patience, but he did not foresee that it could get lost like a river in the sand. He was revealed as having no real aim. Little by little he had ceased to want, in order simply to live. The impact of pleasure had been so strong that his will power had crashed into smithereens. He could influence the King as much as he liked, but he needed nothing any longer except to remain where he was. Ricardo, his Achilles heel, had noticed this at a glance, with cold disgust.

When he had worked for and with João, Manuel had often felt irritated. He well knew that he was, could not help being, and would always remain a parasite, a symbiot at best. João's independent spirit and behaviour exasperated him, but he saw it now, and supported it. With João he was the ivy round a real tree, whereas the King was barely a shrub. Whatever he said was echoed by immediate laughter or servile approval. Manuel was aware now that he would never become a minister by these means, for that perpetual acquiescence had drugged him to sleep. The satisfaction that he experienced from it now was only the paltry pleasure in indulging a habit.

All caution had deserted him. Since he had no precise project left he no longer felt the need to protect his security. Drugs, docile bodies, more or less poetical desires soliloquised in front of an infatuated and admiring King—then the night with two or three selected girls, the pursuit of the senseless gamble of permanent continuous orgasm; these constituted his new routine and were followed as strictly as the rules of a convent. Besides, his maxim was: bring disorder into order. That could be mimed, and the King, delighted to have understood a parable at last, explained fifteen times a day, while showing his penis even to bishops and ambassadors, the superiority of disorder in order. At least to that extent the King was pleased.

Ricardo had known for a long time that it was there that he should and could strike. But how to go about it? Not that Manuel took any precautions, but it was necessary to make his death exemplary, spectacular and of a kind to impress the King's feeble mind. Ricardo began to spin his web. A return to religion would be the best for him. He discovered Manuel's two favourites, the daughters of a merchant in Bairo Alto, rich and capricious. The elder one was married, the son-in-law always away in Goa or Timor. She made love in secret as often as she could. The younger one knew everything about it, and even had the keys of the garden with two gates. She was the cover, but had not as yet the courage to lose her virginity, in spite of her brother-in-law having on his rare visits put his hand up her skirt. She let herself be seduced by Manuel, and actively practised the Aretino style with him, relating every detail to her elder sister, whom it excited madly. The three of them spent entire days in the bottom of the garden, where he had built a cool, delicious little summer house with magnificent glazed tiles on the outside, a closed universe containing a large sofa, a tiny bathroom, and enough to eat and drink.

One of Ricardo's lieutenants, the son of a heavily-indebted family known for some sordid crimes, who had entered the secret service, had originally been chosen by the elder sister, but discarded in favour of Manuel. Having been kicked out, he remained furious and watchful. He shadowed her, and told Ricardo all he had seen. The bird was in his grasp. All that remained was to close the trap.

Manuel did not satisfy the elder sister, and at night she went in search of a carter or a stable-boy for a quick one in a doorway, or two sometimes. When the man put a coin in her palm she laughed her head off. She made Manuel laugh too when she told him about it. The little sister did not understand, but she would soon grow up. One night Ricardo waited for the elder one, called Anna-Lucia, and when she had her skirts lifted up to her ears, and was being attended to by two fellows simultaneously, he appeared with a few of his policemen carrying lanterns. He took the girl back to his house in the most atrocious posture for any lady, however debauched. He told her what he wanted—or almost all of it. She should obey implicitly, await instructions, and hold herself ready every day. It would not be long, and then all would be forgotten. Nobody would know, and she could carry on as before. Without Manuel: that was clear enough. Otherwise there would be immediate dishonour. She would be taken with the two fellows to her father after a short visit to the tribunal. Not being in a position to argue, as an intelligent girl she accepted at once, and with awful menaces Ricardo made sure she would not double-cross him. The deal was made. For the first time in ages he was excited. Women and boys did not interest him. He liked only long, solitary sessions. But humiliated and defeated Anna-Lucia excited him strangely. He jumped on her as if to sign the contract. Anna-Lucia found a sort of pleasure in it which Ricardo noticed and was flattered by. He told her that it had originally been his intention to hand her over to the cuckold who was waiting outside for his recompense. She thanked him, trembling. Ricardo sneered. They left. With one swift movement Ricardo restrained the imbecile who wanted to throw himself on her. One minute.

He made Anna-Lucia leave, then set his thugs on the lieutenant, and they strangled him. 'Throw his corpse and those of the two fellows straight into the Tagus with weights attached to their ankles,' he ordered, and rejoined Anna-Lucia.

'You have nothing to fear,' he said. 'They won't be seen again.'

There was a strange light in his eyes. As she did not understand immediately he took her hand to show her the state he was in. Twice the same night was truly a feast. He took her against a chair, and thought she was properly under his control as he gave her brief orders, describing the costumes and accessories she would have to hide in the summer house, while awaiting a very simple signal: the next thunderstorm. She should not say anything to her sister. She would be attended to after the surprise. Caught in the trap, Anna-Lucia could do nothing. Ricardo saw and took her every day to make her feel the length of the rope. She made everything ready.

The expected thunderstorm came at the end of one afternoon. The Lisbon sky was as black as an Italian painting. Anna-Lucia and her little sister shivered in the little house in the garden, terrified by thunder and lightning. Anna-Lucia was more afraid than her sister. She hoped Manuel would not come, but he came. It seemed as though he had not even noticed the storm. He undressed the younger one, and possessed the elder as was his wont, sodomising with one while stroking the other. It was the beginning of his ritual. He threw himself about, clearly excited by the electricity, the deluge and the moistness of the thunderstorm.

But Ricardo and four policemen, whom he called his wolves, were watching the scene, astounded, forgetting for an instant why they were there and the sinister tools they had carried with them. Meticulously, Ricardo waited until Manuel was approaching orgasm. He gave the arranged signal. The four burst in, and he followed ten seconds later. They felled Manuel and the little one, and overpowered the elder, not without pawing her avidly as they did so.

They were all tied, and the four, as if at a picnic, unpacked their baskets. The instruments consisted of the somewhat ridiculous stuff that had been confiscated from partakers of the black mass. One might imagine oneself in a theatre. Like stage-hands they arranged the scenery. The younger girl, still unconscious, was tied naked to an improvised altar before being stabbed. Ricardo had hesitated about whether he should revive her first to enjoy her fright, but decided not since they had to act quickly and effectively. He examined the edge of the blade while his wolves made a fire in the fireplace, and heated in it a long and narrow iron bar with a wooden handle: a strange tool, the use of which they all appeared to know, and it terrified Anna-Lucia. They gagged her before she could shriek for mercy, a useless change of sides which came too late, and for which she would pay dearly. Now she understood. Ricardo was jubilant at the sight of her. He promised himself to make her last for a long month at least and told her so.

It was ready. The iron bar was red-hot. Ricardo stabbed the little one. Her fetters were taken off so that the corpse should look like a sacrifice. He himself pulled out the dagger, and put it into Manuel's still unconscious hand. He would have enjoyed him seeing his slow death. The pain they were preparing for him would wake him up and kill him at the same time. A pity. But there too efficiency was preferable. Lightning struck the highest tree in the garden. Ricardo had been waiting for it. He gave the signal, the red-hot iron was driven into Manuel's chest who screamed and died in the same breath.

They all left. Soon it would be discovered, this perfect illustration of God's punishment of the sacrilegious criminal struck by divine wrath during the celebration of a black mass and the sacrifice of a virgin. People were already approaching at the run, so loud had been Manuel's last shriek.

'Take the girl to the house and into the cellar,' shouted Ricardo to his wolves. 'You can rape her but do not damage her. I am not jealous.' When they had gone, he waited for a while before appearing in front of the little crowd assembling in the house. The good people were petrified. By a lucky chance, lightning had struck another tree only ten paces away. The awful burn on Manuel's chest, his features distorted by pain, the blood-stained dagger, the scenery round the little girl and her bloody nakedness—this would be the beginning of a fine legend. Modestly Ricardo savoured his victory. Nobody, he ordered, should touch anything. Nobody thought of doing so. One of the King's pages appeared just as Ricardo became impatient because none had come. He departed post-haste to inform the King, and Ricardo had the King's chaplain notified, and His Eminence as well for good measure.

João and the King arrived simultaneously and entered together. The King fainted at once. João was one up. Ricardo's presence immediately revealed the truth. But he could not do anything about it. However, he could mitigate the results of the shock. Taking the King in his arms he brought him back to the castle. The poor monarch was delirious and mad with terror. When he came round, João in his vestments, biretta, purple cassock, and purple socks, laid down in person the rules of penitence the whole court should follow. By sheer luck he had advised the King that very morning to keep his distance from Manuel. The King had objected. But now in his enfeebled mind he did not connect João with Manuel. So as not to waste any time in the turmoil, João obtained from him his full powers.

The Court was like an overturned antheap. It was too good to believe, but there had certainly been a good number of witnesses to what had taken place in the garden. Manuel's burnt chest looked so spectacular, and was so near to people's ideas about lightning, that even the sceptical kept quiet. Above all João himself set the example by celebrating an expiatory Mass, and ordered austerity.

Ricardo behaved discreetly. At Court he was treated like a leper. Nobody would approach him. None the less, he managed to pin down the Marquis behind a tapestry.

'Make haste,' he said to him. 'His Eminence may win all. The King is going on a retreat.'

The Marquis succeeded in overcoming his natural irresolution, and forced his way into the King's presence. João was away, preparing the retreat in a hermitage in Cintra. This was the right moment. The King had always held the Marquis in horror, and feared him. In his present state the Marquis' apparently sincere compassion changed his mind. He confirmed him in his functions: by inadvertance João thus lost the police. Moreover, the King invited the Marquis to come to Cintra whenever he wanted. João returned in the middle of this armistice. He could do nothing. The King left, surrounded by monks and priests. The government remaining in Lisbon had two heads now: João who ruled all the ministries, and the Marquis who held the reins of the police.

João tried in vain to find out the truth about the Manuel business, but could not disentangle the knot. Ricardo had organised a coup that apparently brought him no profit. The Marquis retained his power but could not add to it. Paradoxically he himself appeared the main victor, since the King had left the entire state in his hands. It was urgent to organise a new network of spies. Laziness and Barbara had got the better of him. At the end of three days the whole business was like an aching old tooth that had not been looked after, was not cured; the pain could revive any minute, and the tongue could still feel the exact spot. He was well aware that something would inevitably develop from this affair. But he had given up trying to understand it, and only wanted to forget.

Ricardo summoned the other two that same evening. Angrily, they came, but without even offering the courtesy of complimenting their host. Luciano secretly admired the work. The Marquis feared him. The road forward looked clear. Once Luciano did his bit the Marquis would get everything out of the king as long as a religious pretext could be found for it.

'It will be,' said Luciano.

'When?' asked the Marquis.

'Ten days at the least, twenty days at the most. I still have to set the stage.'

They separated quickly, each profoundly disgusted by the other, disturbed in their search for a clear conscience by the presence of their accomplices.

Ricardo was in no hurry to go home. There were few public places where he felt happy. Always the same void surrounded him. Besides, that night all the places of entertainment were closed because of the King's sudden imposition of austerity. He had ordered expiatory mourning for three days. Ricardo knew where to go. In the port downstream from the church of Madre de Deus, in a sort of district reserved for the curriers (an esteemed, closed guild, cut off from the rest of the town because of the insufferable and persistent smell of all its members—never mind, they lived among themselves), near a warehouse, there was a restaurant-tavern serving the best food in Lisbon, where the leather merchants of Villa Franca, Xira and Santarem stopped on their way home, to take advantage of the next tide.

Ricardo was an habitué. He was assumed to be a merchant from Minho. He came twice a month, holding his nose on entering, but forgetting the smell after five minutes and two drinks. When he was seated the landlady brought to him *dobradas a moda de Porto* a savoury mixture of tripe and dried beans, and wine from Setubal. That was happiness. The woman was pretty and friendly, but he

masons, and on Gianvittorio's order he suffered the ordeal of being the eyes and ears of the brethren in the enemy fortress. The truth was that he did not understand Ricardo's intentions in this matter. He sensed it was not a wanton fantasy, but the real motives escaped him. He would tell Gianvittorio so shortly. Anna-Lucia's story had shed no light. He briefly questioned her. Yes, she said, Ricardo had raped her too, in fact was the first. He found it difficult to believe, for Ricardo had taken neither girls nor boys in the last ten years, just a frantic solitary pleasure to which Joaquim had often been witness.

'You cured him of a strange affliction,' he said. 'It is to be seen whether he bears you a grudge for it.'

He continued to question her. Perhaps, he thought, it was the traces of earlier delights in the girl that had appealed to Ricardo. One could base one's tactics on that theory.

'As far as you can,' he said, 'excite him and prove to him that you like what he does with you . . . If you could really enjoy it, even despite yourself, it would be better still.'

She was not in a position to protest. He continued:

'In that manner we will gain time, and hold at bay the moment of the real irreversible tortures.'

He listened. A door banged upstairs. He disappeared like a shadow through some secret passage, but before going he kissed her on the lips. She opened hers, but his remained closed. Full of respect, yet with a light hand he had touched the smooth thighs and the sex which she offered him.

Ricardo unlocked the door, and entered. The torches were artistically placed. The light fell direct on the opened thighs and raised belly. It played with the thick and dark pubic hairs. Her head had fallen back. The beautiful eyes opened. Enchanted, Ricardo felt his erection. What a feast.

Brutally he pushed his fingers into the openings at his disposal. Instead of a shriek he heard a groan that was also a sound of pleasure. Anna-Lucia wasted no time in applying Joaquim's advice. Ricardo harshly twisted her breasts. The groaning mounted, it was nearly a song. Ricardo lifted her head by pulling her hair. Anna-Lucia swooned. Ricardo brutally entered her, then stopped. There were better things to do.

He returned to the door, and shouted for Joaquim. Let the puritan little fool see how a real man amused himself. Joaquim appeared, unmoved.

'Untie her and turn her round,' Ricardo shouted.

Joaquim did so. Her wrists bled a little. Ricardo played with her for a long minute. From time to time he tied her hair, and pulled her head back. Anna-Lucia shrieked with pleasure. Ricardo exulted. He stopped before the end to spare his virility. He would spend a more exciting night alone.

'You will undress her,' he said, 'and put a collar round her neck and tie her to a post. You will sleep standing up like a horse, fair lady.'

When the collar with nails pointing inside was put around her neck Joaquim turned to Ricardo.

'If you want her to last,' he said, 'she ought perhaps to be fed and washed.'

'You are right,' said Ricardo. 'The moment I go upstairs you will do so before tying her . . . But before that I should like to have a little chat with our guest.'

Anna-Lucia's legs were free, but her hands were chained to her back. He pulled her up.

'You know what awaits you which will make everything more delicious for me,' he said.

He told her everything while he continued to paw at her. As long as she appealed to him—ten days, twenty days—she would only be chained and raped. Afterwards the small tortures would begin: nails, whips. A chain was attached to the collar. He pulled her to the end of the cellar to show her in detail the instruments of torture. An astonishing pair of pliers would be used to pierce her tongue, which would then be pulled out to be cut. That refinement was for the day before the last. On the last day her eyes would be torn out (he showed her the instrument), and she would die shortly after, her insides impaled on a red-hot iron.

Anna-Lucia felt more of a desire to laugh than any fear. The overdone stage-set looked ridiculous. She controlled herself. My girl, you are playing with your life. So she showed respectable fear. Ricardo's suspicion had no time to revive: a sense of humour was not his forte.

He left in a hurry to go to bed. His chosen technique was not to satisfy himself with his hand, but lying on his belly to rub himself against the mattress, his imagination roaming in all directions. Infinitely curious about the ways of human nature, Joaquim had occasionally watched him, and noticed that it never took him less than an hour and often even more to reach the end, with at times six to eight walks one after the other afterwards. He had thought of stabbing Ricardo with a sword at such a moment, but the opportunity to do so and escape unmolested had never come his way. One never knew how many of the wolves were in the house. Moreover Gianvittorio would surely not authorise him to do so. Tonight Ricardo seemed to be alone, but there was Anna-Lucia too.

The moment Ricardo had gone upstairs to wet his sheets, Joaquim completely untied Anna-Lucia. They embraced in earnest. At last Joaquim could caress her. She said she loved him. He did not believe her at once because he loved her already, but she insisted and gave him proof. Naturally not only proof with her body, although their bodies partook of the feast too.

Washed, fed and happy she still had to be tied again. Joaquim gave her a sleeping pill, and penetrated her gently for the last time, while she fell asleep. When the whole house had dropped into silence, he ran to Gianvittorio who was waiting for him. The circumstances in which Manuel had died had struck at the imagination of the entire town. The majority accepted the supernatural, divine punishment through lightning. A minority asked itself how. A few asked themselves why.

Anna-Lucia's story transmitted by Joaquim seemed like a powder keg to Gianvittorio. It could not be revealed without giving away the source. Joaquim's presence in Ricardo's household was too important to be sacrificed. Joaquim trembled a little. Gianvittorio reassured him: he would not allow Anna-Lucia to perish. But Ricardo's plan had to be discovered. With Joaquim he hurried to Kotor. Kotor and Clara listened to them, summoned Laurent and Alexandra, but nobody could explain it. They all saw the logic of a menace, of an attack: but why Manuel, and why in such a manner?

The general conclusion was that caution was necessary; but they practised caution already, as they watched the priests overexcite themselves with what they called a miracle. They were condemned to wait for the enemy to make the first move, as it was only a vague intuition that made them fear an attack.

In any case they were all of the opinion that it was worth losing an informer at Ricardo's to free Anna-Lucia. She had to be liberated as quickly as possible. In that case, said Joaquim, why not liquidate Ricardo? Gianvittorio thought it would solve nothing. It would alert the enemy. An escape would be considered a love story: a murder would not. It was better to make a fool of Ricardo.

'Right,' said Joaquim. 'In that case let me enjoy myself. I guarantee his survival, but not to keep him unharmed.' They all laughed, relieved and delighted by that diversion after their anguish.

Joaquim needed help, but so invisible, so unnoticed that it should leave the impression of his having acted alone. It was enough to get the wolves out of the way. The brethren undertook to deal with this. Ricardo came home next evening without realising that he was alone with Joaquim in the house.

Having returned early that evening he felt in the right mood for a bit of fantasy. He had Anna-Lucia tied by her feet to the beams of the ceiling, and for a good quarter of an hour he amused himself with what he saw.

He thought he was making her swoon with delight, and rushed to his bedroom without asking for more, saying only that he might come back. Joaquim freed Anna-Lucia. She dressed as a man, which nearly distracted them owing to the interest Joaquim took in it, and because it was difficult to find breeches of her size. He armed her. They entered Ricardo's bedroom at the moment of his ecstasy. Anna-Lucia sat on the nape of his neck, and Joaquim on his shins. With a stiletto Anna-Lucia cut the duct that joined the testicles to the penis, while he traced the shape of a penis on each buttock, pointing to the objective. Anna-Lucia's behind weighed heavily on the back of Ricardo's head, smothering his shrieks. The work was done in less than a minute. Joaquim knocked him senseless, and stuck his nose into his sperm. They tied him to the bed-posts—a fair revenge—and Joaquim sprinkled a coagulant with salt in it on the wounds so that they should easily be seen. They escaped. The brethren rescued Joaquim's father the same night.

They disappeared in Alfama like a stone in water. The next morning a decent-looking wine merchant opened a shop near São Miguel. He was a widower, who lived with his young son and his daughter-in-law, a young couple, the very image of happiness. They never went out. They were noticed in the beginning; later they were forgotten. The father found that the bed of the young ones in their bedroom above his made a little noise. He moved up to the attic, and there he remained.

Anna-Lucia's father, shattered by the discovery of what had gone on in the bottom of his garden, kept his mouth closed. The little sister was buried without a religious service, and nobody mentioned the big sister any more. Her husband vanished to Timor.

Chapter IV

Luciano had had a very busy week. He thought he would die of laughter when he heard about Ricardo's mishap. The latter had gone to his house in Cintra to hide his shame. As everybody hated him, joy was general. It was taken as Manuel's posthumous vengeance. Wanting to find out more, Luciano summoned the wolves, who sensing that the tide had turned, were not loath to tell everything. It all pointed to a tale of love between little Joaquim and the beautiful prisoner. Luciano was able to savour the subtlety of the vengeance. For a long time he had suspected Ricardo of leading a curious sex life. Nothing remained unexplained except the mystery of how the father had escaped from prison. There was a smell of conspiracy and organisation about it which did not please him. The duke had vanished. That sort of miracle had some reason behind it. No trail was found. Because of it Luciano was not going to postpone putting his own plan into action, but the possible existence of an adversary of his own calibre on the other side of the chessboard annoyed him, especially as he could not see *who* he was. Not Kotor, and not Laurent. There seemed to be no connection between them and Joaquim. His thoughts moved on.

During that week he could be seen every day with three of his men at the arrival of the fishing fleet at Sesimbra. A curious pastime. They bought fish-heads, though not any fish-heads, only those with large teeth. Anyone following them would have understood nothing about their ichthyological passion. But nobody did follow them. Gianvittorio thought it over, increasingly sure that a coup, of which the Ricardo-Manuel affair had been only a preliminary, was in preparation. But he did not want to be discovered. He made no move.

Kotor worked passionately. Laurent and Alexandra, after prudently waiting for three days, took to their night rides again. João, who had held back too for two days, could no longer resist and resumed his visits to Azeitão.

At the end of the week Luciano appeared to have enough heads of swordfish and eel. They dried in the sun in the yard of his police barracks and stank terribly. Nobody understood what the chief had in mind. When the heads were really dry kitchenmaids were sent for, who applied themselves to work that seemed truly senseless: heads on one side, teeth on the other. Then the heads were thrown away. All the cats of the port passed on the news. There was a feast at Sodre. Then dressmakers were summoned, but alone Luciano saw them, and explained their work to them. When the ten days were up, the Marquis came himself to ask discreetly for news. Luciano was flattered.

'I have said between ten and twenty days, Your Excellency. Ten have gone by, but not twenty. Now I know what I am doing. In exactly nine days' time we will act.' He took a calendar. 'Full moon. If you believe in werewolves then stay at home.' He laughed.

The Marquis was leaving, but turned back from the door.

'What are we doing about Ricardo?'

'I doubt he will ever claim his share,' said Luciano. 'But one never knows. Let us give ourselves the luxury of loyalty. I will let him know.'

'What is becoming of him?'

'He is trying to get cured. It's difficult. He can neither sit down nor sleep on his back. Walking is out of the question. He remains in a hammock, lying on his belly, his buttocks in the air.'

'Is it true that . . .' murmured the Marquis.

'Well, yes. A eunuch. For all the harm he did to girls it is not too bad a fate.'

The Marquis did not want to laugh with Luciano, who resented that. So the latter left it there, and promised himself to be particularly loyal to this imbecile. And in the end it might be he himself who would collect the whole prize.

During the following six days, police agents were recruited in Luciano's name. Forty scoundrels, he had said, but not any of our own men. He took Ricardo's wolves, and a few galley slaves were taken from the chain-gangs, but only assassins and confirmed robbers. Any that smelled of politics or heresy were excluded. The lot of them were put up in a converted stable. They were given all the food and drink they could ask for. Ten healthy whores were caught for them in the port. Only noise and uncontrolled drunkenness were forbidden. Two offenders had their throats neatly cut in front of everybody. The rest grumbled, but calmed down. By the eighth day there were a good forty of them, hounds straight from hell. They were clad in very dark brown breeches, waistcoats, cravates, scarves and hats. They were forbidden to touch the dressmakers.

On the morning of the ninth day, Luciano let the Marquis know that there would be news for him at six in the evening. The Marquis left his house at five. He arrived a good half-hour too early. Luciano did the honours. A Delft clock showed ten to six.

'Come with me,' said Luciano.

He hid the Marquis behind the shutter of a window that gave on to the courtyard. Already the forty had assembled in silence. They looked terrifying. They lined up in ranks of eight. Each rank had a chief. The bells chimed six o'clock.

Luciano went into the courtyard. Behind him four of his men brought a large trunk which they put down beside him. Luciano began to make a speech. The Marquis, who knew his classics, found it as melodious as Tacitus. To start with he spoke about the vampires. At the first mention of the *Name* the men trembled.

Luciano played with the myth and the horror: creatures of night, who drank the blood of the living, beings from the other side of the grave. Then he told them how the vampires had conquered Alfama through perversion and subversion, about the great number of their clients and disciples. How could all this be stamped out. *How*? That was the question. The vampires lived in Alfama like fish in the sea. Everything was life and nourishment for them, aid, home and assistance. Those fish would have to be lifted out of that sea. The thugs' attention was riveted on him. They could not see yet the part they would play.

Luciano gauged his audience. He held it well. He continued. To separate the vampires from the people they had taken advantage of was the solution. With their diabolical trickery the vampires had hoodwinked decent people, had damped the normal, natural horror that everybody ought to feel at the very mention of the accursed *Name*.

To mobilise such a horror, awaken the normal sentiments of self-preservation, and give the curse back its real meaning would be their role. Luciano stopped, and they understood that they had to shout their agreement, total adhesion and enthusiasm. Had they swords they would have drawn them at that moment and waved them above their heads. Luciano continued. He brought forward a priest who guaranteed the Church's approval, the horror of the vampires, creatures of the Devil, and salvation for those who destroyed them. The priest blessed the crowd, which was by now on its knees.

Luciano had the trunk opened. The dressmakers had mounted the sharp teeth of the fish on leather bracelets, turning them into knuckle dusters. There were forty of them, and forty daggers as sharp as razors. 'Tonight, gentlemen,' said Luciano, 'Alfama is yours. Run through the streets. Disembowel them. Rape them. Pierce the hearts of all you meet. I need five victims per man. And brand all their necks with the teeth you will be given.'

He showed them how to do it: to drive in the sharks' teeth at the top of the jugular vein, making wounds similar to the vampires'. If two hundred victims were found in the morning there would be plenty to open the eyes of the most obstinate partisans of the vampires. They could take all, rings, necklaces, watches and purses. All that could be put into pockets and a sack. The dressmakers had sewn sacks for each man. Everything was distributed, they burst with impatience. Luciano held them back. They must wait until nightfall as the vampires live only at night, and *a fortiori* the sham vampires too. Each leader received a map, showing an entrance into the town, and a way out. At the first light of dawn the forty and their loot had to be back in the courtyard. Each would be given a thousand reis, and they could disappear at their convenience. Forty pairs of eyes shone. Their imaginations were working at full speed.

Luciano returned to the Marquis, and drew him aside.

'Congratulations,' said the Marquis. 'But what happens afterwards?'

'Afterwards it is for Your Excellency to enter the game. This is the plan. In the morning you rush to the King to obtain *carte blanche*. Then we take Alfama.'

He took a sheet from his sleeve, a list of military units. The Marquis pouted: the rules did not allow him to touch the army.

'All has been foreseen,' said Luciano. 'At three in the morning, before dawn, I need here fifty rifle-men from the police. You have a hundred, so that is easy.'

'Of course, but for what purpose?'

'Let us go on. Two regiments are needed. Fortunately infantry will be enough. But we must not use the Germans or the Swiss. The soldiers must be Catholics.'

This was all very well. It was easily said, but João was war minister too, and commander-in-chief of the army.

'You will be able to do as you want,' said Luciano. 'He won't be available—not before noon at any rate. I have arranged things. You may have an unpleasant hour or so if our coup fails. But it won't fail. His Eminence will remain prostrated for at least ten days.'

'But what are those soldiers going to do?'

'Their job: killing. It will be an historical massacre. For a long time our officers have been on the edge of history. They will be delighted. Do not worry about anything. You will know what to do tomorrow, I promise you.'

Evening came, and the lanterns were lit everywhere. It had been very hot, but the heat lifted at last. Everybody was out in the streets. From Graça, Castello, and around the quays the groups of eight set out; and a few hours later they began to infiltrate. People had finished their outdoor chores, and were dining or chatting in the taverns. Vigilance had been relaxed for some months. Families who had a vampire in their midst took practically no real precautions. Already for many people the vampire was considered as a permanent guest, pandered to, whom the halo of romantic mystery and prestige continued to surround as on the first day. It just became normal, another standard, but a standard established by a network of disciples and accomplices. They knew one another, and if not they recognised each other by that scar on the neck, as evident as a star on the forehead. Those who were not of them knew and recognised them too, an error which Kotor and Clara had wanted to avoid, but could do nothing about. Some were envious, others curious or sceptical, but there were no more reactions of horror, refusal or even of disgust. In one sense that was all to the good. The old curse seemed to have lifted. 'It has fallen asleep,' said Kotor, the only one who still felt some vague fear. What *was* found astonishing about those travellers who had crossed the Styx from the other side was precisely their normality.

They joked, played cards, made love, betrayed no special knowledge, nor any memories about the dark river and its two banks. They were just like other people. In the beginning it was frightening to see the familiar dead rising every evening from a coffin hidden in the cellar, but afterwards one became accustomed to it in the same way as one grew used to the absence of black magic, witchcraft—secret yet spectacular practices which everybody had expected to find. The simplicity of it all was fundamentally the most difficult thing to accept. In brief, confidence reigned. The vampires, and the friends of the vampires, were no longer on their guard. No vigilance, or almost none; but a flood of recruits, since so many wanted to become vampires.

Hidden in dark corners, the eyes of the forty men nearly popped out. The district was in the throes of a sort of rapture. Songs, not only fados. A man from Madeira recognised a dancing song which he began to hum until he suddenly remembered what he would have to do five minutes later. They saw drunks, girls moving about, others who embraced in the shadow of a doorway, and the whiteness of a petticoat. In the full moon the white or rose-coloured walls gleamed as at noon. The clocks chimed midnight. The milling around diminished. Many shutters were closed. Wherever a light shone, there were certainly vampires in the house. The soldiers were forbidden to touch them. But there remained all the others . . . The twelfth stroke was the signal. There was a brief hesitation. Then the first group of eight leapt forward.

And struck. Two lovers, who were very much advanced in their courting, did not even feel what happened to them. They were knocked down, marked, disembowelled by two crossed daggers, and finished off with a stab to the heart. A big success. On the necks of the two victims the mark of the teeth was like a conspicuous signature. The members of the group panted like hounds. The scent of blood killed all erotic ideas.

They had to force themselves to rape the girl's corpse. But duty is duty.

The groups pounced and stabbed for hours. They lay in wait near the bloody corpses, and woe to him who stopped to have a look. Knocked down, slashed, disembowelled, finished off, and raped if it was a girl. They left them all in the middle of the street so as to be easily spotted.

Soon there were about a hundred corpses. Towards four o'clock a glimmer of light appeared—dawn. The good work was accomplished.

In all the houses of the vampires the lights went out after the family dead had gone down to the cellars. The groups began to withdraw. The sacks bulged with loot, rings, money, necklaces, watches, even silver buckles. Each knew where to go. One of

Luciano's agents was waiting for them, checking their way out; and then in turns they entered Alfama, where it was bright daylight already. All had been accomplished in absolute silence as arranged. Not a shriek, not a groan, only a sigh now and then.

That night Laurent and Alexandra had not gone out. They had drunk, read, eaten, given blood and peacefully made love. Kotor and Clara, involved in an exhausting chemical experiment, had not budged from the laboratory. Gianvittorio and Fernanda had gone early to bed, tenderly and quietly. It was a night like many others.

At half-past four all was quiet with the vampires, and the others had not yet awoken. The groups of Luciano's police advanced into Alfama, some of them curiously supplied with jars of white paint and brushes. They admired the finished work. The forty had done their job well. There were at least three hundred corpses. As though they had already rehearsed the ballet they were going to dance, Luciano's agents made ready for the curtains to rise.

Day came on the Tagus, a haze of heat, the clouds vanishing. It would be a magnificent day. João arrived on horseback with his bodyguard. He had left Azeitão in darkness, but now all was already grey. The boat and the oarsmen were waiting for him. He jumped into the boat. It reached the middle of the river. A *saveiro* in full sail approached at great speed. The crew could already be seen, fishermen preparing their nets, and taking advantage of the tide to get out of the estuary. Suddenly, a plank in the bottom of João's boat gave way. In less than ten seconds the vessel sank. The surprised oarsmen were already swimming with their light clothes off. João's bodyguard, who wore a heavy coat and enormous boots, was dragged to the bottom by their weight before he understood what had happened to him. He drowned without a whimper. Perspiring after the fast ride and fearing the chill of dawn João had covered himself with a large great-coat, and was half asleep. He fought hard in the icy water, succeeded in getting rid of the great-coat and his shoes, but his frock-coat began to weigh him down. Furious that he might die for the sake of a Parisian fashion, he surfaced with the strength of despair. The *saveiro* was almost on top of him. He shouted. A fisherman heard him, and swiftly threw him a rope. He gripped it with all his strength, and was lifted on board without the *saveiro* having to slow down. He collapsed on the deck, and passed out.

From the stern a fisherman sent a message with a powerful lantern: three long flashes, three short ones. From a dark window on the quay a similar lantern replied with two long and two short flashes. Satisfied, the fisherman sat down, put out the lantern, and went to look after João who was still unconscious. He undressed him, emptied him of water, and massaged him. Finally he forced down his throat a huge gulp of *bagoco*, a specially powerful drink.

João came round. It took him some time to understand where he was. The fishermen surrounded him full of friendliness. He drank a little more, then he looked about him. The *saveiro* was already beyond Belem, and beyond Cascais too. She was in the middle of the fairway. João was master of himself again. So he had got rid of the famous frock-coat. He searched his clothes, and found his purse in a pocket. The sight of gold produced not even a sparkle in the fishermen's eyes. João asked them to turn back. They spoke to each other in some dialect, João understanding a word only here and there. And they did not seem to understand what he was saying. The *saveiro* was gaining speed. The fishermen forgot João, to attend to their nets. João saw where they were going: off Cape Espichel, where fish were plentiful. He gave up trying to explain: they would come back with the rising tide in a few hours' time. He fell abruptly asleep, his head against the ropes, happy to be alive. When they reached Cape Espichel it was full daylight.

From the window, Luciano saw the forty returning to the courtyard. They gave the impression of honest and contented workmen coming back from work. A real Persian market. They compared their little sacks of loot, told each other stories about what they had done, and how many they had killed. Luciano sneered. Two hours earlier he had let in the fifty carabineers of the police whom the puzzled Marquis had ungraciously put at his disposal. He had posted three behind each window shutter on every floor. Each had a musket and a carbine, thus two shots could be fired in a few seconds. They were told a story about plunderers and rebels, but, frankly, they were not much interested. They were accustomed to doing what they were told, and that was all. Luciano made a quick last inspection. They were all present, watchful, taking their time.

The signal was simple. Luciano had taken a carbine of great accuracy capable of firing two shots, carefully loaded, an ornamented, beautiful firearm. He aimed for a long time, then fired. Fifty shots were immediately fired, leaving thirty dead, killed outright. The others who were wounded—and two miraculously untouched—could not understand that Heaven was crashing around them. It was arranged that the second salvo would be fired shot by shot so as to avoid the mistakes of the first. Some of the forty had received two bullets, and the others, none at all. Luciano fired at one of the survivors who had not been touched, and blew his head to bits. Sustained fire finished off the rest in a few seconds. All was swept clean.

The soldiers descended, and began to pull the corpses towards an unused cesspool. They threw them in like refuse. Others added, first shovelfuls, then whole sacks of quicklime. They finished by cementing flagstones over the top of it, the whole operation lasting less than an hour. Those who were not busy transporting the corpses washed the bloodstained courtyard, while some of them collected the loot into wicker baskets. There was no theft. It was a handpicked company. When all was done they fell in, and marched to the quay near Madre Deus to assemble. They were to wait there until twelve. Luckily, many had thought of bringing food and wine flasks with them. As they shared them with those who had not, Luciano was already far away.

For he had to be everywhere at once. After the shooting he had left for Alfama. From the terrace of Graça he saw the roofs forming staircases and small squares. He listened. Loud shrieks which were started by his agents rose from Alfama. They shouted near the corpses, vociferating that the vampires had struck. Ah! they had taken off their masks at last, those vampires. Showing the bleeding marks on the victims' necks they denounced the ritual nature of the murders, the bellies slit open crosswise, the pierced hearts. They were joined at once by onlookers, and members of the victims' families who recognised their dead. Shutters and windows opened by the hundred, people called to one another, and a long wail rose from the whole of Alfama.

Luciano sighed with satisfaction. All was going as planned. He only had to supervise. He waited for a moment to see, to gloat. It was ecstasy, orgasm. His plan was a masterpiece of organisation. Everywhere his agents were instigating denunciations, kindling the flames of the old hate of vampires. Wherever vampires slept in the cellars they painted the front door with a large white cross. At nine in the morning Alfama was in turmoil. People got together, arguing or shouting their sorrow. The dead were washed and exposed to the public gaze.

Luciano rushed to the Marquis, who was burning with impatience. Reports had come in: two words sufficed to explain the technique. For form's sake the Marquis pretended to worry about the fate of the forty sham vampires. He had not the slightest doubt about their destiny, but even so wanted to be reassured. Luciano just smiled: he never left any trace behind that could harm him. 'We will continue,' he said to the Marquis, who was a little dumbfounded despite himself. He must go at once to Cintra to see the King, describe the crime, emphasise its ritual and sacrilegious side, obtain the free use of the crack regiments, get *carte blanche* to clean everything up with free choice of the methods to be used. Already Luciano had informed the staffs of the two units about the mission in store for them and prepared a relay of messages from Cintra to the barracks to bring the King's signed order to march. Before ten o'clock a cordon of troops should encircle Alfama, and the advance platoons should be concentrated in front of the chosen entry points.

'Upon my word,' said the Marquis, 'you have been a soldier, and a staff officer at that.'

'I should like the commissariat to follow immediately,' was all Luciano said. 'And I play chess fairly well.'

The Marquis did not wait for the end of the sentence. Already he was in his cabriolet. Hurry, coachman!

It was eight o'clock when the Marquis reached the monastery. The King was finishing his first morning prayers. Less downhearted, he was eating (a little meat again, and some wine). He had had theological discussions with the librarian monk, had gardened with the old prior of the community, learning how to graft and cut, and had reared birds with the youngest monk who was as handsome as a god. He had not yet had to confess sinful thoughts, but that would come in time. The Marquis waited for an instant, then caught him on his way out from the chapel. As always the King made a movement of near horror, then repented at once as befits a good Christian who practises charity. The Marquis told him about the vampires and what they had done, suggesting they were truly the emissaries of diabolical forces that threatened the throne and the altar. He did not have to go on: the King approved immediately.

'Kill them all,' he said. 'Let none survive.'

The Marquis left with the signed order, but even before he reached the cabriolet it was torn from his hand by one of his orderly officers who was Luciano's man, which, the Marquis promised himself, he would not forget. The marching order was swiftly relayed to Lisbon. The regiments left the barracks. The officers learnt only when they were already on their way what the orders and their objectives were, and shrugged their shoulders. A small job, and if it went well not even a shot would be fired.

The two colonels joined Luciano on the terrace of an inn above the cathedral, half-way up from Alfama. Luciano felt great satisfaction, while waiting for the Marquis to show his hand. Drinks were served. The girls of the inn were very excited by the sight of the fine gentlemen. One of the colonels even succeeded in taking off a garter.

Everybody laughed. The *vinho verde* was cool and bubbled. The Marquis arrived, appreciating that they had waited for him. The technical aspects were discussed. They checked their timepieces. It would start at twelve o'clock. It was very hot already. The heat would be insufferable by eleven, not to mention the smell of all the dead and of the blood in the sunshine. Before noon everybody in the district would be inside the dwellings. Besides, that was the order given by Luciano's agents.

The shouts in the morning awoke Gianvittorio and Fernanda. He rushed to determine their cause, leaving her hidden in the house because she was too well-known, and the scarf on her neck was particularly conspicuous. In under an hour Gianvittorio crossed the whole of Alfama, and had seen the length and breadth of the disaster. The white crosses on the doors left no doubt of the objective. He could do nothing against the increasing rage of the townspeople. In any case he ought to spare his strength, which was not very great. He joined Joaquim who with Anna-Lucia had run everywhere too, and they made their inventory of what they had seen. Anna-Lucia told them about the arrival of the troops. They climbed the spire of São Miguel. The priest was entrenched behind the altar, murmuring prayers, out of his mind with fear. From the spire they saw the regiments spreading out.

They climbed down and assembled the brethren. It was not easy. More than half held the opinion that the vampires and their friends should look after their own business. The remainder was definitely hostile, indeed in a murderous mood. Only a very few were willing to help. Despite his influence, his rank, function and prestige, Gianvittorio did not carry the day. His principal argument, namely that if there was persecution and massacre, they too would be persecuted and massacred, and if Alfama fell they too would lose their fortress and shelter, left them unimpressed. The assembly broke up without taking any decision, without even smoothing out the internal squabbles. In any case there would be no armed resistance. Some spoke of mutual help, of saving themselves, but without conviction. One group of them was convinced there had been provocation; another, not a negligible group, believed without saying it aloud in the guilt of the vampires. Gianvittorio was furious. If he survived he would have his revenge. Half-past eleven struck. They had wasted nearly two hours in talk. There remained the hope of the army going into action only at nightfall. Gianvittorio knew from reliable sources that the regiments were very slow to manœuvre.

He went back to Joaquim. What to do? Evidently Clara, Alexandra and their friends must be warned. Clara was not at home: she had been called out by many, but there were no wounded to be saved, only the dead. She came back weighed down with grief. The misery, the tragedies, the youth and beauty of some of the victims had so upset her that she had not grasped the reasons behind it. She was overcome by the individual cases, her heart bleeding and not a thought in her head. She could have killed herself for being such an idiot when Gianvittorio enlightened her. They ran to Kotor's palace, which was silent, deserted and locked. The door, which they could not break down, was as immovable as the walls. They returned to Clara's house. On the side that opened on Alfama, down below under the terraces . . . the incline of the street was very steep. It was badly paved, and there were no soldiers. They had put up a barrier lower down, but were too lazy to climb as far as Clara's house.

There was the underground passage through the cellars. At the bottom of Clara's cellar was a turning wall that gave on the underground passage which led to the hall of the statues and the crypt of the coffins in Kotor's palace. A few lanterns, stairheads, steps to climb and descend. Gianvittorio went to fetch Fernanda, Joaquim, his father, and Anna-Lucia. With Clara there were six of them. They reached the palace. Complete silence reigned. Alexandra had taken the habit of drugging herself every dawn after Laurent's departure, and woke up only towards evening. They gave up the attempt to break in on her. They felt time slipping by. Anguish twisted their bowels.

Clara entered the crypt of the coffins. Barbara's had disappeared. Five remained. They looked at each other: they had to choose. They could evidently carry only one, and caution demanded that they destroy the underground passage after their return.

'Kotor,' said Gianvittorio. 'Without him nothing could survive.'

They agreed. The six of them just managed to carry the coffin. They began their return journey when it struck twelve. They stopped every ten yards for Gianvittoro to let the walls collapse behind them. Advancing yard by yard towards Clara's house they lost all notion of time. They heard nothing any more and could hardly see one another. The coffin was an enormous lump of lead. Every quarter of an hour they had to stop for another fifteen minutes to regain their breath.

At the first stroke of twelve the soldiers quivered. The officers consulted their maps for the last time. The colonels thought they were out hunting, and had the impression of holding back a pack of hounds at the kill. The soldiers had fixed bayonets at the end of their rifles. A number of them, one in five, carried very special arms: sticks made of hard wood and very much sharpened, and mallets too. Before the officers and sergeants had explained what it was about, it had been a huge joke, but now it seemed more an object of horror.

The twelfth stroke of the clock, and sergeants and officers followed by the ranks let out a great shout and began to march. The occasional passers-by were surrounded, bayonets pointed at their bellies, and their necks inspected to see whether they bore the scars of the friends of the vampires. If they did they were tied up, beaten and pushed aside to be attended to later. The houses with the white crosses had their doors battered down. The inmates were treated in the same manner. Then came the rush to the cellars, and the discovery of the coffin. That is where the sharp sticks and mallets came in.

The coffin lid was violently lifted. The sight of the vampire sleeping in his half-death repulsed the first comer. But they grew used to it. For some of them the beginning was very hard. To hold a wooden stick above the vampire's heart, to hammer it in with the mallet, and see the cataract of blood, to hear that desperate groan of the vampire who felt himself dying for the second time, this time the real and irreversible death, was horror itself. But horror loses its edge. The second time it was not as bad as the first, and so on. In the first phase the soldiers treated their prisoners with sacred fear, hardly daring to touch them. And they released all who had no scars, even if they lived in the accursed houses. In that first phase the people of the neighbourhood, folks mostly on the fringe of society, more or less on the run, in equivocal situations, and the others who lived in harmony with them, merchants and artisans, found themselves in the paradoxically thrilling situation of approving of the forces of order for the first time in their lives, and being on the quite unfamiliar other side of the barricade in a military operation whose repressive aims were beyond doubt. In the great game of cops and robbers they turned into cops without being aware of it. Thus for the first time in decades the army and the police began to feel at home in Alfama. Some cheered, others encouraged the soldiers, and some of them pushed one another aside to see better.

But then the situation changed. As the soldiers became accustomed to their gory task, and were covered in blood like butchers, progressively losing all their sensibility, the people of Alfama pounced on them, identifying them as their eternal enemies. There were scuffles, and shots were fired. Unnerved by the smell of blood and exasperated by the unresisted massacre, the soldiers used their firearms.

At last the real battle is coming, said the disgusted officers. This phenomenon repeated itself at every door: the initial timidity of the soldiers, the apparently indifferent, almost approving population that turned afterwards against the invaders. But it was too late; Luciano, in accord with the colonels, had established eight columns which followed as nearly as possible the route of the eight groups of false vampires. The Marquis' hundred carabineers watched over all the possible exits in sections of five, reinforced by groups of two infantry companies. Their order was to let no one enter or leave. At first they had felt frustrated, but now they had plenty to do. Small groups of fugitives tried to escape. When everybody in Alfama had understood that they were encircled, they turned to attack in order to force an exit. The shooting became heavy. There it was at last.

The eight columns converged on São Miguel, on Kotor's palace.

The prisoners were taken down to the quay near an enormous wooden palisade, a hundred metres or so in length, which protected the docks of the Macao and Timor Company. Two improvised buildings for drying tobacco were behind it. There the prisoners were assembled, now truly ill-treated with rifle butts and the points of bayonets. Utterly crushed, they remained silent. Their numbers rose all the time. Soon there were a hundred at least, some of them badly wounded, all of them prostrate.

The advance continued. Luciano tried to follow the advance of the columns. Messengers came and went. The colonels marked the progress of the troops on a large map on the ground. The Marquis was boiling over with impatience. He wanted to go down and mingle with the soldiers, but Luciano held him back. At least an hour was needed to reach the palace. Anyhow, there was no difficulty. They would be there before nightfall.

It was easy to follow the soldiers' advance: they were floundering in blood. Luciano's policemen, supplied with the list of freemasons, Jews, rebels on the run, and escaped convicts, went into action. They entered houses where the petrified inhabitants piled up in the cellars and attics, and selected their quarry. From time to time some heads had to be bashed in. They chose girls too. There was not much rape, minds being otherwise engaged. The girls belonged to a different part of Luciano's plan. Real merchandise. There were specialists among the policemen who seemed to be looking for virgins. They made sure by lifting skirts and pawing them with indifferent brutality. They preferred blondes, but as there were not many they took all whose skins were white. Now and again they took even an experienced woman if she was remarkably good looking. The chosen men and women were not sent down along with the rest, but taken away through another exit near the Castello. Carts were waiting, much like cages, where everyone was counted and checked. The men were sent to the central prison, the girls to a disused convent.

Suddenly the soldiers met genuine resistance. In the end Alfama had understood that although the vampires certainly were the main target, they were not the only one, perhaps not even the most important. People began to face the soldiers; but they were already well advanced, and everyone was surrounded. The houses had to be taken one by one. Seeing their comrades fall the soldiers became mad with rage. They turned into wild beasts, and that well-oiled machine that had worked so well was thrown out of gear. The meshes of the carefully spread net, at first masterfully drawn in, started to move apart, and became entangled as well.

There was a break-through. About fifty determined men and women, who had understood what was happening, first broke through the cordon of soldiers, then violently fell on the policemen, literally tearing them to pieces. The survivors gave way. That whole section of the net was torn, and columns of fugitives escaped along the road to Villafranca de Xira. When Luciano realised what was happening it was already too late. Over-confident, he had kept no troops in reserve, and uncertain of his hold over the war ministry he did not dare send in the cavalry which would have saved the situation. The Marquis began to curse, and rushed to join the advance guard. The western wing, which was the left wing of the troops, continued progressing towards Kotor's palace, but slowly and with heavy losses.

One of the colonels had half his head blown away exactly one yard from where the Marquis stood. He was spattered, and trembled with fear. The other colonel, who had followed him too, decided that the climb was too much to the advantage of the besieged, and that they should withdraw towards the quay. He was satisfied with what they had gained, which was certainly an achievement, but it meant nothing to the Marquis. They discussed the matter for ten minutes, the Marquis remaining in command, but everything slowed down. Despite their orders the soldiers started throwing fire-bombs, which silenced their adversaries but demolished the houses. So the cellars could not be reached. Decidedly it was all going wrong.

The explosions dragged Alexandra from her sleep. She leapt out of bed, and mounted the stairs of the central building. On the top was a sort of terrace-veranda. Columns of smoke rose from the whole of Alfama. Alexandra left her perch. The palace was deserted. The servants who were not sleeping in their coffins had disappeared; at least she thought so. Then she found them trembling with fear in a coach-house. She calmed them, armed them, and reflected about the situation. She had not the faintest doubt about the final aim of the attack. The palace had a main door that was evidently known to all, and a postern gate that was known too; but there was a door unused for many years which had served at one time for the delivery of fodder. She would have it opened. The stableboy, the coachman and two maidservants helped her.

The door moved. It gave on to a very steep street which led down to the quay. The street was deserted. Alexandra had a horse harnessed to a light carriage made for that purpose, and took herself to the cellar where the coffins were. She saw that Kotor's coffin had been taken away. There remained the others. She called the servants, and four of them carried Laurent's coffin to the carriage.

Alexandra put beside her on the box two carbines, each loaded with two bullets. Also two pistols. She would not have minded having more firearms, but some had to be left to the others who would try a sortie, each attempting to get away on his own. Dressed as a man she pulled her felt hat down to her eyes, and hid the rest of her face with a scarf. Two of the stable-boys asked permission to escape on horse-back, taking Mithras and Lili. She sighed, but agreed. They all embraced. Outside the shouts and the firing increased. They were approaching.

The fine organisation of the attack had blown to pieces. Generally the resistance collapsed, but the breach down at the river had not been closed. A human wave, growing ever larger, broke through it; their watchword: escape along the river.

The stable-boys quickly opened the coach-house gate. Alexandra whipped the horse drawing the carriage. The horse bounded forward on the cobbles of the steep street. The others started running beside the wall, and disappeared in the first alley they saw. Two horsemen charged, and everybody got out of their way.

Alexandra drove down the slope like one demented. Some soldiers, who were climbing painfully under the cross-fire of hidden marksmen, found themselves face to face with her. With her two pistols and her carbines, each capable of firing two shots, she hit three heads and grievously wounded two more infantrymen. Five shots in six got their targets—not too bad. The rest of the soldiers threw themselves into the streets they had emerged from. Later when they were severely interrogated they could describe nothing. The street ended almost in a cul-de-sac on a kind of terrace. To the left was a *ladeira* even steeper than the street which had an outlet above the river. The troops had already passed through, and had come through again when they were put to flight. There was not a soul about. Window-frames banged, corpses lay on the cobbles, and the flies were busy with them. Lower down, already outside in Alfama, were the wine docks. Vast empty barrels were waiting to be loaded on flat-bottomed barges with *latine* sails which would take them to Palmela and Setubal across the Sea of Straw. Alexandra stopped the carriage and got down. Where to go and how? The barrels drew her attention. An elegant and indifferent young man came past, and his expression changed as he quietly counted the barrels. He raised his head and looked at Alexandra, at her startlingly blue eyes which were all that could be seen between her hat and scarf. He climbed up to her.

'So you got away,' he said.

'For the moment.'

She could not disguise her voice. At once the young man grasped that it was a woman on the run.

'What do you carry?'

'My husband.'

She pulled down the scarf, let him see the scar on her neck, took off the felt hat, and threw it far away, and down tumbled her mane of hair. He had never seen anything so beautiful. In two seconds he was at her side.

'José de Andrade,' he said. 'I trade in wine. Ask whatever you want from me.'

'Do I fill you with horror?' she said. 'This is the day of the great massacre.'

'I know how to recognise the truth. I have an idea.'

'Let me hear it.'

'Is there a coffin in the carriage?'

'Yes.'

'Would it fit inside this empty barrel?'

'Yes. But there is the matter of the weight.'

'The slope will help. I am a Hercules.'

She looked at him more carefully. He could be. He rushed to his warehouse, and came back with a rope that he put round the coffin.

'I will pull it, and you will guide it,' he said.

She came down. The coffin just fitted into the barrel. José put the lid on.

'The first round is ours,' he said. 'But what about the next? They must have noticed you.'

'Excuse me,' she said. 'My name is Alexandra von Hoffburg.'

'I begin to recognise you. I have often talked about you with your uncle. But enough of worldliness. You will have to resign yourself.'

'I know,' she said. 'The carriage and the horse into the river. A splendid disappearance.'

'The only way,' said José. 'If they find no explanation they will look for one.'

'The idea of sacrificing my horse horrifies me. I do not want to.'

'I will do it for you.'

'Then you will fill me with horror.'

'I will take that risk.'

He literally pushed Alexandra behind the casks. Then he took a small pistol from his pocket, and fired it near the horse's ear. The horse bolted down the slope. At the end of the *ladeira*, tangled up in the harness, pushed by the weight of the cabriolet, the horse was already running at great speed. At that instant a small group of soldiers appeared on the scene. The horse, and carriage and some of the soldiers were thrown high, and fell back about fifteen yards lower down, half on the quay and half in the water. A fine confusion: blood, bowels, broken wood and torn leather, soldiers crushed by the struggling horse, and the cabriolet sinking into the muddy water. A detachment, arriving at the double to close the breach, nearly received all this on their heads, and quickly dispersed.

José pushed Alexandra into a barrel, and he followed. They could hear each other's breathing in the dark.

'Is my horse dead?' she asked.

'Certainly. And in a manner that will remain in the memory of those who saw it. They will believe you drowned in the cabriolet.'

He came nearer to her.

'I think you are superb.'

'I feel the same, but do not take advantage of the situation.'

He laughed. 'It would be the first time I should get paid in kind.'

She relaxed, then collapsed. He took her in his arms, and she sobbed, furious with herself because of her weakness. He stroked her hair, gently massaging the nape of her neck and the bulging forehead. She embraced him forcefully. He felt her breasts in his hands. They were like marbles. He pushed her away. She found that surprising, having felt no doubt that he was not indifferent to her charms.

'Another time is another life,' he murmured. 'It does not amuse me in the dark and in anguish. I am not a medicament, I am not a tranquilliser.'

'Even so I owe you everything . . . Why? You know who we are.'

'I know the legend, and I have no belief in what is happening today. He who cheers the hounds can easily become the hare.'

She embraced him once more as a reward. All was quiet, so they climbed out of the barrel. She looked at him more closely: a young middle-class chap, a Hercules as he rightly put it, ready to take over from the aristocracy. I could easily have fallen for him, she said to herself, and he knows it. A trifle melancholic, surely romantic, perhaps a poet, but a man of action too. He took his decision very quickly. He lent Alexandra his hat, and summoned his dockers and their foreman, none of whom had any desire to work that day. They all grumbled about the army and the police. They loaded the extra barrels José pointed out to them without murmuring, and accepted goodhumouredly the news that they would be leaving at once. The overloaded *fragata* left the dock less than half an hour after Alexandra's entrance into José's life. They were already far down the river when the police succeeded at last in closing the torn net. It was about four o'clock.

The Marquis and the surviving colonel, having taken their troops in hand again after they had heard from the police that the breach had been closed, arrived at last near Kotor's palace. Sappers had been sent for to blow in the huge front door. The Marquis drew his sword as if posing for a *genre* painting. Light infantrymen raced all over the place, breaking into every room. Not a soul anywhere. An idiot of a sergeant, fiddling rather too vigorously with the material in Kotor's laboratory, blew up part of the wall, which crushed ten soldiers as it collapsed. A column of smoke rose, looking rather like a small mushroom. The door of the crypt flew open on its own.

The Marquis chased round the landings, kicking doors in. The colonel and his officers thought he was showing off. The Marquis saw that Alexandra had vacated her bedroom only a short time ago. He pulled out a nightdress which he cut into two with his sword; stockings, underclothes, face creams and combs followed. He swept everything before him, breaking scent bottles. They came to fetch him, and the young ensign sent to him would remember for a long time the red-faced man, his wig askew, frothing at the mouth in the middle of the broken glass he trampled on.

The Marquis reached the cellar as the coffin lids were taken off. There was no Laurent, no Kotor and of course no Barbara. The Marquis cursed furiously, and nearly fell on Luciano who arrived out of breath. It was apparent that without proclaiming it Luciano was delighted at the Marquis' discomfiture. The sleeping vampires were swiftly despatched. It was the first time that the Marquis and Luciano themselves witnessed the death of vampires. Spattered with blood, the Marquis fainted away, and was despised even more than before. On the other hand Luciano was absorbed, and approached with almost scientific curiosity, to see better. He watched attentively as the boar-spear was driven in, and the blood spurting as if it were kept in some kind of pocket. In a low voice the colonel asked for explanations, which Luciano gave him in a complacent voice. He spoke of the first death of the vampire and his second death.

'In fact,' said the colonel, 'if we liquidate the prisoners we have to kill them twice.'

'Perhaps not,' said Luciano. 'I have ideas about it. Let us finish here first.'

In an instant the ruins of Kotor's palace became the headquarters of the forces of intervention in Alfama. Once closed again, the net was pulled tight, and some big fish struggled in it: one of the kings of the Lisbon underworld, a long-searched-for printer, a convict who had escaped five years ago. Even if the military operation was a complete failure from the Marquis' point of view, it remained extremely fruitful for Luciano. It only remained to cover up. Since João could still not be found either in the ministries or the Archbishop's palace, they sent for his coadjutor, a fanatic who had always exasperated His Eminence. Everything was settled in a few minutes. It was unnecessary to consult him: the coadjutor accepted all responsibility. The vampires could be liquidated. Reanimated, deep in a dark reverie, the Marquis, the colonel, the coadjutor and Luciano went down to the quays to the spot where the prisoners were assembled and concentrated. Any that were not vampires were taken to the central prison or the jails of Caxias and Peniche. They were all ill-treated, beaten up, ribs broken, skulls squashed in, arms and fingers broken, and sometimes legs too. The even more ill-treated political prisoners were all sent to Peniche.

Near the long palisade of the Macao and Timor Company stood the accomplices and disciples of the vampires, with their hands tied behind their backs, their collars torn, conspicuously showing their scars. They had not been beaten too much because they continued to inspire some kind of terror.

The Marquis looked at them one by one, but none seemed familiar. A corporal, who had seen the cabriolet leaving Kotor's palace, and a soldier who had survived the collision on the quay, as well as two policemen who had seen from below the carriage falling into the river, easily explained the route the supposed escapers from the palace had taken. It was good enough to convince Luciano, but not to lift the Marquis out of his burning doubt. It was time to begin the liquidation.

Luciano's reasoning was simple: by pushing a boar-spear directly into the heart of a disciple of the vampire he would be killed twice, first as a human, then as a vampire. A brilliant idea, once one had thought of it. All were convinced, yet all regarded Luciano as another monster. Even the Marquis moved away from him. Luciano gave the signal. They began.

Twenty at a time the vampires were pushed against the palisade. They were literally nailed to it as the sharp boar-spear entered the palisade after piercing the heart. Blood flowed copiously. The corpses were unhooked. Part of the palisade had been taken away in order to give direct access to the river, into which everything was thrown. That took only a few minutes. The blood, washed with plenty of water, ran in the gutters to the sewers. After that it poured into the Tagus which turned violently red for some distance.

With shining eyes the vampires fraternally comforted one another, embraced one another when they could, and died without a sigh or a cry. They were more fanatical than Luciano would have believed. From mouth to ear they whispered the news of Kotor's and Laurent's escape and probable rescue. Some openly laughed at their executioners, none of whom dared to hit them. Quite the contrary: they kept them at a distance, almost politely. None the less a great deal of blood ran. One could have believed it was a slaughter-house. The officers were disgusted, the soldiers nearly sick. Luciano felt there was a risk of weakening. The policemen got their carbines ready, prepared for every eventuality. Then Luciano had to resign himself to sending the troops away, and letting the police finish the work. But soon a wave of horror swept the whole town. The martyrdom of the vampires had lost them all respect.

For the town had gone through different stages. The attack on Alfama in the wake of the discovery of the vampires' 'crimes' was at first thoroughly approved of. People assembled in groups on the Rossio or the Chiado, in the cafés and in the taverna where *ginginha* is drunk in the morning, a liqueur of cherries that brightens the day. But very quickly, when they saw the convoys of prisoners—especially those who were taken to Peniche—many came to understand the general purpose of the operation. At first they could not explain João's disappearance, but they came to explain it only too well. Everybody thought it a *coup d'état* by the Marquis. Excitement grew to the extent that the entire town became paralysed. It was a barrel filled with gunpowder.

The Marquis, who had not had the strength to remain until the end of the killing of the vampires, had to take notice of it as he imprudently crossed the town. He was recognised, insults flew, then stones. He swiftly turned back to seek an escort from the delighted Luciano: it had never been the operation's aim to provide the Marquis with a stepping-stone to power. Luciano was waiting for João's reappearance, and found he was late. Reality did not match the plan altogether. That would have to be dealt with. The regiments returned to their barracks covered in blood. Swearing, the people saw them march past, but they looked so fierce that not a word was uttered against them. The day was dying. Policemen and the auxiliaries requisitioned from the municipality began to clean up Alfama, where the survivors began to reappear.

The *saveiro* with a resigned João on board, arrived at the quay of Sodre around that time. João, who had mostly slept after having gaily taken part in the fishing, woke up when they reached Jeranimos. He was intrigued by the unusual movement of the barges on the river. Something, the nature of which he could not guess, had upset and increased the traffic. He jumped ashore without bothering overmuch about the *saveiro*, which he was to regret, for he would never again find any trace of it or be able to explain the secret of his miraculous meeting with it.

The moment he put his foot on shore he was caught up in the drama. Smoke was still rising from Alfama. The crowds were agitated. In shirt-sleeves, without his wig, and tanned, nobody recognised him. He joined the loudly-talking groups, and soon learned everything. He could have gone to the Archbishop's Palace, or the War Ministry or the Ministry of the Interior, but he chose the Army. The General Staff was waiting for him. The three generals and the colonels were old friends of his. Orgies and boozing together had sealed their friendship. General Fabio de

Carvalho, the chief of staff, had just decided to impose unofficial martial law. His cavalry had just encircled the town, and the Marquis and his escort were locked into the Palace of the Annunciation for their own protection. Like a gust of wind, João entered the map-room of the General Staff, where Carvalho was explaining the state of things on an unfolded map. Generally they were against the operation which, having no information, they could only see as a *coup d' état* by the police forces. João did not hesitate for a second. He could not go it alone, and if one had to share power for power's sake it might just as well be with Carvalho, a good soldier, hardly corrupt, hardly a bigot, and liberal in his own way. He explained it cynically, and the others accepted at once. None of them really wanted power. The compromise suited all of them.

They would have to see the King, whom they decided to retain on their side so as to smooth their path. Little news had reached Cintra, and the King was cutting out pious pictures in the company of the youngest monk. On seeing the two of them beneath a lamp João was struck by the thought that in certain exceptional cases conjugal happiness was possible. The King seemed even to have forgotten the Marquis' visit in the morning and the consent bullied out of him. The little monk found João appealing and sympathetic, so different from that mangy dog of a Marquis whom he had hated on sight.

João explained the whole business as an attempted *coup d'état* by the Marquis and Luciano. A trifle crestfallen, the King refused to let the Marquis be broken on the wheel. Kicked out, yes; exiled to his estate, yes; but nothing more. They could do whatever they wanted to Luciano, and as far as power was concerned they were free to take it.

João left for Lisbon deep in thought. Everything would fall into place. He had only grasped very late in the day the true identity of Kotor and his children, and he had only his own stupidity and weakness to blame: not for the first time, and it would not be the last.

On reaching his house he did not have to start looking for Barbara. The bailiff from Azeitão was waiting for him. After rising at the end of the day, as was her wont, the Meninha had just simply vanished after hearing the news from Lisbon. She had gone back to her room, and no one had seen her since.

Luciano was announced. He did not lack audacity, that one. He entered, and bowed ceremoniously. João did not move, and looked at him unblinking.

'I could say like Regulus to Your Eminence that I bring peace or war in the folds of my toga.'

'Spare yourself the use of vain quotations. You are under arrest. You will go before a court martial tonight, and you will be shot tomorrow morning. You will be spared torture.'

João turned away as though he had nothing more to say or listen to. Nevertheless, Luciano's complete impassivity intrigued him. So he looked again: Luciano was smiling.

'A serious mistake, Your Eminence. I understand your annoyance. Yesterday it would have been justified. Today it is rancour, a useless sentiment. All power is in your hand—the army, for instance. News travels fast. I know the situation.'

João took his measure of the man.

'I am defeated,' continued Luciano. 'My allies were just incapable creatures.'

'A better word would be accomplices,' said João, realising at once that it had been a mistake to answer. The conversation was begun.

'A matter of vocabulary,' said Luciano.

'What have you to propose?'

'Thank you for not saying "to sell". I should like to make the point.'

João could not resist a gesture of admiration. Absolute dirt, yet what courage. It would be easier if one could always despise one's adversaries.

'The Church,' said Luciano, 'approves of the liquidation of the vampires. If you punish me, a man whose position proves his lack of power-seeking, you are going to start a serious conflict. The coadjutor, your coadjutor, officially authorised me to act . . .'

'He can drop you, now that he has what he wanted.'

'He won't do it. He is in my power, but I prefer to come to an understanding directly with you, instead of obtaining mercy through his intervention. You will have the scalps of Ricardo and the Marquis in this adventure. That is a great deal to have at the end of a defeat caused by your blindness, leaving aside the dropping of Dom Manuel. It is not too good being one of your protégés . . .'

João felt cold sweat running down his back. Either he stopped this at once or he was obliged to discuss it.

'I can prove your links with the vampires,' Luciano went on. 'Nobody will believe for a second that you were so near to them without knowing, without knowing *everything*. It is my turn to speak of complicity. An ecclesiastical court would not be more indulgent with you than a court martial with me. You will be burnt, and you won't be saved from torture.'

'I'm lost,' said João to himself. Luciano hid his triumph.

'Countess Barbara. Nobody would believe that you did not know what she was doing at Azeitao, and without you at Caparica.'

'None the less I was unaware of it,' sighed João.

'Happy are the innocent,' said Luciano, laughing.

João sat down in an armchair, and motioned Luciano to sit down.

Luciano chose a stool.

'You see I do not let myself be carried away by success. Let us talk. The Marquis you are exiling to his estate. That suits me well.'

'Careful. Do not provoke me. I can still decide on destroying us, you and me. I liked Count Kotor very much.'

'A noble attitude. Be reassured. I believe he is safe and sound.'

'Where is he?'

'I do not know. And certainly I shall not know. In my hands he would be dead by now. But as I have not found him among the victims he must be safe.'

'And my niece?'

'Apparently drowned in the Tagus with her lover. Ten reports affirm it. But I do not believe in the drowning of vampires. We will act as if we did.'

'What do you propose?'

'My conditions will be very gentle,' said Luciano. 'I leave you the Marquis' police and Ricardo's. Admit you could have done with them. I keep the secret services. You need fear nothing as I have no chance of reaching the King. I keep my domain, my means of action.'

'The prisoners at Peniche must be freed. I have many friends among them.'

'That depends on the Ministry of the Interior, and you are the minister. But I keep the female prisoners except those you might fancy. I expect to sell them to the Sultan of Miquenez. I shall have to pay the bill for your mistakes.'

João shuddered, wanting to speak, but remained silent in the end.

'I also want to protect myself,' Luciano went on, 'from one of your sudden changes of mind, and for that reason we will draft a secret protocol. There will be two copies which each of us will sign. Thus you will be protected too. Is it not reasonable?'

João did not have the strength to put his agreement into words. He only made a sign, and got up. Luciano remained seated.

'We must placate the annoyance of the military,' he said. 'That court martial needs a victim . . . There was after all a conspiracy, illegal use of two regiments, with several dead, one of them a colonel.'

'The other colonel will speak if he is accused. He will crush you.'

'I had no thought of accusing him.'

'Then who?'

'Ricardo will make the perfect guilty party. His lower-class origin will protect the nobility from all suspicion.'

'He will speak too.'

'No. I have just had him arrested. In the course of his transfer the carriage met with an accident. He cut his tongue in the collision. And as the smashed carriage crushed his hands he cannot write either. He has lost the balance of his mind, as you can well imagine.'

João shuddered, and left the room. Luciano stood up to salute him, three deep bows as prescribed.

Ricardo was sentenced during the night and was shot at dawn. He was spared torture.

Chapter V

Once again Kotor read aloud the tenth poem of Pindar, which told the story of Castor and Pollux, one mortal, the other immortal, who shared one immortality between them. For Kotor it was a familiar incantation. He was installed in a little room, harshly prepared for him in the attic of Clara's house, on the site overlooking Graça. A brick dividing wall had left enough space for a table, books and papers. Nobody could have believed that it was a hiding-place. A spiral staircase led straight down to the cellar where the coffin was. Clara, Ursula and Fernanda had built and bricked it up all on their own, with material brought successively along by Gianvittorio, Joaquim and Anna-Lucia. Total secrecy. Kotor did not put a foot outside.

Perhaps the precautions were exaggerated, for normal life had resumed in Alfama. The police and the army had withdrawn like water after a flood. There were no regulations, no patrols. People were back, especially the freed prisoners from Peniche, but no more vampires or disciples were seen. Those who had not been butchered disappeared. Nobody pronounced the *Word* any more. One could even doubt that the thing had ever existed. Fernanda's parents had escaped the massacre, but her sister, who was found in the cellar, shared the fate of practically all the sleeping vampires. Some had managed now and then to escape. But it was not easy to transport a coffin.

Cautiously, the brethren returned. Alfama had kept undamaged the network of two different front doors and underground passages. The alarm signals were improved. But for a long time the neighbourhood remained dead. At first Clara gave up receiving the sick, but in time her house was visited again. It was Ursula who almost always attended to the ailing. Clara was present on occasions, but everybody began to understand that she was slowly handing over the succession to Ursula.

A curtain of silence had descended. Joaquim, Anna-Lucia and the father had become drapers in Lapa. Their neighbour, a merchant importing lace from Malines, was none other than Gianvittorio, who gave himself out as being Flemish. Fernanda, whose neck was hidden by point-lace—the scar was disappearing—missed the times when her sister had taken her blood. She became very friendly with Anna-Lucia. Both of them had made and wore very short lace chemises which hardly reached the pubic hairs, leaving between stocking-top and chemises large areas of thigh. Naturally, they walked about like that the whole day long. The husbands were like stallions; Joaquim's father also had pleasant hours of reverie.

The destruction of his laboratory and the almost total loss of his archives had paralysed Kotor at first. The death of so many disciples, his brothers, gave his imagination and sensibility an awful shock. A whole army had perished in battle, and the battle had been lost. Luckily not everything had vanished, for many disciples survived who after their first death would open the cycle again. That permanent fight had its ups and downs without ever ceasing. But victory was no longer in sight, perhaps it no longer existed. Already Kotor had accepted his role as a military Sisyphus, for ever recommencing with a handful of indomitable adherents an endless fight. However, now all his research had to be started from nought again, and his work reconstructed with the sole aid of his unsure memory. A wave of discouragement washed over him. If it were only a case of existing, lasting, prolonging without finality a precarious, sickly and limited life, then the very meaning of the fight became blurred. The conquest of the right to the light of the sun, perhaps immortality too, this alone had any real sense. But in the malediction of the night, without the hope of getting out of it, taking a little blood from a keen disciple, all that turning into routine and mournful habit, was more than enough to discourage him. He did not succeed in mobilising his enthusiasm and remained seated at his table the entire night, answering Clara in monosyllables, lost between the vain effort of re-creating his work and a growing moodiness. The ritual gift of blood hardly soothed him. He partook of it only from a dry and deliberate need to survive, but without passion or fervour.

'I have become an official of longevity,' he said to Clara.

'Let us leave, in that case. You will never find here the energy which is so necessary for you again. Alfama is for you the image of defeat and death.'

'Yes, I have thought of leaving. But where and how? Our brothers have become strangely silent.'

'True. I do not receive messages any more, as though the

network that united our spirits were broken. Besides, even with us words have become necessary again . . . We have to speak to understand each other.'

'Perhaps the meeting of so many spirits, all seeking the same goal, produced a form of subtle energy that nourished our souls without our knowing it. We have suffered a cruel amputation.'

'That does not explain Swedenborg's silence. Before knowing you we did meet at times . . . In vain I have used my crystal sphere ten times at least . . . Nothing appears any more.'

'We are entering a dark tunnel. I asked the numbers.'

'And I the stars. I am afraid of hearing the same answer.'

'Departure, death and rebirth. All is severed again.'

'Your daughter Barbara . . .'

'What? Has she escaped the disaster?'

'She has been saved by the Blacks from Bahia. They treat her like a goddess. I just received their message, and that gave me an idea, namely to escape with them.'

'I do not know whether Africa . . .' Kotor began.

'Oh, they are slaves of the fifth generation . . . Bahia is their homeland, Africa only a distant nostalgia. Even their language is used only in their religious rites. Among themselves they speak Portuguese. They eat, sing and make love in Portuguese.'

'Bahia,' murmured Kotor. 'I will consult.'

The ritual of geomantic consultation began, inspiring with a new envy and desire Kotor's hibernating spirit. For the first time since the massacre something interested him again.

Jean-Pierre hit the kerb as he parked his car. 'The traffic in Rio is terrible,' he raged. One should never go out during the rush hour. It was still daylight, but all the street lights came on simultaneously. He got out of the car, and looked round. He felt lost. Diplomats seldom went to the northern part of the city, an enormous industrial district in a working-class neighbourhood. It was like a tropical version of the run-down outskirts of Paris. The *tenda* he was looking for was bound to be there. Yet he hesitated, finding it rather odd to look for a religious centre between a garage and a tyre-retread workshop. None the less it was there: a little mill-stone house belonging more in the countryside than in an industrial suburb. In front was a garden, and a courtyard was probably behind. In the garden were five or six little kennels which turned out to be niches for household gods. At the bottom of each one candles had been lit in front of primitive altars, and naïve and simple statues which Jean-Pierre recognised as various incarnations of Exus. He stepped forward. A small girl disappeared at the sight of him, and soon came back with an old man whose white hair accentuated the blackness of his skin. Jean-Pierre introduced himself. He carried voluminous letters of introduction. Ever since he had arrived *en poste* in Rio he had taken a keen interest in the cults of African origin which proliferated everywhere, *macumbas*, *ubamda*. He was writing a book on the subject. In two years he had learnt quite a lot.

'Is "Mae" Clara in?' he asked. 'I have a letter from Senhor Jorge for her.'

'She is never here in the daytime,' said the old man, 'but she will soon come. Sit down.'

He ushered him into a room with flowery wallpaper, furnished with a few divans and unmatched armchairs (no doubt sent out to Brazil by Levitan, the Parisian cheap furniture store, around 1932 and abundantly reproduced by the local furniture industry). They brought him coffee. Dressed in velvet, her eyes large, the little girl smiled at him timidly. Night fell. A hanging lamp which would have cost a fortune in an antique shop was lit.

Somebody was moving in the room next door. The little girl listened.

' "Mae" Clara has arrived,' she said. 'I will let her know.'

She disappeared behind a curtain, and returned to fetch the visitor who entered a large room which was utterly different. It gave the impression of luxury. On the wall were the expected pious images. Every religion takes along its St Sulpice or its Guerassimov, and Jean-Pierre was not surprised by its being the same with the African-Brazilian religions. The lady interested him far more. She was not really black, only her parchment-like skin was very brown. Jean-Pierre thought it might almost be dyed. Large, very black eyes, snow-white hair—she could as well be fifty as a hundred.

'I have read the letter our friend Jorge sent us,' said 'Mae' Clara. 'Without his recommendation I would not receive you. My *tenda* wants no notoriety whatsoever. I do not like being spoken about. I do not allow any photography. There are very few of my ceremonies at which you will be permitted to assist.'

She was like ice. Nevertheless, they talked, and it took a good hour for 'Mae' Clara to admit she understood French; hers a strangely old-fashioned French. Her *tenda*, her parish, was not attached to any of the big federations of the *Ubamda*. She was of the Bahian rite, nearer to the *Candomblé*, but a bit on the margin in her relations with the orthodox *Yoruba* cults. It was difficult for Jean-Pierre to place her. But there was strong mutual sympathy. She seemed to understand Jean-Pierre's purely sociological outlook, a convinced atheist, but passionately moved by the 'four hundred years of resistance' of the African religions that had held their own in Brazil. Clara appeared to grasp his point of view perfectly, which other 'Mothers of Saints' or 'Fathers of Saints' were often loath to accept. Yet she dropped a curtain of silence on her own beliefs, Pantheon and Olympus. She only generalised with some new notions like the syncretism of the Greek gods and of the Yoruba Olympus. It was known, described and written by everybody that the African gods had hidden behind the masks of the Christian saints for centuries. But 'Mae' Clara's constant reference to the polytheist Greek, Egyptian and Chaldean mythologies he found even stranger. Iemanja-Aphrodite, Exu-Hermes, the Eguns and Osiris, Ogum and Mithras—very curious. The two of them talked more than they had intended to, Clara saying more than she had expected, and Jean-Pierre exceeding his role as the objective inquirer.

They chatted well into the night. Dinner was brought in. The servants were handsome, happy and immensely respectful, mixing family affection with the disciple's devotion to his master. As a sign of belonging all wore a scarf round their necks. A staircase led to a kind of cellar. Someone could be heard moving about in the cellar, and then the stairs creaked. A giant of a man came slowly into view, not at all astonished to see Jean-Pierre, as though some mysterious signal had already informed him about the presence of a guest who was a complete stranger. The man was tall, uncommonly fat, not black but perhaps a mulatto; and he too gave the impression that his skin was dyed. A patriarch, a Leonardo.

'My husband Ladislau,' said 'Mae' Clara, 'the *Babalorixa* of our *Terreiro*. Monsieur Jean-Pierre Rémy, diplomat and French writer.' She completed the introduction.

Where have I seen this face? Jean-Pierre asked himself. They spoke about the past. Even André Malraux could not have juggled better with the epochs of gods, beliefs and myths. A sorcerer speaking about Cardinal de Bernis in the depths of Bom

Successo, an industrial suburb of Rio . . . They were pleased with one another's company. More than that, perhaps. They spoke about divination. From Peking, where he had been stationed, Jean-Pierre had brought back curious views on the techniques of divination of Pa-Kona and geomancy. He had fallen among specialists. He asked if they would carry out the rite of *buzios* for him. He trembled slightly when he found they had divined too much, and the misfortunes of his unreciprocated loves burst forth from Ladislau's and Clara's divination. The whole night went by. A servant came into the room, and opened a shutter without speaking. The thin line of dawn could be seen in the heart of the night. Clara rose.

'Come back,' she said. 'You are always welcome.'

They embraced, and Jean-Pierre saluted Ladislau with the traditional embrace. Only then he remembered. That sorcerer was the portrait in negative of Orson Welles. He laughed, which prevented him from seeing the long glance Clara and Ladislau exchanged. It also prevented him from seeing the glance they threw on the jugular vein on his neck.

It was still day when Alexandra awoke. She looked at the labyrinthian shape of the barn's rigid beams above her, very beautiful, and her eyes rested on them. A hymn to geometry and physical strength. Ordinary craftsmen had made that work of art with the great simplicity of their souls. It was a long, tall and very narrow building with double windows placed very high up, perhaps twice the height of a normal man. Alexandra could not guess the reason for that strange shape. They had arrived with José after an unbelievable barge voyage of two days. Their barge had anchored deep in the countryside, in the middle of a marsh, to the amazement of the water buffaloes standing in deep mud, which lived there by the dozen in a half-wild state. When night came, with Laurent helping to carry his coffin, they moved under olive trees, sleeping the whole day. José seemed to know exactly where they were going. He told Alexandra that the range of Arrabida was their goal. Above the Portinho of Arrabida, a fishing village with about ten dwellings, was a hamlet, with a monastery with ten hermits according to the rule of the closed orders. There a little lane led on to a barn, all on its own in an abandoned olive grove, overgrown and returned to the wild, invaded by small thick cork-trees. The barn had been in his family for a hundred years, left to rot because of now long-forgotten law cases. José had neither the intention nor the desire to start it up again. Thus he was the owner of three unploughed wild mountains. In the middle was the barn (at least three centuries old), showing that oil once had been made there.

José had helped Alexandra to move in. An immense curtain cut the only room in two. On one side the shutters were fastened for Laurent's coffin, on the other were a sort of bed and two supports and some planks to make a table. And there was a sink-hole, a kind of kitchen, and a well outside under a porch.

Every second or third day during the first month José came, bringing a few pieces of furniture, books, candles and crockery. Lost in the forest, invisible to human eyes, the fugitives established a rustic life. Alexandra and he coldly discussed the situation. The question of food. The fall of Alfama had traumatised Alexandra. Furthermore, she received a vague message: hide, disappear, pretend to be dead. Laurent's gift was more developed. He knew that Kotor, Clara and Barbara were safe. But his messages were very weak too. For the sake of prudence they should hide until the results and consequences of the Alfama massacre could more clearly be gauged. Barbara seemed nearer. Indeed she was.

When she had woken up on the evening of the massacre, her spirit was invaded by calls of distress and fear. She was the most receptive of all of them. Telepathy was not equally given to the vampires and their disciples. With Barbara it was really the gift. She knew immediately what was happening, and she sent out appeals to be calm, to escape and to hide. She was the only one to know exactly the state the few survivors were in. In agreement with Kotor she took the decision to go totally underground, stopping all outside manifestations, and even abstaining, though only provisionally, from all form of retaliation.

From Alexandra she received only hazy messages. 'We are in safety, I exist.' However, with Laurent she nearly had a kind of conversation—although without words. 'This is where we are, we do not know how to survive without giving ourselves away, we certainly are the prey they are looking for.'

José, Laurent and Alexandra were in despair because they could find no solution. Every unusual movement of people or goods would be spotted like a lighthouse. A black slave appeared with a letter from Barbara. She put him at their disposal, she guaranteed him, and the scarf round his neck was ample proof of their relationship. At once José saw how to make use of him. He could put him into livery, and give him official work, namely the repairing of the oil-press to give the impression that he was vaguely thinking of restarting the olive plantations on his mountains. That would explain the fishermen bringing him food and sustenance and his going to Portinho to buy fish and bread. So they did. The Black worked nonchalantly, and went about unseen for much of the night. He was their feeble link with the outside world. He brought back the necessities, so that José could space out his visits. First he feared he might be followed, and then he saw that his passion for Alexandra could have no results, and would get him nowhere. Every call tired him out despite the mutual friendship and the night-long fabulous discussions.

A routine was born, a monastic rule of life of the besieged. Laurent and Alexandra had never loved each other so much. Tristram and Ysolde in the forest, they said to make themselves laugh, except that there was no sword in the middle of their bed to separate them.

They never tired of each other, never tired of love and words. They believed that the cycle of their days was an island in time; their forest a sort of island too.

A lyrical fluid was born in Laurent. He prophesied. In the heart of the defeat he invented marching songs and hymns of victory, as if Kotor's unrealisable dream were on the threshold of victory.

For Alexandra time ceased to exist. That was what she said to herself at the end of the day, gazing at the network of beams above her bed. Since childhood she was accustomed to live only for the present with the idea of taking from it as much as was possible. But now she could not hold back a vague fear and worry about the future. The few rare contacts which she or more often Laurent had with Kotor received but one answer: hide, wait and survive. This was certainly wise counsel. Naturally, Alexandra could not imagine what she would decide to do if she were in Kotor's shoes but she did know the depth of his despair. Her thirst for action remained unimpaired and unquenched.

She got up, dressed as a man and went out. It was still the hottest hour of the afternoon. Cork-oaks, conifers and enormous century-old olive trees in a state of wildness. A multitude of insects, hares and rabbits. They caught some in the night. For her amusement she had forced Laurent to take the blood of a fat and splendid hare. She was fascinated, hypnotised and madly amused by the notion of the immortal hare-vampire, which would rise on its own in the night from the poulterer's slab to start chasing round the warrens. An innocent joke that almost provoked Laurent's anger before it ended joyfully in bed. She arrived near the monastery. Twelve little chapels were spaced out on an unbelievably steep escarpment, a masterpiece of the Baroque style, forming the stations of the Cross, and marking a frontier. For beyond them began the domain of the monastery of the closed order itself. The monastery was stuck to the top of a cliff looking on the sea from a great height, and resembled, thought Alexandra, the Eremo dei Carceri in Assisi which had so much impressed her. Here was no town nearby, only solitude. She heard the bells chime five o'clock. A few monks, who worked in the garden, returned to the monastery. Alexandra found herself horrified at the sight of those living dead, automatons of the Faith.

That prevented her from noticing that she was discovered. A figure hidden behind a tree was observing her, in a monk's habit without a cowl, a novice who probably still had a little freedom of movement. She retraced her steps to the barn without realising that he was on her heels. While she had been looking at the monks he had looked at her; and then discovering the barn he thought it had surely more than one inhabitant. When night fell the novice gave up his surveillance, vowing to return to see who was the new arrival in that wilderness. Outside the monastery there was a small outhouse, a sort of shed, for the novices. They were four, preparing themselves to become monks of the closed order. They ran essential errands, and were admitted to the religious services. In the feeble light of a lantern on the wall one could see more clearly the face of the prying novice: he was Antonio, the fiancé of Lavinia, Kotor's first disciple in Alfama, who had left the world when she became a vampire.

However, curiosity was not dead in that simple-minded soul. Next day he returned to the barn. They were all sleeping, but Antonio was patient. His habit was the colour of the tree trunks. He stood motionless like a fakir. The flies themselves mistook him for a rock. He could have been mistaken for a stone when Alexandra came out, and he managed not to flinch when he saw her washing herself naked with the water of the well. All day long and the next day too he played the role of peeping tom, suspecting some inexplicable adultery. As he had to return at dusk evidently he could not discover the essential secret. During the two days that he followed Alexandra she vaguely sensed a climate of hostility and of pursuit which she attributed to some hunter running around the hills. The telepathy of their group consisted only in receiving messages consciously and personally sent. As regards the rest, some of the vampires succeeded in finding access to the spirit of third parties in the shape of a kind of perfected intuition. Alone Barbara succeeded—and only at rare moments—in reaching the mysteries of thoughts, but always subject to jamming, often as unconscious as the oyster's impulse to shrink when the lemon juice is squirted on it. Kotor had always been somewhat timid about that gift of hers, afraid to study it, develop it, and use it as a system.

When the novice had persuaded himself that the she-hermit living in the same forest was lovely and desirable, and nothing explained her presence there, he lost all restraint, and began to prepare a nocturnal expedition with exceptional care. It took him two long days to organise everything: break the padlock of the outhouse and be able to put it back, a dark lantern, a truncheon, a dagger, a gag and ropes. He set out on a moonless night, not without preparing himself for landmarks and broken branches—the art of the poacher. Thus he blindly advanced as far as the barn, where only a thin line of light could be seen between two imperfectly closed shutters. He approached, saw, and collapsed in a dead faint: Laurent was taking Alexandra's blood.

Laurent felt a strong pain. It happened, or so he believed, that he could feel the terrible pain of an animal caught in a trap or captured. Then he knew how to close his spirit, to make it more difficult to sense what was going on around him. Otherwise the suffering and pains of the whole animal world, of which there is so much, would have tormented him to death.

'Imagine,' he said, 'a person feeding himself on the anguish of living people, especially the anguish they experience at the instant of death . . . Every minute, every second is like a shriek of pain from all who feel their lives escaping.'

He could not explain the melancholia that seized him. He knew death, the universality of death, its omnipresence everywhere at every second. He had felt it for centuries, and Kotor's gamble was precisely that. Any other victory than that one seemed derisory, and that victory was out of reach. Men would throw themselves on their tyrants, which was all to the good, and once again cut themselves loose from the old order. But already it could be seen that while they remained slaves of their feudal lords, the middle classes were not at all prepared to free their own slaves. Gods and religion lay in wait for man and his fears, more thirsty of anguish than the vampires of blood. Laurent sought to cut loose.

'I do not want to become like Father,' he went on. 'A bureaucrat of immortality, with centuries to wait for his equation to be solved. Kotor drops his arms, and hides like a tracked animal.'

'We are tracked. We are hiding too.'

'There you are. We drop our arms too. We let the old malediction and the old legend be reborn. We have become the enemies of humanity again. Our forces are dispersed.'

'Perhaps we are condemned to be dispersed. To go on frightening little children for centuries.'

'And credulous grown-ups, that is to say everybody.'

'Kotor will recover his patience,' she said. 'He knows how to wait.'

'No. He likes waiting, which is not the same thing. Waiting for a privileged, opportune moment which might never come or which he would not recognise when it did come. Spartacus did not distribute arms to the slaves to bury them until the right moment came. He told them how to hold them and how to use them.'

'But at least Kotor has survived. Spartacus was defeated.'

'Especially by his friends. His Liberated City crumbled under its own weight. Besides, there were even freed slaves who wanted to keep slavery for their own benefit. Kotor should take his troops in hand.'

'They are yours too,' Alexandra said. 'Speak to him. But who do we fight, and how? In which world do we want to live? An eternity in this one hardly appeals to me. Survival has sense for me only if life is transformed.'

'Marching proves itself through marching. The fight against death involves another style of life.'

'Defeat stuns one.'

She threw herself into Laurent's arms. Neither of them could explain the wave of anguish and uncertainty that overcame them, the impression that nothing had any meaning left. They escaped into love-making as if it were a drug.

On the other side of the shutters Antonio, the novice, slowly regained consciousness. Mastering violent nausea he had another look, but a tide of sheer hatred overwhelmed him even more than before. Alexandra and Laurent were making love with unparalleled fervour. He escaped into the night. Brambles and the branches of oaks tore him as he passed. He regained his breath only as he reached the door of the novices' outhouse. His temples and ears were throbbing. He hardly had the strength to reach his litter of straw and pass out. Next day he did not get up. A father brought him broth. He was in delirium.

Towards dawn Laurent (now satisfied) tried for a long time to approach Kotor's spirit. Alexandra held his hands, helping him with all her strength. But their anguish struck an obstinate refusal to communicate, or to share their pain and fear. They felt more alone, and for the first time found it insufferable to be unable to sleep in each other's arms because of the malediction. During the day they were walled up in incommunicable loneliness. It was difficult to resign themselves to it, and they embraced like lost children before Alexandra closed the coffin lid.

They found each other again after night fell with true and devouring passion, which prevented them from paying any attention to the *terzo incommodo* whose eyes were glued to the opening between the shutters, feeding the fever of his fury—or perhaps the fury of his fever. Alexandra had invention, and Laurent was inexhaustible, a fine balance. The novice would make a good confessor after having seen them. They questioned each other for hours about the structure of their bodies, that machinery that made them different from the bodies of other people, that elusive mysterious change of process already more advanced than in the old human species, but not yet on the level of consciousness and comprehension, which it would surely reach when the vampires took in hand the inheritance of *homo faber* and *homo sapiens*. That new man, *homo immortalis*, they endowed with a harmonious life from which slavery and lies, races and castes would be banished. That utopian delirium, a drug like any other, was calming, relaxing and produced a euphoria that made them laugh till tears came into their eyes. Longevity, a span of life lasting two or three thousand years, would surely produce a delightful society. Nursery schools until the age of one hundred, university to the age of three hundred, inevitable polygamy, new moral rules and ethics. The evocation of those delights brought them nearer to happiness than they had ever been before.

The novice suffered most from the sight of that joy and their evident and provocative happiness. Tortured by the thought of sin, which had become the key to his mind and the major obsession of his whole existence, the sight of those two who apparently lacked it was like a challenge to him. He avidly listened. First it was difficult to understand even the words. Alexandra and Laurent understood each other even before they formulated their thoughts, waiting for the answer before the question was put as in a poem when one finds it unnecessary to write some of the verses. What he heard shocked the novice even more than what he saw. The liqueur was too strong for such a weak soul, yet he returned every evening like one drugged who cannot live without the drug and his nightly dose any more. That lasted for about ten days.

Barbara perceived a hostile and dangerous presence around Laurent and Alexandra. She repeatedly warned them. As the novice had overheard Laurent and Alexandra speaking about those warnings, he made his mind a blank, and during the day he did not leave his paddock, where Alexandra saw him at his usual work without suspecting anything. She put it down to Barbara's over-acute sensibility. It is often like that between sisters-in-law. However, the warning did some good in one sense. For the first time in Laurent's very long existence he started to evolve a coherent theory about his own position as a vampire that was scandalous for his time, even for his spirit. What Kotor had striven for, and tried to live for, minute by minute in the circuitous ways of his uncertain knowledge, Laurent felt he could one day grasp and define. It was an audacious synthesis of alchemy, astrology and medicine, combined with the virulent criticism of a certain sort of life in society. A bridge could be erected between a scientific and a social utopia, resulting from the crisis of conscience in a man whose precarious existence had made him too short-sighted to establish even a fragile relationship between himself and the Universe. Ever since her first meeting with Laurent, Alexandra had been waiting for the poetical strength of his imagination to find a project, an interpretation of life, sex and history. Thus they had to return to the forest of Tristram and Ysolde for a movement of the spirit, similar to the *coagula* of the alchemists, for the vampires—one of them at least—to dedicate himself to the exploration of their singularity. Gently he recognised the limits of his identity, a beautiful lyrical movement towards accepting his condition. She had never loved him so much. She tried in every possible feminine manner to help him with all her strength.

Precisely at this moment in the novice's mind the horror and the scandal found the only possible answer: an act of refusal, negation and destruction.

Antonio asked to be received by the prior, an austere man animated by fast and voluntary abstinence, who wanted to hear nothing, and lived out of his century. He was neither interested nor curious. He was tired of the visions of his monks. There remained the secular arm. The mountain of Arrabida and the land of the monastery belonged directly to the duchy of Palmela, the duke possessing everything including the jurisdiction from Sesimbra to Setubal. The Marquis, now a recluse in Palmela, exercised the privileges of the deceased duke whose inheritance was the subject of ten law suits, which had dragged on for years.

Stunned by his defeat, and conscious of having lost everything because of his flight, he had given up the fight, for power, and all ideas of a career or a future. He did not even want to go to his estates in the Minho, but chose Palmela as his place of exile. He hunted and mortified himself. He was unwilling to receive the novice, who said he had something to reveal. The novice had forgotten to say what it was about. The Marquis was not in the mood to listen to anyone, especially local petitioners, until the moment when as an aside Antonio pronounced the word vampire. The castle was in turmoil.

The Marquis had the map of the estate spread out, and had everything explained to him. This time he knew without any doubt that he had Alexandra in his grasp. José's property was indubitably in his fief. Thus he could act unhindered. He held himself back, and managed to conceal his immense sense of triumph. He told nobody that he had recognised the fugitives, letting the others think that he accepted the novice's idea, namely that they were survivors of the great massacre of the vampires. He ordered complete silence, and mustered his forces, ten to twelve reliable men, no more. They had remained loyal to him because they were too compromised after the great shipwreck. The idea of calling in Luciano did not even enter his head. He had seen with deep disgust that Luciano kept his place, without being able to explain to himself the kind of bargain Luciano and João had struck. He kept silent. A letter from the King, which he did not even unseal, let him know of his decision to relieve him of all his duties. It was followed by a *lettre de cachet* signed by João ordering him to remain on his estates. Nobody at Court knew what became of him. There were no regrets, no questions.

Alexandra's arrival on his estate was really a gift from heaven. He had to account to nobody. Moreover, the events of Alfama were glossed over. Legally a great veil had been drawn over that day, and nobody wanted to hear it mentioned again. Some officials of the ministries of justice and the interior tried to settle the problems of property, damages and inheritances in a general desire for silence, but without ever uttering the *Word*, the *Name* more forbidden now than ever before.

The Marquis decided to be a better strategist than Luciano. Hatred and a thirst for vengeance had erased all desire in him. He was not even sure whether he needed or wanted to rape Alexandra. Torture would suffice if the agony could reasonably be prolonged. Not to give the alarm, but strike like lightning at dawn when the vampire was in his coffin and the girl in bed. He must keep his men in complete ignorance and confusion. Keep watch on the novice. An idea came to him. He made Antonio repeat everything several times, describe the exact spot, and make a drawing of it. Then, unsuspecting, he stabbed him. Throughout the night his horsemen were locked up with him in a chapel. They fasted, and went without water, and they endlessly recited the entire missal together. Thus not even a thought could escape from the chapel. The Marquis was afraid of the most unimportant thoughts too. The twelve horsemen, besotted peasants with no intelligence, did not understand what was happening. They thought they were to hunt the father of all the wolves in the forest because of the multi-shaped boar-spears which the Marquis had ordered them to cut. Barely half of them could read. The others mumbled after them. They were told to sit down. Their heavy hobnailed boots scraped the flagstones. Their fat arses shook on the rough benches. Most of them slept with their eyes open, which hardly changed their expressions.

Of course, neither Laurent nor Alexandra suspected in the least that they were living their last night. Yet death was in the spirit of their conversation. Laurent had just harnessed himself to the hard work of disentangling the skein of contradictions and fears. 'Hope not, dear soul, for immortal life, throw yourself into action.' More and more Pindar's cry seemed to him the only issue, or old Faust's with his *Am Anfang war die Tat*. Alexandra thrilled in his arms. He spoke about the ferociousness of the gods, and of the Christian West, covered with the blood of the entire world, marching with giants' steps towards the destruction of the world instead of building a new one according to the ancient promise of their Founder, the emblem of whose agony became the worst of all the arms of massacre ever employed by man. To Laurent, only the Nidanas could appeal, these twelve instrument-makers whose harmony could make life bearable. Alexandra laughed at him: men surely killed in Buddha's name too, and the gods of India dripped with blood. She told him—he knew it so well—about Zeus striking Asclepion with lightning, as a punishment for bringing a dead man back to life. Thus, with the same strike of lightning, he killed both the healer and the healed. Laurent deplored the bad luck of men who chose the horror of the blade of monotheism against Æsculapius and Mithras. But how could the fire be stopped?

'One can light a fire with a match,' she said, 'but one does not put out the fire by withdrawing the match. What is one to do?'

They thought of the golden age, another golden age, of amiable pastoral nations without violence or weapons. They laughed at their illusions. Virgil surely had his slaves whipped when they did not serve the milk and honey correctly for his friend Horace. All ended in derision. Life, gaiety and verve, said Laurent to himself, the marble breasts of his mistress cupped in his hands. They made love non-stop, held back indefinitely their orgasm with star-like calm, already far from everything, becoming perhaps, if Zeus had been right, a new constellation, a new sign of the Zodiac, obeying wisdom and grace, making men obey the laws of harmony and gentleness.

'We will be the gods of tenderness,' said Alexandra.

With Laurent inside her they hardly moved, sure of eternity which at that very moment would be taken from them for ever. That night appeared to them a night without end. It was the image of happiness. Laurent was the first to see the little streak of day in the East under the black velvet curtain. The sparkle of the stars began to fade. He sighed. They rose from the large bed, and with their arms around each other they went to the other side of the large room. He sank into his coffin, appeased and happy, once again ready for the deep plunge into the ice-cold world of his daily death. She tucked him up in his coffin as she would her first-born in his cradle. He slipped into sleep. She kissed his icy, beautiful forehead, and closed the coffin lid. Nuptial music accompanied her to her bed. I hope I am pregnant, she said to herself. The first rays of the sun appeared as she closed the shutters. She lay down, shivering with cold, for the mornings are cold in the mountains of Arrabida. She pulled up the blankets, and fell asleep at once.

The Marquis woke his horsemen, befuddled with prayers. They reeled with sleep as they gathered the horses in front of the chapel. In silence, stuck in their saddles, weapons in hand, and the wooden boar-spears tied to the webbing, they continued to doze without understanding what the Marquis was waiting for: for the sunrise. The castle of Palmela dominates the whole of the alluvial plain thrown by the Tagus against the small hills of the Arrabida chain. To the East one could see as far as the mountains of Spain. The sun appeared between two peaks. The Marquis gave the order to leave.

He had divided his little army into three sections. He himself was leading the one taking the road below the monastery, and another crossing the crest would rush down when the Marquis gave the signal with his red-plumed hat. The third would come from behind through the forest. They would be guided by the noise made by those charging down from the crest.

A powerful signal of danger reached Alexandra a split second before she heard the sounds of the charge. She burst from her bed with one leap, and pushed open a shutter. She saw nothing, heard only the sound of the horses, and the shouts of the horsemen coming from every direction. Evidently the house was encircled.

With kicks, carbine butts and the boar-spears' handles the Marquis' horsemen started to break open the shutters in the part of the building where the vampire slept.

Alexandra rushed to the coffin. She had no weapon near at hand. They had only one pistol, useless against such an invasion, and in any case it was in Laurent's jerkin inside the coffin. Instinct impelled Alexandra to climb to the girders of the roof, and hide in the network of the beams which she had so often looked at from her bed.

At the sight of the coffin, and with the boar-spears in their hands, the horsemen now realised the work that was expected from them. They drew back. All had taken part in the killing in Alfama, and not one of them wanted to soak in blood again.

'Run to the side, get hold of the girl,' shouted the Marquis, filled with fury by the hesitation of his henchmen.

While they pulled aside the large curtain he took a mallet from his pocket and seized the largest boar-spear. He himself tore off the coffin-lid, cruelly breaking his nails. He swore so loudly that some of the men decided to help him, but they jumped back with a movement of fear when they saw Laurent, immobile, his eyes closed, happiness written over his face, lying in his coffin, so handsome that it struck their imagination for ever.

The Marquis was paralysed too, not daring to move. Light, which in any case was deadly for the vampire, streamed into the room. The Marquis shook himself and pointed the boar-spear at Laurent's heart. Then something happened that had never happened before: the vampire opened his eyes as though he wanted to see for himself his own second death. He moved. Alexandra among the beams, and the horsemen, were frozen with horror. But not the Marquis. To see that creature alive his hatred became boundless again. With all his might he hit the boar-spear with the mallet. The boar-spear entered Laurent's chest with an awful sound of splintered bones. Blood did not burst forth at once. Now quite conscious Laurent held his breath, holding for a second more the fluid of life. He moved his arm, took the pistol from his pocket, and fired at the exact second he let out his breath, and his blood gushed forth like a geyser. The bullet, fired at so close a range, blew off half the Marquis' head. He did not even have the satisfaction of seeing Laurent die. After dropping the pistol Laurent tried to pull the boar-spear from his heart, but as he pulled so the blood flowed stronger. In despair he abandoned the impossible struggle, and raising his eyes saw Alexandra in the network of the beams. He had just enough strength left to smile, and the extreme courtesy to die smiling.

The Marquis' men had not seen Alexandra. They had been splashed with the brains of their master, and were covered with the stream of blood from that person with the ecstatic smile who was dying so happily. It was too much for their weak brains and dark souls. After a brief silence, together the twelve let out a loud shriek of horror. They ran away without taking the trouble to jump on their horses, who bolted too, and riderless they rushed pell-mell with their former riders rolling over one another through the boulders and the trees. The whole business had taken no more than three minutes, surely an eternity, a slow-motion action but of surprising brevity.

Silence returned quickly. Disturbed for a moment, the cicadas continued their music. Her mind a blank, Alexandra tumbled down from her perch. A tardy warning from Barbara or Clara—she did not know which—reached her full of anguish.

'He is dead,' was her message. 'I am dead too. Goodbye, my sister.'

She closed her mind to all communication, and with a dry eye, her will strained, she coldly examined the situation. It was impossible to live without Laurent after their magic days together. But to live indefinitely after her first death, which would now be her fate, she refused to imagine. She wanted to die, therefore had to die twice simultaneously, otherwise she would be forced to drag out her widowhood for hundreds or even thousands of years.

For a long time she stroked Laurent's gentle and peaceful face. Dead for ever. She believed in no kind of beyond, did not think of joining Laurent in another disembodied world, but simply admitted she could not live without him. If I kill myself tonight with this dagger, she said to herself, I will be reborn as a vampire. The solution looked a terrible one, and produced enough sweat and anguish to make her will and spirit writhe.

But Alexandra had always been energy itself. Nothing had ever resisted her. Especially not my carcass, she said to herself. I shall make you jump that hurdle, she said, speaking to her body as she spoke to her horses.

The Marquis' mallet had blunted the edge of the boar-spear it had struck. Even so I am not going to die beside the corpse of this dog, she said to herself. By the legs she dragged the corpse, with only half a head left, and threw it outside. Let the blood spread everywhere. She would do no cleaning. With the dagger she sharpened the blunted edge of the boar-spear that had entered Laurent's chest until it was sharp once more. She touched the new point with her finger. It pricked. It will prick even more in a while, you fool, she said to herself. She looked round: she felt herself weakening. I must do it at once, or I won't have the strength left.

She took off her chemise, and holding herself by her elbows she lay down full-length on top of Laurent's corpse. Then she kissed his frozen lips. Under her left breast she searched for the exact spot where her heart was. She felt it beating hard, a frightened animal aware of its fate. She leaned against the boar-spear's point. It pricked her, and a little blood flowed. Then with one movement, using all her strength, and holding on to Laurent, with all her passion she drove the boar-spear into her chest without a groan or a cry. The spear pierced their two hearts. A stream of blood, as abundant as Laurent's, burst forth and ran like a river. There had been no unnecessary movement. Alexandra's strong will and pure energy prevailed. She smiled. So she succeeded in killing herself twice at the same moment, once as a woman, once as a vampire, dying her two successive deaths at one blow. Her already frozen face dropped on to Laurent's face. They made the strangest recumbent figures, as if they had been sculpted so.

Chapter VI

When they awoke simultaneously at sunset, Kotor and Barbara knew at once what had happened to Laurent and Alexandra. Kotor had suffered a lot from his wordless confrontation with Laurent. The death of his partisans, the destruction of their shelter, and the dispersal of the survivors had obliged him to take heartbreaking decisions. The fall of Alfama was the defeat of his efforts to create a fraternal society of vampires, the defeat of his attempt to be accepted by mankind, the defeat of the hope of lifting the old malediction and the old repulsion. He would have to fall back on himself, base everything on the success of his work, which seemed to be fated to become the sad parallel of Sisyphus. Laurent had reproached him with a taste for withdrawal and secrecy, an absence of perspective and of a generous outlook. That tragic double death had proved he was right, and Kotor faced a sudden crisis almost of disillusionment, a temptation to suicide and abdication.

Luckily his close circle faced him, first Clara and Ursula, then Fernanda and Gianvittorio, who on his own initiative, and without consulting the brothers or the chiefs of the Rosicrucians, decided to put those of his organisation who had resisted at the service of the surviving vampires. He found only half a dozen. If any more remained they were surely in haggard and frightened groups seeking perilous refuges. Gianvittorio heard that some had reached Algarve, the sea towards Morocco, and others Spain.

Gianvittorio was going through a very violent crisis too. He had been touched by the great vampire dream. The grand upheaval he had believed to be near, he saw, would now be postponed. The brothers and the small group he led doubted they were ready for it, and their plans were less than coherent. The quick end of feudal tyranny, however certain it was, seemed further off. The contradictions of different interests came into the open, and the centre of gravity of the movement was moving to England and France. He had long discussions with Kotor and Joaquim. The women, Clara, Fernanda and Anna-Lucia, acted in concert too. To save Kotor from madness, preserving the essence of the project of the group, seemed the first necessity. Kotor would never find his primitive strength again in Lisbon, nor even in Europe.

A small but sturdy, well-built and rigged ship returning from Timor and Goa was for sale. She was too small for ordinary commercial operations to Angola, Mozambique and Brazil, and it was certainly not the season for voyages of discovery. Her owner was ready to sell at a good price. Strolling on the quays Joaquim noticed her. He rushed to tell Anna-Lucia. The other women were summoned. So was Gianvittorio. But where should they go, and with what sort of crew, he asked.

The answer came from Barbara who, from her retreat in Caparica, talked every night to Clara. Barbara's Bahian folk, the old mother of the saints and the small group of slaves, wanted to go back. Going back was no longer to Africa, but to Reconcavo, the Bahia of all the saints, the town of Salvador, and in the town to the secret neighbourhood, the Pelourinho, the faraway twin of Alfama.

A goal, a refuge and a crew. They even found a skipper. José, Alexandra's unsuccessful lover, had discovered her and Laurent's corpses. Without separating them he buried them as they were, riveted by the boar-spear that had pierced their hearts. Then he disappeared in the mountains, weighed down by his grief. Barbara had sensed that burning sorrow, and received him at Caparica near Cape Espichel. She sent him to Clara who introduced him to Gianvittorio. José was a sailor who had few equals. The idea of the adventure, the group, and the gamble delighted him. The expedition began to take shape. The ship was called *Flor de Mavo*. Gianvittorio bought her, and renamed her *Santa Alexandra*.

José received his orders. Gianvittorio had contacts everywhere. Barbara's Blacks were the crew. They knew by instinct. They were mustered: Kotor, Clara (Ursula remained to assure the succession), Joaquim, Anna-Lucia, the old father who discovered a strong liking for little black girls, Gianvittorio and Fernanda. Barbara hesitated for a long time. On the eve of the departure she took her decision, said goodbye to them, and disappeared without accepting Ursula's hospitality.

So they left. By luck the tide was running out in the night, and the moon was at the end of its first quarter. It was as light as day. The small sailing ship left her anchorage in silence with all lights out except the navigation lights. She reached the middle of the river, and the tide took over. The wind was favourable. She slid along the surface like an arrow. There had been no trouble on the quay. The brothers' influence remained strong. Leaning in the shadows on the rail in the stern, Kotor and Clara watched the lights of Lisbon disappear. A little before the tower of Belem they saw the windows of the small rose-coloured mansion, where João now resided, brilliantly lit up. The minister was indulging in an orgy of work which astounded the whole town.

Clara's eyes widened. It was too far to see. However, she could feel the halo of anguish, remorse, guilt and bitter regret that surrounded João. She sent him a calming thought without knowing whether he would receive it.

In the bows, seated on the rail with their legs dangling above the water, Gianvittorio, Fernanda, Joaquim and Anna-Lucia watched the prow tear the dark water apart, cutting it into two silver furrows. A small lightship was anchored on the sandbank facing Caparica. They were soon past her. On the other bank the last lights of Cascais were seen one instant more, then were swallowed by the night. They had reached the sea. A strong wind rose. The four young people embraced, and smiled at one another. Their hearts were filled with great, undefined love. Lips met as if by chance. Happiness, perhaps. Yes.

João sat writing at his desk. He had taken off his frock-coat and waistcoat, and loosened his lace cravat. His pen raced along the paper: a plan for draining the marsh of Ribatejo and building a model village that would be run by the villagers themselves. It was on an estate confiscated from the late Marquis.

The corpse of the Marquis was discovered three days after his disappearance. The horsemen had never gone back to the castle of Palmela. They split up, each going off on his own. None would ever forget. Their panic had been so great that none would ever mention it. They were suspected of firing the pistol shot that had blown off half their master's head. The corpse was found by a poacher just after he had killed a gigantic hare, the largest and finest he had ever seen. In order to hide it he took it to the deserted barn in the forest. He literally fell on the corpse. In his surprise he dropped the hare into a hole. Then he ran to warn the bailiff, who had been worried about his master's absence and arrived at once. Nobody managed to explain the prodigious quantity of dried blood covering the floor. Nobody touched it. And nobody could explain the presence in the castle of the stabbed corpse of the novice. The bailiff did not search further. The horsemen had killed their master, but had not robbed the corpse. The more cold-blooded among them had corrected that mistake by taking all the Marquis had on him. Thus everything became clear: a foul crime during a shooting party. The Marquis had no heirs, so João simply took possession of his estates.

He tired himself out in unsuccessful searches: no trace of Alexandra or Laurent. They were lost for good. Owing to his respect for family ties José sent him one of Alexandra's necklaces with an anonymous note: they are dead, they avenged themselves. The missing piece of the puzzle fell into place. Now João knew who had killed the Marquis.

He was so miserable that he engulfed himself in work, and left the ducal palace for a delightful little rose-red palace near Lapa above the river. It became the seat of government. He was sure that Kotor was hiding somewhere. Looking by chance at a maritime register—nowadays he wanted to look at everything—he saw the announcement of the change of owner and change of name of the *Flor de Mavo*. He thought of discreetly assisting her departure, and when he found out that others had done it he admired the work and said nothing.

On that night he worked with the windows on the balcony thrown wide open. Without guessing its source he clearly felt the message of remission of anguish and grief coming from Clara, and understood it as a last salute. He raised his eyes. On the dark river a little light was gliding along. So they have left, he said to himself. He sighed. What idiocy, what blindness and what defeat. He missed Kotor. He guessed everything about him and the bitterness of an unrequited friendship rose in him. He thought of Barbara too, guessing what she had been, and the bitterness of lost love rose in him even more strongly. The little light disappeared towards the high sea.

He continued to work. There was a movement behind the curtains, which were brightly lit by the moon. He raised his eyes again, and could not decide whether his imagination was cheating him or whether he was really seeing what he saw.

Barbara, who had moved from the balcony to the curtains without João seeing her, took her time in leaving the curtains in a somewhat theatrical manner. She had put on a long, full and simple white muslin dress, and her fair hair flowed freely down her back. She was well aware that her flaxen, almost white, hair, her pallor and the white dress, also her very light blue eyes and the moonbeams, produced together an impression of the unreal. Since His Eminence loved the romantic, it was perfect in every sense. She looked at him fixedly.

The two remained immobile for a long instant, then she took her decision and slowly advanced towards him. He stood up, went round the desk, and leaned against it. They held each other's gaze. Barbara's eyes were alight with promises. João felt that the course of time was suspended. She continued to advance very gently, moving even more slowly. It was more gliding than walking. She was barefooted.

Equally slowly, ritually, João raised his hand to his collar, and with an infinitely slow gesture took off his cravat, which he let drop on the floor where the lace spread out like petals. With the other hand he opened the collar, freeing his neck entirely like a condemned man before he is beheaded. And firmly, without his eyes leaving hers, he offered his neck with the jugular vein throbbing. She had reached his arms when with the same gentle slowness she began taking his blood.

The little sailing ship was already four hours out when a faint light appeared on the horizon. The land had vanished, the wind was strong, and all the sails were set. The ropes were sighing, the prow cut the waves with the same precision and sound as a pair of scissors cutting a piece of satin. The four young people rose, and went aft to join Kotor and Clara, whose arms were still round each other.

'Day is breaking,' said Gianvittorio.

Kotor came out of his meditation, and with a majestic smile gave each of them a long kiss of peace.

'Thank you,' he whispered into Gianvittorio's ear. 'I do not know anything about our future, but nothing is lost. Thanks to you, Gianvittorio.'

Gianvittorio's eyes were smarting. Fernanda ardently embraced the grand old man, who had to disengage himself, laughing.

'I will accompany you,' said Joaquim.

'I too,' said Anna-Lucia.

Kotor stretched out his arms, and held them. At last they could all breathe freely. They were saved; not really since that word meant nothing; but on the verge of a long voyage. They smiled gravely.

Helped by Joaquim and Anna-Lucia, Kotor began his descent to the hold. The three of them were almost of superhuman beauty, which wrung the others' hearts. It took them a time to regain their composure after the group had disappeared into the depths of the ship.

The hold of the ship had been specially fitted. A dark space contained the coffins of the three real vampires on board. The first two were occupied by Blacks from Bahia who, initiated by Barbara, had died their first death and become vampires. Their coffin lids were closed already, and they were both asleep. That area was separated from the rest of the hold by an empty space that was the anti-chamber. Joaquim and Anna-Lucia helped Kotor to lie down, and closed his coffin, heavier than that of the others and as old as time.

Then they came out, smiling at each other tenderly. The hold smelt of tar and resin. They closed behind them the coffin compartment's door. The anti-chamber, which took up the whole width and a good part of the length of the ship, was faintly lit by portholes very high up. The sun rose, and started drawing strange figures on the partitions. They had the feeling, like new Jonases, of being inside the stomach of a whale. Anna-Lucia leaned against the pleasantly smelling wooden partition. Joaquim lifted her skirt and the famous chemise of Malines lace. I shall have my buttocks full of splinters, she said to herself. They embraced, rocked by the waves. He entered her. She was happy; he also. She looked into his eyes. She understood that he wanted something he did not dare to ask for. If it was what she thought the posture would not be comfortable: she would try.

Yes, it was that. Their love-making became a little fiercer. There was laughter in their eyes. And love.

'Being a whore,' she said, 'gives one the advantage of impeccable technique.'